A
Christmas flower

ALSO BY BRYAN MOONEY

Been in Love Before
Christmas in Vermont
Once We Were Friends
Love Letters
A Second Chance
A Box of Chocolates
Indie
The POTUS Papers
Eye of the Tiger

A
Christmas Flower

BRYAN MOONEY

LAKE UNION
PUBLISHING

Text copyright © 2017 by Bryan Mooney
All rights reserved.

Published by Lake Union Publishing, Seattle

www.apub.com

Amazon, the Amazon logo, and Lake Union Publishing are trademarks of Amazon.com, Inc., or its affiliates.

ISBN-13: 9781477808993
ISBN-10: 147780899X

Cover design by Danielle Christopher

Printed in the United States of America

CHAPTER ONE

Logan Mitchell worked the overheated chain saw hard, trying to help contain the growing forest fire. The searing heat from the blaze scorched his back and neck. Rivers of sweat drenched his clothes inside his protective work suit. He finished clearing a patch of trees and scrub grass, stopping long enough to survey the ground around him. It was then he thought of her. She was intruding on his day-to-day life more and more, and he thought of her often. He wondered how she was doing back home since the funeral. *Home.* It would be snowing this time of year, he mused. He missed her, but now was not the time. *Focus, Logan, focus,* he admonished himself. *You got a forest fire to fight.*

As he pulled to restart the chain saw, his trained ears heard the loud, unmistakable snap of a splitting tree behind him. Firefighters called it the death splinter—the last act of a dying tree before it cracked in two and crashed to the ground. He looked around. Jeff, the rookie of the team, had not heard it in the gulch below.

"Look out, Jeff! Look out!" Logan shouted to the young firefighter, trying to be heard above the din of the huge fire's exploding rage. The harsh, acrid smoke filled his lungs when he called out, but it was no use. Jeff kept working. Without thinking, Logan dropped his chain saw and ran at full speed over the burning brush, stumbling over loose rocks as the wind whipped the fire up the hillside. Even without the saw, he was weighed down by the forty pounds of firefighting gear he wore. Logan tackled Jeff to the ground and away from danger as the massive flaming tree came crashing down behind them, hot flames and cinders blowing across his face and hands.

Jeff stared at him, shock registering on his face. "That was close," he stammered. "Thanks, Capt'n," said the twenty-four-year-old recruit.

Logan still thought of Jeff as a rookie, but he had been on the fire line as a smoke jumper for the past two months. He was no longer a rookie.

A female voice rang out over the din. "You guys okay?" It was Sharon, one of his squad leaders. "Come on, we got a fire to contain." She rushed farther down the fire line, using her ax to clear trees and shrubs. They had just begun using drip torches to start the back-burn, hoping it would take away the fuel from the fire to starve it—kill it.

Logan looked at Jeff and said, "Let's go. We got work to do."

He stood. His back was tired and sore from the long shifts fighting the fire. At forty-two, Logan realized that maybe he was getting a little too old for all this. If he had been a second slower, that crashing tree would have killed them both. But he loved the work. He loved the challenge.

Grabbing his saw, he went back to work clearing a fire lane. They needed a break in the weather—a wind shift, rain . . . something. Anything would help.

A few days earlier, his elite team of smoke jumpers had parachuted from a plane in front of the fire, landing near the summit of the mountain. They had worked their way toward the inferno. Logan had landed hard, hitting his head and back on a tree limb, but he had shaken it off. Their equipment had landed two hundred yards away, dangling from the treetops.

It was tough and demanding work. They had not slept in beds, showered, changed clothes, shaved, or eaten a regular meal in nearly two days. Now his team was dead tired, having worked night and day with only short breaks from clearing the woods with axes, shovels, Pulaskis, and chain saws. The winds were hot as a hellfire inferno, blowing flaming cinders at them at over thirty miles per hour.

Today the fire was raging toward them from the valley below, forcing them back up the hill toward the peak. On the other side of the mountain, ten miles away, was the small community of Trenholme. The only thing that stood between the town and the raging wildlands fire was a small group of dedicated smoke jumpers. They were trying to clear a red zone of dirt in front of the fire. *But would it work?* Logan asked himself. The thick smoke burned his eyes and throat like tear gas.

"Straighten out that fire line over there. Look alive!" he bellowed at them, then coughed. He looked to his left. "Gary, you okay?" he asked the young redheaded firefighter from Tulsa. Logan noticed Gary's bunker gear was torn and shredded at the back of his legs.

"I'm good, Capt'n."

"Stay safe. Watch yourself. Your suit's ripped in the back, on your legs. Careful."

"Thanks, Capt'n."

The fire burned at over eight hundred degrees, and the noise level was like that of a freight train roaring straight toward them up the mountain. They shoveled dirt on the grasses to contain the flames and provide a firebreak. Suddenly, with his shovel in midair, Logan heard it . . . silence. Sweet silence. The fire was weakening. The wind had shifted, turning the fire back onto itself and killing the flames. It was running out of fuel and oxygen. Now it was time to hurry to make sure it did not come back to life again. His crew worked for hours to shovel dirt onto the smoldering flames and the burning brush, cutting in larger fire lines to starve it even further.

As the sun set, the skies opened, and it started to rain. Soon it began to pour. Rain. Heavenly rain. Glorious rain. It was a welcome relief to all the firefighters as they took off their helmets and looked to the sky above. Their faces were black from the soot and smoke, but for now their job was finished. They had contained a monster.

Hours later, another group of firefighters, Hotshot Team Seven, came to relieve them from the valley below. They were a welcome sight as Logan and his crew climbed into the back of waiting trucks and headed down the mountain. This was what they trained for—to fight forest fires.

Logan was glad it was over, at least for the moment. "You guys did a good job," he said proudly as they bounced around the back of the truck. Then he added with a laugh, "Oh . . . and merry Christmas." His firefighters were tired and aching, all glad to be going back to their base station.

Christmas was coming soon, and most of the team would go back to their day-to-day lives—until the next alert called them on their ever-present red beepers. All except for Logan. His off-season job was to continue clearing out dead trees and grasses for the US Forest Service, trying to prevent huge fires from occurring in the future. He would always be watching and waiting for the next fire to appear.

CHAPTER TWO

"Mom? Can you hear me?" Silence.

"Mother? Mother?" Again . . . silence.

"Judge, can you speak to her . . . please? I really need to talk to her." Her father—she had often called him Judge like everyone else in town—was silent as always.

Beth knew she was on her own. At home in years past, the retired judge usually sat in his favorite chair in the corner by the fireplace, reading his newspaper and smoking his pipe. She would always remember the sweet aroma of the cherry- and honey-flavored tobacco as he puffed on his well-worn pipe. She had loved to watch the small wisps of white smoke rise, swirl, and linger above his head before disappearing.

Still silent.

She sat on the cold bench at the foot of their graves. Years ago, shortly after her father died, she had arranged to have the cemetery staff strategically place it at the foot of his grave. Now, with her mom joining him, she could sit and talk to both of them. She usually found comfort sitting so close and talking with her mother, but not today. She rose and looked around in silence. A large snowflake tumbled against the grayish-red granite headstone, falling to the ground in front of her.

It was getting colder as Christmas neared. She felt the chill in the air as another snowflake fell, this one even larger. She pulled her wool coat and scarf tighter around her to protect herself from the cutting wind causing the scarf to flap wildly over her shoulder. After gently whisking away the freshly fallen snow from the top of the bench with the back of her hand, Beth sat down again. The white stone memorial bench felt colder that day as she sat looking at them. Her parents usually had all the answers.

"I don't know what to do, Mom . . . Dad," she began again. "I'm trying to keep the family together, but Claire has a mind of her own. She has her own life, and now she's moved to an apartment in Boston. I haven't heard from her about Christmas Eve yet. She seems to have a new boyfriend every time I speak with her. Logan's in California . . . maybe he'll come home for the holidays." Her mind wandered. "It would be good to see him again. I miss not having him around to talk to, like old times."

She watched the snow fall, even heavier now. Her mother was quiet. Beth told her, "It's not like when you were here, and you and I and Claire would bake Christmas sugar cookies and fruitcakes together, then decorate the house and the hospital and . . ."

Not able to hold it in any longer, she looked at the headstone, desperate for an answer. "Mom, the board wants to close the hospital by New Year's . . . starting on Christmas Day of all days. I thought for sure I could stop it. But it's not like when you ran the hospital. The town council doesn't want to spend any more money for the new equipment we need to stay in compliance with the state regulations. Without it, we have to close. It'll cost lots of money, but we desperately need the hospital, Mom. The people in the community need it; they need this hospital. If we don't get the funding, we will lose our certification and be forced to close. That is unless you or Dad have a spare couple of million dollars lying around the house that you never told me about."

Silence.

"I didn't think so."

The silence was broken by the sound of a bright-red cardinal flying to a nearby snow-covered branch. The snow fluttered off the tree to drift to the ground below. Beth smiled at the sight of it and then felt another flake brush against her face. It was getting colder. Again she tightened the scarf around her neck. It was her favorite scarf; her mom had made it for her years ago for Christmas, and now she cherished it.

"I don't know what people around here will do if it closes. This is home. This is why you came back here to River Dale. This town needs this hospital. Am I the only one here that sees that?" she said, nearly shouting, the anger slowly rising inside.

Dr. Elizabeth Harding was the acting administrator of the River Dale General Hospital. She had quit her job in Chicago to return home to River Dale when her mom had become ill. Her mom had passed away earlier this year, the day after Mother's Day. Beth missed her so. She looked at the cold granite slab facing her. Looking and hoping for answers. Mom always had all the answers. But not today.

"Mom, the new regional hospital in Winston is over forty miles away. People can die in the time it takes to travel forty miles.

"And now . . . Rory, who's been very good about me being away, wants me back in Chicago. I go back every month or so to see him and be with him, but it's not enough. He wants me to join him at the company he works for, Ascot Pharmaceuticals. They offered me a lot of money and a nice job, but the position involves a lot of traveling. Sales. And before you ask, no, we haven't set a date yet. Something always seems to come up." She twirled the engagement ring around her finger. "Not yet anyway," she whispered with a smile. "But I'm still working on him. Yes, and I know I'm not getting any younger." She stopped talking, then lifted her face to the heavens. It continued to snow larger and larger flakes. Beth playfully opened her mouth and closed her eyes to catch some of the chunky snowflakes as they scattered about her face before she turned back to talk to her parents.

"And to top it all off, the hospital is getting overloaded with flu cases, so it's all hands on deck. I had to pull supervisors and administrators from their desks in all departments to try to help out on a rotating basis. Sidney is adamant that the board wants no more admittances. Between now and Christmas Day, he wants me to begin discharging or transferring patients so we can start the closedown. I don't know if I can do it." She paused to gather her thoughts and took in a deep breath.

"Drake and I make our final emergency appeal at a special board meeting later today. Of course you remember Drake . . . thin, youngish face, blond hair, and tiny reading glasses. British. You hired him for that special copper project. I don't know what I'd do without him. He has some great ideas. I've always said I should just practice medicine and let him run the hospital. I loved being a pediatrician." She laughed and stopped for moment. "But I think the board liked the cachet of the name *Harding* on the marquee. He's just thankful to have the job to have his visa renewed every year. He's really great in research and administration."

Silence.

Beth watched the snow fall. "Mom, I need your help."

Silence as yet another snowflake brushed against her cheek. Then another.

She lowered her head and whispered in desperation, nearly begging, "Mom, give me a sign or something, anything. Let me know I'm doing the right thing. Please."

Silence.

Beth waited and waited, then glimpsed her watch; it was late—time to get to work. She smiled grimly. "It's late. I gotta go, Mom. Can't be late for work." She knew it would be a busy day at the hospital; slick, snow-covered roads always brought in accident victims—new patients.

"We'll talk later," she said, and blew her parents a goodbye kiss. "Time for me to go." She stood to leave, but turned back to say, "Merry Christmas, Mom, Dad. I love you both." Beth paused and sniffed the air and smiled. The distinctive aroma of sweet, fresh caramel floated in the air. Her mother's favorite. *Thanks, Mom.*

She walked to her car, and as she threw her purse on the seat beside her, it fell to the floor. She leaned over to pick it up and saw a family picture of the three "girls." Her mom stood in the center, Beth and her younger sister, Claire, on either side of her. They were all standing in front of the Christmas tree on Christmas morning. Her mom looked good in the picture, even though she had lost so much weight. Mom's last Christmas.

God, how I miss her. Why did she have to leave? I had so much more I wanted to learn from her and so many other things I wanted to know.

Her thoughts were interrupted by the insistent text alert from her cell phone. She had a message. It was from her sister, Claire:

Sorry Beth, can't make Christmas Eve.
Got a party to go to with my new boyfriend.
You'll love him.
Maybe see you on New Year's.
Love ya!

This must be the new boyfriend of the month. For years it had been a tradition in the family that on Christmas Eve they would get together to bake cookies, fruitcake, and apple crisp. She had promised her mom she would keep the family together. At their mother's funeral, Beth, Claire, and Logan had promised to be home in River Dale for Christmas. But now Claire was staying in Boston with her boyfriend, and Logan was in California fighting forest fires. *We have fires here he can fight,* she thought with frustration.

This year had been difficult as they all had drifted apart. They all had their own lives to live, she reasoned, but it hurt nonetheless. Well, there was nothing she could do about it. She could call and lay a guilt trip on both of them, but what would that accomplish? Nothing. It would just make everybody feel bad, even if it felt good to her at the time. *Maybe I can talk Rory into coming to town for Christmas.*

Snap out of it. I'll still have a great time. I'll bake cookies, drink eggnog, listen to Christmas music, watch Christmas movies on television, and light a fire in the fireplace.

She had returned home to River Dale to be with Mom, family, and friends, and now everybody was deserting her. She was itching to tell Claire exactly how she felt, how disappointed she was, but her mother seemed to whisper to her from that photo—*Don't take it out on her. Let it go, Elizabeth. It's okay. Let it go.*

Looking at it, she had to smile. *Time to go to work.*

It began to snow even harder. *Looks like we'll have another white Christmas this year,* she thought as she pulled her coat closer around her. She loved Christmastime, but her boss's words still rang in her ears: "No more admittances! No more." *Easy for him to say, but where are all these patients supposed to go? Winston? Forty miles away—a place where no one knows them or their families.*

It was a short drive to the hospital, and she soon pulled into the spot marked RESERVED—HOSPITAL ADMINISTRATOR—DR. ELIZABETH HARDING, MD, MHA. Her phone rang. She searched frantically through her purse and answered it on the fourth ring without checking the caller ID. "Hello," she said quickly.

"Hiya, darlin'." It was Rory.

"Boy, just what I needed—a familiar, comforting voice."

"Hey, it can't be that bad of a day; it's only eight o'clock in the morning in New Hampshire," he said, clearly trying to cheer her up. "How's the remodeling going?"

"Dust everywhere. The contractors took out another two walls in the other bedroom because of the water leak in the bathroom next to it. Just what I want to do at Christmastime, stir up all this dust. I'm sneezing like crazy. Driving me nuts. And they're only working sporadically because of the holidays."

Rory sneezed once, then again. "With my allergies, I'm sneezing just thinking about it. But that's what you get for living in an old house."

"You should be glad you're not here. You'd be going crazy with all the dust."

"Right. Other than that, how are you?"

"Well, it doesn't get any better. My sister just contacted me and said she can't make it for Christmas. And I have one last shot at making the board members change their minds about closing us down."

She heard his trademark laugh. He offered, "Hey, any time I make a sales presentation, I always think to myself beforehand, *What's in it for them?* Then I go from there."

"Right," she said glumly. "All they're interested in is money. That's what it all boils down to for them. ROI—return on investment, French is always reminding me."

"French?"

"Yeah, he's the finance guy on the board. All he thinks about is money—fund-raising bond issues, city credit ratings, stuff like that."

"Perfect. Show him how not closing the hospital makes sense from a monetary standpoint. It saves time, because your hospital is closer than the one in Winston. And it saves lives."

"Yeah," she responded. "I should have you come here and make the presentation for me. Drake is good, but he gets way too technical and analytical. He gets bogged down in the details." She stopped for a minute, then blurted out, "Hey, that's a great idea."

"What? Make your presentation for you? I don't think so, darlin'. I already have a job."

"No, I know that, but come here for Christmas. Moral support. You'll love it here at Christmastime. It's the best place in the world. We could sit in front of the fire and have some hot rum and cider. Or eggnog and rum. Attend the town's traditional Yule Log observance. Watch the tree-lighting ceremony. Sleigh ride in the snow. Open gifts on Christmas morning. And if Logan comes into town, you would finally get a chance to meet him."

"Right."

She had talked so much about Logan, Rory almost sounded jealous.

"So you'll come?" She knew the mere thought of living in a house filled with dust, even for a few days, was enough of a deterrent for him.

He paused. "No can do, Elizabeth. How many times have I told you? I have a lot of year-end sales numbers I gotta hit before January first. This is still a busy sales time for me, sweetheart. You understand, don't you?"

"Yes. I know, I know. I just thought—"

"Another time. Another year, okay? I promise. Okay?"

"Sure. I understand. Maybe next year."

"Gotta go, Beth. I got a call coming in. Talk to you later. Bye for now."

He hung up so quickly he never heard her say, "Bye, babe. I love you." The line went dead.

CHAPTER THREE

Claire finished texting, still not feeling right about the message she had sent to Beth. She had always looked forward to celebrating Christmas Eve at home in River Dale with her big sister. But this year would be different.

She glanced around their apartment. It was bare, with no decorations at all. No tree, Christmas cards, nativity scene, music, or mistletoe. Roger did not care for the holiday time of year and said he only wanted to spend the time with her. *Sweet and romantic,* she thought, but she still had a nagging feeling of regret as he joined her in the kitchen.

"Now see, that wasn't so tough, was it?" he said with a smile, folding his Boston newspaper and sitting down in the chair by the window.

Claire loved his smile. His sense of humor. He could always make her laugh—or at least he used to, before he lost his job. But she was certain this was just a bump in the road. He was always so witty and fun. She looked outside and saw that it was snowing again. Just like home.

"Yeah, I guess," she responded. She poured them each a cup of coffee, and then, sipping hers, she watched him. He was so strong in his convictions; he knew exactly what he wanted to do with his life. And he would hold out for just the perfect job, no matter how long it took. He always seemed to have all the answers. She liked that; it made her feel safe, secure . . . comfortable.

As it began to snow harder, her smile grew. A playful smile. "Rog, what do you say we go for a walk in the snow? Just you and me. Fresh snowfall. You can see your footprints on the sidewalk. We can walk down to the park and feed the birds, then stroll over to O'Riley's Pub. You know, see if any of the gang is there. We haven't been there in ages." Her smile of anticipation grew larger. "Then we can come home and have some cocoa, sit in front of the fireplace, cuddle, and read some—"

"Nah," he said, making a contorted face. "It's cold out there, not like LA. Let's just stay inside. Do you mind?"

"Of course it's cold. It's snowing. It's winter in Boston. If it was hot, we would have to change the name of the city to Miami." She chuckled to herself; he never seemed to appreciate her quirky humor.

He stood and set the paper down slowly as he walked back into the small apartment's living room. "Maybe later, okay?"

Claire's smile dimmed. When he said that, she knew that it would never happen. "Okay, but I'm still going to make some cocoa. You want some?"

He mumbled something unintelligible from the other room. Then he said aloud, "I'd love a beer."

She looked outside and watched neighborhood kids playing, dragging their sleds behind them as they headed for the nearby hill in the park. *A good day for sledding,* she thought.

"Claire? Beer?" he said again.

A picture on the wall of her, Beth, Mom, and Logan brought back so many memories. "Merry Christmas, guys," she whispered. It began to snow harder—big, fluffy flakes falling fast. Christmastime. Her smile returned, this time only larger.

CHAPTER FOUR

The special Friday board meeting in the hospital's executive conference room started promptly at four o'clock. In attendance were Dr. Elizabeth Harding; Dr. Drake Corrigan; Sidney Milner, chairman of the River Dale Hospital Board; board members Ronald French, CPA, and Royce Wilson, mayor of River Dale; and two other part-time members of the board, both of whom lived outside the city limit. Beth was nervous, again, as she stood to address the group. She clenched her fists to gain control of herself and calm her voice.

"I want to thank all of you for taking time today to listen to the proposal that Dr. Corrigan and I have put together to outline a plan to save and revitalize the hospital." She was anxious; she was fighting for the life of the hospital, much as she would fight for the life of one of her patients.

"You each have before you an outline, which lists a new direction for the hospital and for the community intended to broaden our appeal and outreach. Years ago, my mother came back here to her hometown of River Dale to make this hospital a leader in its field. I ask the board to remember that we are the nearest rural general hospital for forty miles and . . . we are also one of the largest employers in River Dale." She looked around the conference room to let that last fact sink in further before continuing. "What we propose is buying the updated equipment required to meet the state requirements and then outfit a sorely needed specialized critical care unit within the hospital. It will provide a much needed—"

"Your mother made wonderful strides in making River Dale General a hospital to be proud of; however, what we have to focus on today is what the hospital needs now to survive. Let me be frank. Do you have the two million dollars for the equipment updates, Dr. Harding?" asked Ron French, the financial secretary for the board. He peered down at her over his horn-rimmed glasses as he slowly rubbed his pencil-thin mustache. His jacket appeared too small and snug for him. Beth had gone to grade school with Ron and had never liked him. At the board meetings, he was always the first one to object to spending any money to keep up with the needed improvements. Today was no exception.

"Well, no . . . not exactly. I think if we ask the county voters for a bond issue to fund this, then—"

"Bond issue? Absolutely not! We want to keep the city's triple-A-plus bond rating, and I can't support a bond issuance that might jeopardize that. You understand, don't you, Dr. Harding? That's all that matters here. In addition, it would take months to get a special ballot before the voters. Besides, the county just opened a new regional hospital in Winston, in addition to ours here in River Dale. I'm sorry, I just don't think the area can support two hospitals," he said with authority. To him the matter was settled.

Royce, an influential board member, interceded. "As mayor of River Dale, I think we should let her talk. I don't think this board has given full weight to the fact that this hospital is critical to the community to be of—"

French cut him off. "Royce, it doesn't matter what she proposes. If we don't have the money for the state certification, then it's a moot point. Right?" Turning to Beth, he asked, "Well? Do you, Dr. Harding? Do you have two million dollars for our hospital?"

She was quiet at first and did not answer him. Finally she said, "No, sir, I don't. But if you and the rest of the board would please take a minute to read through the proposal that we put together for you, I am sure that you will see—"

"Dr. Harding," said her boss, Dr. Sidney Milner, the chairman of the board, "we are sure that you and your staff have made great progress and spent a lot of time in putting together this proposal. Is this the same proposal that you and Dr. Corrigan presented to the governor in the state capital earlier this summer? That crazy copper thing?"

"Yes, sir, it is," she said reluctantly.

"And what was their response to your proposal?"

"Unfortunately, sir, we never heard back from anyone."

"I see," he responded. His voice softened. "Dr. Harding, even if we were to come up with the money to do what you propose, we now have a new hospital in Winston that has taken our place regionally. So, in addition to the needed funds, we would also need to find a new mission for our hospital. I just don't see that happening."

He paused and looked at her, then closed the folder she had presented to him. "We will review it overnight and give you our decision soon. But I must tell you that the board has already met in private session to discuss this matter and . . ." He stopped to look around the room to confirm the consensus. "Let's just say, it does not look good. But I assure you, we will give it a very thorough vetting. Thank you."

French chimed in. "In the meantime, Dr. Harding, in accordance with state laws, we would like you and your staff to start transferring patients from River Dale General and accept no new admittances. None. Direct them all to Winston Regional Hospital. Do you understand what I am saying, Dr. Harding?"

"Yes, sir."

"Furthermore, any deviance from this directive will result in the loss of your separation bonus . . . and your year-end bonus. Is that clear?"

"Yes, sir," she said in a whisper.

Sidney stood and said, "The board would like to thank you and Dr. Corrigan for all your efforts. That will be all. This meeting is now adjourned."

And with that, the meeting was over. They never even gave her a chance.

She walked to the elevator with Drake. They had worked long and hard to put together their presentation, and it seemed the board would not even consider it, much less read it.

"Maybe tonight, after they read through it, they'll see what we see—a resurgent River Dale General Hospital. What we have done with the ICU is spectacular and bound to be noticed sooner or later," said Drake, trying to reassure her.

"Yeah, I'm sure," she said. "But Drake . . . unfortunately, *later* doesn't help us." She smiled at him and saw the compassion in his eyes. "We'll figure something out, trust me."

He smiled weakly and started to say something, but he stopped when Sidney approached them.

"Dr. Harding? Beth?" He appeared out of breath. "Don't count on the board members changing their minds. Not with French leading the way—he only thinks of dollars. I think he wants to be on the state hospital board or something, and he thinks this is a good way to show he can act tough financially. It's over, Beth. Trust me. Let it go."

He leaned in closer. "This is just between you and me, but the board of directors at the Winston hospital has made some confidential inquiries asking if I would be interested in joining the board there once River Dale closes. The chairman also made the concession that I could appoint my own hospital director if I so choose. I don't know what your plans are after you leave here, but if you think you might be interested in moving to Winston—"

"Thank you, Sidney. I just don't know what I'll do if . . . when the hospital closes."

"All I'm asking is that you think about it. Just give it some thought. Let me know soon. I'm leaving for an anniversary cruise in the Caribbean with my wife for a few days and have instructed the movers to see you to . . . start the process. Please begin transfer procedures as soon as possible. I expect to see everything implemented by the time I return. I'm sorry, Beth, but it has to be this way." He pressed the elevator button and turned to her as the door closed. "And French meant what he said—no more admissions, starting now. Send them to Winston Regional." He offered her a weak smile, then said, "Merry Christmas."

CHAPTER FIVE

The River Dale fire station, officially known as RFD 17, was on New Hampshire Route 4 just outside town. The two-story red-and-gray-brick building had been built more than forty years before but was well maintained. It held two fire trucks and one rescue vehicle, along with an ambulance. RFD 17 was capable of housing nearly twenty firefighters when it was at its full complement, which was not that often.

Christmastime was sometimes slow, but they often had their hands full with hunting and fishing accidents, house fires, car accidents, road spills, heart attacks, and the inevitable calls to respond to fires caused by Christmas trees. In addition to these normal duties, the longtime chief, Bruce Devlin, had started a campaign to visit each home in his jurisdiction to make sure residents had working smoke detectors and a carbon monoxide alarm properly installed on the premises. And for the past three weeks they had been contending with an active arsonist on the loose in their region. A very dangerous situation.

Inside the old station house, a tall, green, brightly lit Christmas tree stood in the corner of the recreation room surrounded by wrapped gifts that had been donated by the firefighters for homeless families. Another large pile was stacked high with gifts—mainly toys—for kids at the hospital.

Jack, Yancy, and Chief Devlin—affectionately known as "the Colonel"—had cut down a donated tree at a local tree farm. A group of them had decorated it late one night on their shift the prior week. Then they had added long pine needle garlands around the rec room and inside the office and training rooms and hung a fresh-cut wreath on the front door. Margie, the station's longtime dispatcher, had pinned a huge, handmade red velvet ribbon to the bottom of the wreath. The smell of fresh pine needles filled RFD 17.

Margie loved to play Christmas music over the sound system. Her favorite, "White Christmas," seemed to get more play than many of the other songs. From her front office window, she could see the freshly fallen snow and would occasionally take her break by walking along the river, many times accompanied by the Colonel.

"Are you going to the Yule Log ceremony next week, Colonel?" asked young Zack Roland, one of the company's newest recruits. Zack was one of the two new probationary firefighters. He was a kindly sort, with a full face of reddish-brown freckles and blond hair that stood straight up in the back regardless of how much gel he lavished on it, trying to get it to cooperate.

The Colonel, a tall man with snowy-white hair, bushy eyebrows, and an ever-present grin, smiled and grunted. "Wouldn't miss it for the world," he said with a hearty laugh. "I love it. It's my favorite time of the holiday."

The Yule Log burning ceremony was held every year at the town square. The fire was started with logs kept from the prior year's event to pay homage to its long history. The whole village met at the town square, and each person would lay a ceremonial log on the fire, dedicating it to a missing family member, friend, or loved one.

The fire chief started to say more, but just then he looked up at the wall of honor in the station and was saddened to see the list of fallen firefighters. The wall held the names of the five local firefighters who had lost their lives in service to the town. They had always been the silent heroes in the community. He had known them all, and he walked to the wall to read their names.

JAMES "JIMMY" CIVILETTI

MARK RODON

THEODORE "TEDDY" MCELROY

JUAN NORMS

PATRICK JANDERSON

The quiet was interrupted by a blast of the loudspeaker as it blared, "RFD 17, RFD 17. Please respond to a red zone alert—Century Alarm is reporting a fire alarm at 630 West Elm, just outside the River Dale zone. Come in, RFD 17."

The fire chief rushed to the office, trying to glean as much information as he could from the call.

Margie went to reply and turn down the call, directing them to another fire station. The Colonel reached her office and held up his hand to stop her. *Just what we need,* he thought with dry determination. He had to make a quick decision. Problems: their other truck was out on another fire call, they were one man short, and the call was outside their service area. But without hesitation, he was ready.

Bruce stopped her from transferring the call to another station. "Tell 'em we'll take it," he said to her.

"But, Colonel, we're short men and a truck. State fire regulations say—" Margie began.

"I know what they say, Marge, but we can't wait. People's lives could be in danger."

"What about Clark? Maybe he can help. He's certified," she said, jutting her thumb toward the young man sitting at a desk preparing grant paperwork for the city and administrative paperwork for city emergency services.

"No. He's on medical leave and classified as 'Desk Duty Only,' and I need somebody at one hundred percent. Besides, I know that address; it's a small apartment building. Somebody could die if we don't go. We'll respond. I'll ride truck thirty-one."

"Bruce . . . are you sure?" she asked him, lowering her voice.

"Yes, I'm sure."

"Your call, Colonel," she said, knowing there was no arguing with him once he had made up his mind. An arsonist working in the area had already ignited three fires in the last three weeks, causing them to be even more vigilant.

"Be careful," she said quietly. Then she grabbed her microphone and bellowed, "Central, this is RFD 17. We will respond." She watched the Colonel shuffle away, favoring his right hip as he walked.

"Suit up, Zack," he said to his driver.

"But, Chief, we only have two—"

"Let's go," he commanded, his impatience showing.

As chief, he did not usually respond to alarm calls, but he borrowed spare bunker gear and began suiting up for their response. He slid inside the truck, strapping on his helmet. He had no choice; they were down to two firefighters for the truck instead of the required three. Regulations called for three firefighters on every call. One firefighter to drive and run the pumper truck, one to spot, and one to go inside and fight the fire. Now they had only Zack as the driver, who doubled as the water pumper, and Bruce as a firefighter. With men on holiday leave and others who had resigned to join the big city fire departments, they were chronically short staffed.

"Let's roll!" he shouted as Zack Roland jumped behind the wheel.

"Are you sure about this, sir?" Zack asked.

"Yeah, I'm sure. Hit it."

The huge bay doors rolled up toward the ceiling, and soon they were on their way out into the snowy afternoon. The siren wailed into the crisp winter air as the massive red fire truck made its way down the icy highway toward Rumney.

The harsh wind whipped the snow into a white frenzy, reducing visibility. They sped past the River Dale Diner and the whitewashed, one-story River Dale Memorial Library on their way to the fire. They passed snow-covered fields, glistening in the late-afternoon light. Chief Devlin was lost in thought as he finished tightening his gear and oxygen tank. He knew he needed to be extra careful with a crazy arsonist on the loose. If not, somebody might die.

CHAPTER SIX

Logan Mitchell had served multiple tours in Iraq and Afghanistan with the Army Eighty-Second Airborne Division. After his third tour, he was sent stateside—just when the US Forest Service called for help as a result of a series of devastating fires in the West. He was the first to volunteer.

He and his unit were assigned to the Third Army Special Battalion for sixteen weeks and helped fight the Sedgewick fire, the deadly Bear Run fire, and the notorious Santiago fire. His battalion commander was an old army buddy from his hometown named Bruce Devlin. He would walk through fire for that man, and many days, he did just that. New England was filled with four generations of proud and hardy firefighters named Devlin, and Bruce was one of them.

Logan found he loved working as a firefighter, and when his temporary assignment with the US Forest Service was over, he took advantage of an early release program from the army. He trained for six months at the Arizona National Firefighter Training School. After he finished his training, he went to work as a local firefighter in Phoenix before being promoted to station manager in the small town of Yarnell, Arizona, where he served for four years. But Logan yearned for something more. He had joined the elite Southwest Hotshot team for three years until there was an opening as a smoke jumper in Southern California. He loved this work more than anything he had ever done.

When the Colonel finally retired from the army, Bruce went back home to New England—to their hometown of River Dale, New Hampshire—and took the job as the local fire chief. Logan had gone home once for Doc Sarah's funeral earlier in the year, but he had not stayed long. Too many memories. Too many feelings. Too much for him to . . .

He lay on his bunk among the other thirty men and women, kicked off his boots, and carefully unrolled his socks as his crew gathered around him.

"All over, Capt'n?"

The title was more a sign of respect than a rank. He was the crew chief for their rotation—the top man, the one everybody looked to for direction. Everyone called him Captain.

"I think so, but we'll know better after they send in a spotter plane or drone to look over the valleys to see if we have any other hot spots. But I think we've licked it; the heavy rains really helped. Get some rest and something to eat." If the word came in to move out again, they would need to suit up, grab their equipment, and be on the plane ready to roll in less than six minutes. Timing was everything in firefighting. For now, all he wanted to do was massage his aching feet, close his eyes, and grab some sleep in the hut.

"The hut," as everyone called it, was a long, one-story wooden building that served as a staging and resting area provided by the US Forest Service. All these huts looked the same, with small windows, dark wooden floors, rows of bunk beds, and lockers to store personal gear. An impromptu mess hall occupied one end of the building, and there they ate hot food trucked in from a nearby town. Showers were at the other end of the building—but only cold-water showers. Sometimes the water was so cold that the men and women joked they found ice in the running water.

As the team settled into its temporary base station, Logan surveyed his injured crew members. Gary, two bunks over from him, had sustained bad burns on the backs of both of his legs. Michelle had a cut down her back after being hit by a falling limb. *Overall, not bad,* he thought. At least everybody had come back alive. Team Six on the north ridge was not so lucky, having lost two firefighters. There were only three hundred smoke jumpers in the entire country. Theirs was a close group, and any loss was a tough one for them to take.

Sharon walked by, nursing a bruise on her face and a black eye but trying to act as if nothing had happened.

"Get some ice on that before it swells shut," Logan told her. "You're going to need both eyes if this thing starts up again."

"I'm good. I'll be okay."

"I know that," he said, but then paused when he saw her touch her face and wince. "Just get some ice on it. Okay?"

"Yes, Capt'n." She managed a pained grin.

He watched her walk away and thought to himself, *She's a stubborn woman, but a great firefighter.*

Josh approached and tossed him a bottle of water. It was ice cold and tasted better than champagne ever did. "Thanks, Josh."

Josh leaned in and said, "Got a call from the hill, and they wanted me to tell you. They just got an early spotter confirmation—our fire is officially dead." The Los Lobos fire was out and now a part of smoke jumpers' history as the fire season finally wound to a close. Their backup, the Hotshots, would stay in the area checking to make sure it stayed out, but for the smoke jumpers it was finally over.

"Hallelujah," Logan said, slapping his hands together and making a loud clapping noise. He lay back in his bunk and thumbed through the pile of transcribed messages his battalion chief had dropped off. Two messages caught his eye. The first one was from Royce.

Colonel injured in a fire. Not good. In hospital.

27

Royce had been a volunteer firefighter in upstate New York before he retired and now was the mayor of River Dale.

The second message was . . . from her.

> Logan—We admitted the Colonel to the hospital tonight. His situation is serious. I think you'd better come home.

Beth. Logan breathed in deep, then reached inside his wallet, pulled out a picture, and slowly unfolded it. It was a picture of the two of them from so long ago. He studied her . . . her face, her hair, her eyes—the eyes that saw everything—and lastly, her smile.

"Nice picture," Sharon said, coming up behind him and looking at it as she held an ice pack on her swollen eye. "You were so young." She elbowed him slightly. "Who's she?"

"An old friend," he said, handing her the picture.

She held the photo in her hand and peered closer, noticing his arm around Beth's waist. "Pretty lady, but sure doesn't look like an *old friend*."

Logan smiled. "She and her family lived next door to us when we moved to River Dale. After my mom and dad died in an accident at our lake cabin when I was sixteen, my aunt and uncle thought it was best if I stayed in school in River Dale. So the Hardings kind of adopted me. I moved into a small apartment they had over their garage out behind their house until I went away to college and then to the military. She was my best friend."

"You see her lately?" she asked, shifting the ice bag around on her eye as she handed the photo back to him.

"Went back for her mom's funeral earlier this year. Just for a short time. I was tempted to stay longer but . . . too many memories." He folded the picture and returned it to his wallet.

"Pretty lady. I wouldn't let that one get away if I were you."

"She's just a friend, Sharon. Best friends."

"Yeah, I'm sure," she said, leaving to get a fresh ice pack.

Later, he reread the message and thought to himself, *Maybe it is time to go home. Spend some time there.* He suddenly realized how much he missed it. New England. River Dale. People. Home. Snow. Christmas . . . Her.

That night he could not sleep as he thought back to all the Christmases he had spent in River Dale and all the great memories he had there. The Yule Log ceremony. Cutting down their annual Christmas tree from Morgan's Tree Farm in Whitney. Then decorating it that night with the family. Cross-country skiing with Beth in the snow-filled valleys of New Hampshire. Making homemade Christmas decorations. Cookies from Schmidt's Bakery in town. Sledding down the hill in the backyard. Winter fly-fishing along the Baker River . . . with Beth.

The next day, he said his goodbyes to the group, packed up his things, and headed home. Back to New England. Back home to River Dale.

CHAPTER SEVEN

It had been a long flight from Los Angeles to Boston and a very long night for Logan Mitchell. He still had miles to go before he could sleep on this cold New England Sunday morning.

"Good morning, ladies and gentlemen. Please fasten your seat belts and bring your seats into their full, upright position. On behalf of the captain and the crew, we would like to welcome you to Boston."

It's good to be home, he thought as he deplaned and walked through the airport, then grabbed his bags off the slow-moving luggage carousel.

While waiting for his rental car, he dialed Beth's number again. His face brightened when he heard her voice, then dimmed when he realized it was a recording.

"Hi, this is Beth. Please leave me your name and number and a short message and I'll get back to you as quickly as I can. Merry Christmas."

"Hi, Bethy. It's Logan. Just landed in Boston and should be home in a couple of hours. See ya soon. Call me when you get this message."

In his rental car, he turned on the GPS, more from habit than any actual need of directions. He would start in Massachusetts and drive north on I-93 toward Plymouth, New Hampshire, then take Route 25 until he was home. *Not long now. Home? Good question. Where to stay? Last time, for Doc Sarah's funeral, I stayed with the Colonel. Can't stay there now. Maybe Heuser's B&B? First things first—gotta see the Colonel. The rest can wait. It'll be good to be home again.*

During the drive up through the mountains, he had time to reminisce, and the memories came rushing back to him. Christmastime. Peanut butter cocoa. Maple sugar cookies made with fresh local maple syrup. Homemade ornaments that he and the Judge had whittled from old pinewood they had found in the forest. German *Pfeffernüsse* cookies from Schmidt's Bakery in town. Fresh maple syrup bought from nearby tree farms poured over homemade biscuits and pancakes. Doc Sarah made the best homemade biscuits and gravy, just like his mother used to make.

He smiled as he remembered the times they had searched for that perfect Christmas tree at Morgan's Tree Farm. He and Beth would bicker and tease each other over which one looked the best, the most perfect, until Doc Sarah would step in and make the final decision.

He remembered the huge pinecones they found in the forest and saved in the old apple bushel basket in the garage. Later, he and the Judge would dip them in wax and something the Judge called *sparkle*, which changed colors when thrown on the fire in the fireplace. For a yellow or green effect, the Judge mixed in borax or boric acid. For a red flame, he used some Epsom salts mixed in with the wax. The Judge knew just what to do. The miles and time passed quickly as Logan sorted through these memories.

Five stockings always hung from the fireplace mantel. One for each of them with their names stenciled along the side—Mom, Dad, Elizabeth, Claire, and Logan. Beth had showed off her sewing skills, creating them from a simple pattern she had ordered from the newspaper.

Logan missed the simple things, especially visiting the Yule Log burning ceremony; everybody in the village called it the log of memories. He remembered the last time, standing there beside Beth, his arm draped around her shoulders to help keep her warm. It had just seemed so natural. He was still lost in memories hours later as he passed a sign—**RIVER DALE, EIGHT MILES, NEXT EXIT**. He turned off the nearly empty state road and was immediately transported back in time as he drove along the narrow two-lane river road. *Life never changes here,* he thought. The familiar road, the mountains rising above him, and the forest of snow-covered pine trees far off in the distance all served to welcome him home.

He drove alongside the Baker River, the rapids churning the water a frosty white as it rushed over the rocks in its haste to hurry down the mountain. He could tell it was getting colder. Ten minutes later, he passed a sign that said:

WELCOME TO RIVER DALE
POPULATION 3,809

Home.

He saw two red foxes running across the field through the snow. An old wives' tale said that meant more snow was coming. He remembered his mom saying, *Two foxes a runnin'—more storms a comin'.* His neck was beginning to ache—his own indication of a storm brewing.

The small town of River Dale was elevated on a hill not far from the fast-moving river water below. But sometimes the river road, which ran along the waterway for miles, would flood out during the spring thaws and become impassable. Today the water was rough. *Too rough and too cold for fishing,* he thought. He loved fly-fishing for trout in the springtime here. So did Beth. It was the best.

He slowed as he reached town and decided at the last moment to make a quick, impulsive detour off to the right through the village. It would take only a few minutes, and it was on the way to the hospital. The road through town, Main Street, was a horseshoe, running from the river, up and around through the village center, and then back down to the river.

He drove past the town hall with its tall decorated Christmas tree out front in the town square, past River Dale hardware store, and past Alice's ice-cream parlor, now closed for the season.

The road curved in front of the church with its high white spire and a huge wreath with a red-and-green plaid bow hung on the front door. Out front, the snow-covered nativity scene was barely visible. Farther down a side street, he saw the marquee for the River Dale Theater touting a Christmas movie marathon. The list included *It's a Wonderful Life, Christmas in Vermont, The Nutcracker, A Christmas Carol, Miracle on 34th Street*, and of course, *A Christmas Story.*

The town was decorated in all its Christmas finery. Every store had white lights in the windows and wreaths, bows, and bells on the doors. The poles of the streetlights were covered in pine garland with big red ribbons adorning the tops. A chalk signboard in front of the River Dale General Store listed the week's events. This week there would be a children's hayride, caroling practice at the hospital cafeteria, a wreath-making contest, a wassail punch festival, and the Yule Log ceremony.

As he drove past Schmidt's Bakery, he quickly hit the button to roll down the car window. He stopped in front for a minute and took in a deep breath to smell the memories. He could almost taste them, too. Beth also loved the German delicacies there. The cookies, cakes, and pies were so good—some of them almost as good as Mom's. *I could live right here in front of the bakery for the rest of my life,* he thought, taking in another deep whiff. He saw the clock on the car's dashboard and thought sadly, *Time to go,* as he slowly raised the window and shifted the car into gear. *Time to see the Colonel.*

He had been unable to reach Beth both times he had called, and they had been vague at the front desk when he had called the hospital, saying only that the Colonel was in serious but stable condition. They repeated the same message when he arrived at the reception desk to get the Colonel's room number.

Outside the Colonel's room, he met the longtime mayor of River Dale, Royce Wilson. Tall and distinguished, he wore his trademark dark-blue suit, white shirt, and maroon tie along with rubber snow boots unceremoniously covering his dress oxford shoes. His graying hair was brushed back to cover the emerging bald spot on the top of his head. His face brightened when he saw Logan. "You got my message, I see. Good to see you again, Logan."

"Hi, Royce." Logan respected the man. He had been a firefighter for twenty years before retiring, returning home to River Dale, and running for mayor. He had held the elected office for the past twelve years.

"How's he doin'?" Logan asked.

"Better. But still touch and go. Doc Harding has been checking in on him personally."

He raised his eyebrows and casually asked, "How's she?"

"Just as smart and just as pretty as she ever was. And oh, by the way, I'm doing fine, too, thank you very much. Just in case you're interested."

"Sorry. Just got a lot on my mind, that's all. I'm going to see Bruce."

Royce chuckled. "I understand. Let me know."

"Thanks. I'll be back. Talk to you later." Logan turned to walk away.

Royce stopped him. "Logan, you still . . . smoke jumpin'?"

"Yeah. Been doing it for a long time. Gets in your blood, so to speak. You know? Why?"

"How long you stayin' in town?"

"Don't know," he responded, wondering where this line of questioning was going. "A week. Ten days. Maybe longer. Wanted to see the old coot and some friends in town, and besides, it's the end of the fire season out in California. So I guess I'll probably leave some time after Christmas. Why?"

"After this latest fire we just had, I'm down a couple of men at the fire station, including the Colonel. For a small detachment like ours here in River Dale . . . well, that's a lot. I could really use an extra hand on the ladder, so to speak. Bring you on the payroll as a regular employee, if you're so inclined. I'd consider it an honor to have you on board. You can even bunk at the station. Decent food. Good group of guys. Couple of veterans, but most of them are rookie firefighters. Maybe you could even do some training for them, if you like. What do you say?"

"It's been a while since I've worked structural fires, and I'm not sure I have—"

"Logan, let me level with you." Royce walked closer and lowered his voice. "I got some crazy arsonist, a firebug, out there, and until we stop him I'm going to need every man or woman I can find. I think he's the one who put the Colonel in the hospital. I could really use you here, even if it's only on call. What do you say?"

Logan relented. "Okay. Sure. Count me in. I'll pull a rotation at the fire station for as long as I'm here. I'll check in later once I'm finished here at the hospital."

"Thanks. I appreciate it. You can grab a bunk and locker at the station and start on the rotation Monday. See Margie when you get there. I'll let her know, and she'll have all the paperwork ready. Roll call is at ten."

They shook hands, and Logan entered the quiet hospital room alone. The room with its cold green tile floor and plain white walls seemed so antiseptic. It was quiet and empty with the exception of the lone figure on the bed. It gave Logan the chills to see the Colonel that way—quiet, motionless.

"Hey, old man. It's me, Logan," he joked, walking closer.

The Colonel did not move, and his eyes remained shut.

Logan reached for his hand. He could feel the rough, worn calluses on his palm and suddenly whispered aloud, "I came back for a visit. Just to see you. Okay?" He sat beside the Colonel, watching his chest heave high, then low, then back again. The room was filled with the sound of the continuous monitors, IV poles, and oxygen machines running in the background. He stayed with him, hoping in some way he could help. The old man's eyes never flickered.

Logan stood and rejoined Royce in the hallway. "I see what you mean. What happened?"

"He responded to a fire with just one other firefighter, and his oxygen tank malfunctioned. He tried to make it back outside but got hit with some falling debris, tripped, and fell. Hit his back, got hurt pretty bad. There was no one there to help him. The other firefighter finally got the computerized *down alert* signal from his equipment and rushed in to help him out. But as you saw, he's not doing well."

"Damn fool for going in shorthanded like that," Logan muttered.

"Yeah, but what would you've done? Same as me—you'd go in," said Royce. "By the way, you got a place to stay tonight?"

"Well, I'm not really sure. I guess I could bunk at the station house if—"

"Yes, he does, Royce. He's stayin' at home and sleepin' in his own bed, not at some old firehouse," said an authoritative voice. It was Beth. "Is this what it takes to get you to come back home to River Dale?" she asked with a grin.

He smiled. Same old, take-charge Beth. He looked at her; she was beautiful. He could not stop staring.

"You been in to see him?" she finally asked.

He nodded. "Yeah. Royce and I were just talking about it." The three of them stood in silence in the quiet hospital hallway before Royce said his goodbyes and left them standing there . . . alone.

Beth turned and gave Logan a long, friendly hug, kissing him on the cheek to welcome him back. "You've been gone too long, Logan," she whispered. She took in a deep breath and stood back, looking at him. "But still handsome as ever, I see. Welcome home."

"Thanks. Good to be home," he said warmly.

"Regarding where to sleep: you're home now, so why don't you sleep in your own bed?" she asked. "I insist." Then she paused. "I figured you'd be coming home, so I already have fresh sheets out on your bed and clean towels. I bought all kinds of foods, just for you. So it's settled, right?" she said firmly. Then she added with those pleading eyes, "Please?"

He had stayed with the Colonel the last time he was in River Dale, and he did not relish the thought of sleeping full time in the bunk room at the fire station during his visit. He did not mind it so much during his shift rotation, but it would be nice to sleep in his old bed again. "Okay, okay," he spluttered. "I'll stay. It's good to be home."

"Thanks, Logan. I can use the company. It's good to see you. I haven't seen you since . . . Mom's funeral. You were here for a while, and then you were just gone." Her voice trailed off. "We have so much to catch up on, that's all. I understand you may need to sleep at the station for your shift; that's okay, too, but when you're done with your shift, just come home. Have you eaten?"

"Airport food. It was a long flight from California, then a long drive from Boston."

She made an awful face. "Ugh! Meet me at home tonight after you check in at the station. I have to get a bit of work done. After that, I have some steaks in the fridge you can grill up. We'll have some wine and talk . . . just like old times. Okay?"

"Sounds good to me."

She kissed him on the cheek. "That one's from Mom. See ya later."

Logan watched her walk away and heard her humming a Christmas tune. He could not take his eyes off her. *Maybe this wasn't such a good idea after all.* He belonged out there fighting fires, he tried to tell himself. What was he doing here? He walked to the elevator and hit the "Down" button. As the doors closed behind him, the monitor inside the Colonel's room sounded one long, steady beep that brought the nurses running with the cardiac cart swinging wildly behind them.

CHAPTER EIGHT

Logan drove down the river road and pulled into the fire station parking lot. He winced when he saw the empty parking spot marked RESERVED—CHIEF.

As he walked in, the scent of the fire station washed over him; the smell of cleansers and equipment brought back memories. All fire stations he had ever worked in had that same special smell, and this one was no different. A whiff of fresh pine needles also rushed to greet him.

"Merry Christmas, Logan," a chipper voice said from behind the counter. It was Margie.

"Hiya, kiddo," he said, and gave her a big bear hug.

"You saw the chief?" It was a small town, and news traveled fast.

"Yeah."

Her face lost its cheeriness. "He suffered a minor heart attack right after you left."

"What?" he said, visibly shaken at the news. "That can't be, I was just there and—"

"Yeah, I know. He's okay now; they put him on some new heart medication."

"A heart attack? I can't believe it. Not the Colonel."

"Yes," she said, lowering her voice. "And it's not his first heart attack. But he's been doing really good, up until now."

"I didn't know."

"He didn't really like to talk about it much. You know the Colonel. He's fine now." Then she paused before changing the subject. "Anyway, it's good to see you. Welcome home, Logan. I got you all set up with a bunk, gear, and locker upstairs. Bunk number seven."

"Thanks, Marge. I'm just going to drop off some stuff in the bunk room and say hi to whoever's up there."

"Sure. See you on the way out."

He walked past the equipment that lined the wall and saw that she already had his boots and bunker gear on the rack with his name above it.

Logan walked down the long hallway past the rec room filled with overstuffed leather chairs and a big-screen television on the one side. Two long, rectangular dining tables sat across from a stove and refrigerator on the other side. He looked inside—the room was empty. So was the weight room.

At the end of the hallway, there was a bathroom with a shower on one side and a room with bunk beds on the other. He introduced himself to the guys on duty and made his way to his bunk.

"You must be Logan," said a young man as he opened his locker. "I'm Johnny Ray Mason. Marge has you bunkin' next to me. Welcome to RFD 17."

"Thanks. Good to meet you." They shook hands as Logan stashed some of the gear he would need for his rotation.

"You're on the rotation startin' tomorrow, right?" asked Johnny.

"Yep. What's the schedule?"

"The usual. One day on, two days off." He looked barely old enough to shave, but he had the familiar tattoo of a parachute on his arm.

"Airborne?"

"You bet. Me and Yancy—he's off duty now—were both in the 101st Airborne—Iraq. Loved it. You?"

"Ranger, Seventy-Fifth—then airborne training at Fort Benning, Georgia. I got out a while back, and I've been a smoke jumper out west for the last couple of years."

"I heard. That's cool." The young firefighter looked at his new bunk mate with respect. "You bunkin' here tonight?" he asked as he plopped down on his own bunk adjacent to Logan's.

"No, I'm stayin' in town when I'm off duty. I used to live here in River Dale and—"

A deep baritone voice bellowed behind him, "Welcome, Logan. Been waitin' for you to show up. I'm Fletch Morgan. Colonel's told us beaucoup stories about you, and I wanted to see if any of it was true." They shook hands, and Logan could feel the strength in Fletch's hand. He could tell from the calluses in the big man's hand he had never worked a desk job. He was a muscular man with a thick blond-and-reddish mustache, carefully curled at the ends. Logan liked him immediately.

"I'll see ya tomorrow, Logan," said Johnny Ray as he headed for the rec room.

"Hey, JR, stick around," Fletch said. "You don't have to leave on my account."

"Gotta go. Remember, I'm the new guy in town. Time to cook dinner. Maybe we'll even be able to eat some tonight while it's still hot. See ya later."

Fletch chuckled as he plopped down on the bunk next to Logan's. "Good kid. You wouldn't know it from lookin' at him, but he's tough as nails." Fletch watched JR leave.

"Fletch, were you Airborne like Johnny Ray?" asked Logan as he stowed his gear in his locker.

"No, marines. *Semper Fi.* Recon. Still miss it, though. Got out for a couple of years, then tried to reenlist; they said I was too old . . . You know how that goes."

Logan was impressed with the men he had met. Solid citizens with military backgrounds—the best that America had to offer.

"You been out west I hear . . . smoke jumper?" asked Fletch.

"Yeah."

"We could've used some smoke jumpers here this past summer," he said.

"What do you mean?"

"Big fires in the national forests—White Mountain and Green Mountain. Lost a lotta acreage. Smoke jumpers need a bigger presence back east."

"Didn't really have time to notice what was going on here in New Hampshire," Logan said as he unpacked his gear. "It's so busy out west. But you're right. I never thought about it that way."

"We got a lot of forestland right here in New England. The West gets the big fires and all the press attention, but every year it gets worse here. Old forests, lots of dry shrub, and no forest management. We get bigger and bigger fires every year, especially here in New Hampshire and Maine. There's a lot of dry brush and timber that needs to be cleared out. We're two thousand miles away from the nearest smoke jumper location. It all comes down to money. We need to have our own fire-fighting operation right here in New England."

He then leaned in and said, "And around River Dale it's getting even worse. The city, the county, and the state have been cutting our budgets for everything from training and trucks to communications gear, bunker gear, and oxygen equipment. You name it. The air pack the Colonel was using in that fire was over twelve years old but has a life span of no more than ten years. That's why it went bad, and that's the reason he's in the hospital. Most of the new stuff you see around here he bought with his own money. But the air packs are expensive—a grand or two a pop." He shook his head. "Our staffing is down twenty percent. We're short six firefighters. Chief Devlin made a presentation to the county council to have four- or five-man crews on every call.

Safer that way, but more costly." He stopped and looked around. "They turned him down."

Logan grunted. "Yeah, man, everybody knows you gotta be crazy to run into a burnin' building when everyone else is running the other way, but that doesn't mean we're stupid." He glanced at his watch. "Gotta go."

"Date?"

"Nah. Going to grill up some steaks. Stayin' with an old friend . . . Beth Harding."

"Wheee. Doc Harding? What a babe. How do you know her?"

"She's an old friend. I lived next door to her growing up, and when my parents died . . . well . . . her folks kind of adopted me. Nothing official. Just moved into the apartment over their garage one day, and I've been part of the family ever since."

"Man, no disrespect or anything—but she is one awesome honey. Whew!" He paused for a minute before asking, "Are you . . . and her . . . you know?"

He grinned. "No, man. Just close friends. Best friends."

"Sure," Fletch said in disbelief.

"Really. I promised her I'd grill up some steaks tonight and then catch up on old times."

"I heard she has one hot temper. Hot temper for a hot babe," he said with a chuckle.

"Really? Never saw that side of her."

"This summer I heard she made a presentation to the city and county councils for more emergency room medications. The hospital has had a chronic shortage of antibiotics, pain relievers, and sedatives. She wanted to go outside of the usual suppliers to get what they needed from a place in Boston at a higher price. They turned her down flat, and I understand it got pretty heated in the meeting."

"Yeah. When she's fighting for something she really believes in, you don't want to be standing in her way." Changing the subject, Logan asked, "You on call today?"

"Nope, I'm here tomorrow with you. By the way, even though you're the new guy here, Royce appointed you as acting team chief as long as you're here."

Logan shook his head. "No, man. I'm not the senior guy here; besides, all you guys have been around much longer than—"

"Man, after everything the Colonel told us about you, we feel we already know you. So, today we took a vote of the guys here, and it was unanimous . . . Chief."

"What does the union say about all this? I don't want to bust into anybody's party, if you know what I mean."

"Union's fine with it," said a voice behind him. "And so is Mayor Wilson, especially since it was his suggestion."

An older man with salt-and-pepper hair approached him with an outstretched hand. "Hi, I'm Carl. On-duty station manager and part-time union rep here at RFD 17."

"Good to meet you, Carl."

"Heard you talk about being acting chief. I think the consensus was that maybe if you worked the job again, perhaps you'd stick around for a while. So they put you officially on the payroll as a temporary employee. If you like it, we'd love to have you . . . permanently," Carl said with a grin. "We really need the staff. And the Colonel said you worked as chief once before in Arizona. So it's settled."

"Well, I don't know about that. I been jumpin' out of planes fightin' fires for so long, it may take some getting used to fightin' a fire from a truck again. You know what I mean?"

"I know, but both jobs are important, my friend. Either way, it's good to finally meet you. Welcome aboard."

"Same."

"Oh, you're my relief tomorrow, so don't be late. I gotta take my wife and kids Christmas shopping at the mall in Winston."

"I'll be here. I'll come in early if that helps, but in plenty of time for roll call."

"Great. See ya tomorrow. Good to meet you, Logan."

Logan headed for his rental car and started the drive toward home. It sounded funny to him—*home*. He had lived all over the world, but he always thought of the house on Riverside Drive as *home*. He turned up the familiar street and pulled into the driveway. He sat in the car and looked at his old homestead on the left and the Harding house on the right; he loved them both but now considered the Harding house his home.

He gazed at the house while the windshield wipers intermittently pushed away the falling snowflakes. The house looked the same. The same two-story stone exterior, the now snow-covered hedges around the front walkway. The wide front porch with the swing hanging from the ceiling, swaying gently in the winter breeze. Just as he remembered it. Home.

He remembered when he had first come to live here with Harding family. His folks had accidentally left the car running in the attached garage at the cabin by the lake. His mom and dad were asleep in the next room and died from the carbon monoxide buildup.

The Hardings took him in as one of their own, and over the years they raised him, clothed him, fed him, nurtured him, and sent him off to college. Doc Sarah was a nationally recognized physician and hospital administrator who had come home to River Dale. Frank was a highly respected retired county circuit judge. Everybody affectionately referred to him simply as "the Judge." Logan loved them as he had his own parents.

In May, Logan had come home for Sarah's funeral and comforted Beth throughout the entire ordeal. While he was there, they had grown close, and as time went on they had grown closer than ever before. *Maybe too close,* he thought.

At the time, he had realized his feelings toward her were changing but could never tell her how he felt. What had once felt natural and everyday to him—holding her hand, a gentle hug, a kiss on the cheek—took on added, complex feelings. She was his best friend, and she never knew. After a few weeks, he had left to return to California. Since then, he had not been able to get her out of his mind. He would be driving to work, fighting a fire, shaving, and from nowhere she would appear with her smile, her laugh, her hello. He took in a deep breath. *Tell her, Logan. You gotta tell her how you feel. Your feelings have changed, and she needs to know that . . .*

He saw her car pull into the driveway next to his. She turned and saw him, then smiled and waved as she got out of the car. "Hiya," she said with a grin, holding up a bottle of wine.

"Hiya, Doc," he said with a laugh.

He watched her walk in the snow in front of his car, her long brown hair gently swaying behind her. After combing his hair with his fingers and tucking in his shirt, he opened the car door.

Maybe this wasn't such a good idea after all, he thought to himself as he swallowed hard. *Let's go.*

She hugged him tight and close. "Come on, let's get you situated," she said with smile, reaching for his hand.

He grabbed his duffel bag and followed her up the steps to his old room above the garage. It still looked exactly the same. The pictures on the wall of the family, his baseball bat and glove, his broken hockey stick, his football from Dartmouth. So many memories. Then he turned and saw her standing there behind him.

"I didn't change a thing," she whispered. "It's just how you left it. I was hoping you would have stayed longer after Mom's funeral, but . . . I understand . . ." Her voice trailed away.

Logan did not know what to say. He was shy around her, and he could never explain it to anyone, not even himself. He had been a leader in college, in the army, and with the smoke jumpers, but with her . . .

They were the best of friends. Friends. Yes, old friends. That was what she had told all her classmates at college when he had gone to visit her one weekend at school in Boston. Just friends, that was all. She had no idea how much he . . . His mind drifted.

He smelled her perfume. It smelled so good. Her hand lingered in his hair as she brushed it away from his forehead. He wished she would not do that. At over six feet, he stood taller than her, but with just the flick of her hand through his hair he was reduced to a bumbling idiot.

Steady, boy. You're just here for a couple of days. Remember, this is Beth. Your old friend.

She looked up at him and said, "You unpack, and I'll get the steaks from the fridge and open some wine. Later you can throw some logs on the fireplace. Then we can talk. So don't be long."

Good old Beth, he thought to himself. Always the take-charge type.

She kissed him on the forehead and said, "Welcome home, Logan. This is going to be great. I can use some cheering up. You're the one bright spot in my day today. I've missed you—missed having you around to talk to."

"Me, too, but I have to be at the station house early tomorrow, so I'll have to make it an early night. Or else I'll fall asleep on you. And I don't want to do that."

She turned to him with a twinkle in her eye. "You're not getting off that easy, my friend. We have a lot of catching up to do. I've missed you."

He smiled and watched her walk away. He had missed her, too.

CHAPTER NINE

The old woman in the bright-green coat and festive red hat hobbled slowly through town, admiring the many Christmas decorations that the cheerful little hamlet of River Dale had to offer. Her bad hip was bothering her again, causing her to walk slower to maintain her balance.

Oversize pine wreaths with immense red-and-green plaid ribbons and bows adorned the streetlights and were now covered with a dusting of gently fallen snow. Every business along Main Street in the small town sported long, fresh pine garlands around their doors and twinkling candles in the windows, all trying to outdo one another. Wreaths of fresh-cut holly were everywhere.

In the center of the square, she stopped to admire the full-size nativity scene, complete with the three wise men. A plastic star shone bright above the manger. As was her custom, she said her silent prayer and wished for a better tomorrow after depositing her donation into the nearby red kettle.

"Ho ho ho. Thank you, ma'am," said the cheery man dressed in a red-and-white Santa outfit as he rang his bell. She loved this little town and its quaint, old-fashioned ways.

"You're quite welcome, young man." *He appears to be the same man from last year,* she thought to herself.

The old woman smiled as she watched young families roasting marshmallows over the bonfire on the town square and singing Christmas songs.

She sniffed the air and followed the scent toward the middle of town and the bakery. Elsie Schmidt's German-style bakery was filled with holiday customers picking up their orders of Christmas sugar cookies, shortbreads, fruitcakes, pies, and pink-powdered *Springerle* cookies with pink, red, and green sparkles on top. Bright-red poinsettias lined the wall from the front door to the glass case displaying all the freshly baked goods. The tables at the rear each had a decoration in the center. A noisy, whirling fan above the entrance door gently broadcasted the baker's sweet, enticing smells out onto the street, inviting even more customers inside in search of holiday goodies.

"Can I help you, ma'am?" asked the young girl behind the counter. She had a pleasant, smiling face and wore a sprig of mistletoe pinned to her white uniform. She was no more than fourteen and looked very much like Elsie, her mother, who stood watch behind her. The tag she wore proclaimed her name as Ansa. She had the same round face and fresh, puffy cheeks as her mother. Her long blonde hair was tightly braided and neatly wrapped and tucked on top of her head under a hairnet.

"Yes," said the old woman. "I would like to place an order. First of all, to eat here, I would like two *Springerle* anise cookies and a cup of cocoa. Put in a few of those small marshmallows and some maple sugar, please. Then to take home with me, I also want another order of twelve cookies. And put those in a small bag, please."

"*Ja, ja,* I give you thirteen, a baker's dozen, ya know," the young girl said in a singsong German fashion.

One by one, the old woman pointed to the cookies she wanted. She would take those home with her and save them for later. When she was finished, she smiled to herself, enjoying the moment as she sat at a table near the rear of the busy shop. She enjoyed watching the steady stream of customers coming and going as she finished her cookies and cocoa. *Wonderful,* she thought. *The cinnamon-sugary aroma rising in this small German bakery is heavenly.*

She loved this time of year, and she loved her annual Christmas visits to River Dale. It was such a quaint village and reminded her so much of her childhood home in the old country. Her family's longtime chef and other household staff would bake Christmas specialties all weekend just for her. Even the chauffeur would pitch in from time to time and help with the baking. She treasured those memories of home.

When she was finished eating her cookies, she cleaned her table, pushed the chair in, and waved goodbye to the young girl who had waited on her. Ansa and Elsie waved and smiled in response.

Outside, the fresh snowfall and the ringing bells from the members of the Salvation Army only added to the holiday feel. As the sun set, ice began to form on some of the steps and sidewalks.

The old woman loved this time of year, and she tightly clutched the small bag of tasty white *Pfeffernüsse* cookies and other assorted delights she had just purchased. She could hardly wait until tomorrow; her mouth was already savoring the sweet taste of the German delicacies. She would have them for breakfast, she promised herself. She laughed. *Yes, if they last that long.*

The sound of Christmas songs drifted in the air from the carolers singing in the town square. It was getting colder, so she pulled her long, frayed silk scarf tighter around her neck to stop the draft of cold air, which was stinging her skin.

She prized her once-a-year visits to the small little town by the river to relive her childhood Christmas days. She was smiling, lost in thought. She had just stepped off the curb when a pickup truck roared by. She gasped, then moved backward to let the truck pass. Suddenly she felt the ground beneath her begin to give way as her shoe stuck in the grate. She searched frantically for support, grasping in the air, but found none as she slipped on the icy street and fell, striking her head on the curb. In the turmoil, her purse slid from her arm and disappeared down the drain. Her handbag was gone and unnoticed as a concerned crowd drew close to help her.

"Ma'am, ma'am, are you okay? Somebody call 911, she's unconscious," a voice said urgently around her. Her head was spinning out of control.

The paramedics arrived in minutes, examined her, and then gently lifted her onto a stretcher. Soon the sound of the rescue vehicle rang throughout the village, hurrying on its way to the hospital with its newest patient.

CHAPTER TEN

Logan fired up the gas grill on the deck outside the kitchen and soon had the steaks sizzling. The smoke rose high overhead and disappeared into the white-gray sky above. The aroma was wonderful, as he had rubbed a mixture of seasonings on them: garlic salt, smoked Worcestershire pepper, Italian seasoning, and some oregano. He had also found an almost-empty bottle of bourbon and some brown sugar in the kitchen and mixed them together to form a paste, then gently rubbed it all over the steak.

Steaks at Christmastime . . . on a grill . . . in the snow . . . That just seemed so perfect. Standing there in the cold, he looked at his old family homestead next door with fond memories. His childhood home. Suddenly, he ached for his mom and dad. His memory of his parents was fading. He could still remember them, but each year their faces dimmed more and more.

Maybe it was the season—Christmas had been his mom's favorite time of year. Maybe it was the rush of feelings he had being back home in River Dale. He did not know why; all he knew was that he missed them even more at this time of year. Doc Sarah must have known that, because she had always spent more time with him around the holidays. "Merry Christmas, Doc," he said in a whisper as the snow began to fall again.

Life is simpler in California, he thought; just yesterday his life was fighting back the roaring flames of a massive forest fire. Now today, here at home, he was fighting back memories.

He flipped the steaks, closed the lid, and looked out over the back-yard, where he saw row upon row of snow-covered rosebushes. Sarah's roses, that was what he always called them. Sarah's red roses. Grand prize winners year after year at the county fair. How she loved her roses. Big ones, small ones, yellow ones, red ones, pink ones—all the colors. He did not know the names of them like Sarah and Beth did. All he knew was that Doc Sarah loved her roses—or any kind of flower, for that matter. She also loved her forsythias in the spring, her tulips in April, her peonies in May, her lilacs and her dogwoods, and her mums in the fall. But he knew it was the roses that she held dearest to her heart.

The door to the kitchen swung open wide, and Beth stood there waiting on the porch, barefoot and wearing jeans and a baggy sweat-shirt. She wrapped her arms tightly around her, trying to stay warm. "Salad's done and on the table. Wine's poured. Hope you like it. I don't drink a lot of wine, but the clerk at the store said it was very good. Now I'm just waiting on the steaks . . . slowpoke."

"Few minutes," he said with a frozen grin. "Be right in."

"Okay. Don't be long." Just before she closed the door, she glanced outside to the rose garden. She sighed but said nothing, closing the door slowly behind her.

Five minutes later, the steaks were done, and so was he. It was cold outside.

"I'm ready!" he shouted as he plated the steaks and went inside.

She had the table set, and everything was in its place. He set the steaks on the table and took in a deep whiff. *Yes! Steaks in the winter, the absolute best.*

"The rest of dinner will be done in just a few minutes. Have some wine," she called.

"Thought you were done?" he shouted from the other room.

"Always remember, perfection takes time," she said with a laugh. "Asparagus with slivered nuts. Garlic smashed potatoes with olive oil and bacon. You'll love it."

Logan was so hungry he could eat them raw. But he would wait.

He took his glass of wine and ambled around the living room. The Christmas tree was in the corner; five stockings were hung in front of the fireplace, as usual. Logan looked around and saw Beth had wrapped the long staircase with fresh garland; he breathed in deep. He smiled, thinking some things never changed—and Beth was one of those things. The smell of the pine needles took him back in time.

"Soup's on," she hollered from the other room, setting down the veggies and smashed potatoes on the table.

He poured more wine and sat down.

"Great steaks," she said, holding up a piece on the tip of her fork. He was amazed at her transformation. One minute she looked the part of a highly paid hospital chief executive; the next moment she was a tomboy wearing an old college sweatshirt and jeans with her hair pulled back, held tight with an oversize brown hair clip.

"Yes, indeed."

She raised her glass and toasted. "Welcome home, Logan. So good to see you again."

"You, too," he seconded as their glasses clinked together. It was then he noticed it . . . third finger of her left hand . . . a ring. An engagement ring. *Engaged?*

"Is that new?" he asked about the ring on her finger.

"Yes, I got engaged . . . in Chicago." For some reason, she could not explain why she had never called to tell him. He was her best friend, and she had not called to tell him. It just never felt like the right time. Now she felt ashamed for not saying anything. It had all happened rather quickly.

"His name's Rory Daniels. I met him at a fund-raiser in Chicago. We hit it off and then dated for a little while. He works for a pharmaceutical company there. His company sells to hospitals and government agencies. They offered me a job in their hospital division in Chicago when I finish up here. It seemed like a natural fit."

"You make it sound more like a corporate merger than a love affair if you ask me," he said with a chuckle as he sipped his wine. The words did not sound right, and he regretted saying them as soon as they left his lips. *Damn. Keep your mouth shut if you don't have something nice to say.* "Sorry. I didn't mean it to sound like that," he said apologetically.

"It's okay," she whispered. "I guess I never thought about it that way. But he's nice; you'll like him. I can't wait for you to meet him."

"Great, me, too," he said, trying to make it sound as if he meant it. "Have you set a date yet?"

"No. We're still working on it. It seems every time I bring it up he . . ." She stopped, smiled, and took a drink of wine.

He looked at her and knew something else was wrong.

"What's up, Doc? What's botherin' you?"

"I don't want to bore you with all the details . . . but the board is forcing me to close the hospital."

"What?" He set his fork down on his plate. "That's outrageous. I can't imagine this community without River Dale General."

"Well, the closing starts Christmas. Sad to say, all the patients will be transferred elsewhere. My mother worked hard to build and maintain the reputation of that hospital, and now some pencil-pushing accountant is saying we don't need it. They say that because we have a new hospital forty miles away we don't need this one."

They continued to eat in silence for a while until Logan looked at her. "This hospital closing is hogwash, and you know it," he said in disgust as he reached for the bottle of red wine, refilling both of their glasses. Then he said in a serious tone, "Beth, I work as a firefighter, and time is everything, just as it is in your business. Minutes count. Minutes save lives." He shook his head. "I don't understand people sometimes."

"Me, neither, but what can I do? My assistant, Drake Corrigan, and I worked for weeks on a presentation to save it. We had a special plan that documented what we had accomplished in our intensive care unit, and they wouldn't even read the plan we put together."

She talked for a while, and he listened, taking it all in, trying to help her strategize another plan to save the hospital.

When they were finished eating, he stood and began stacking the plates to carry them into the kitchen.

"We have tried just about everything," she finally said, sounding defeated as she leaned back in her chair.

Logan stopped and nearly dropped the plates he was holding.

"Beth, what would Doc Sarah do? Show them. That's what the Beth I know would do. Don't take it lying down. Fight fire with fire."

"That's a lot of clichés, my old friend. Easy for you to say."

"Show the board how it would impact them if they didn't have the hospital around to service the community."

"You're right! That's exactly what Mom would do." She smiled, stood, and took the plates from his hands. "You start the fire in the fireplace, and I'll take care of the dishes."

"Sounds like a good deal to me."

He put some large and small twigs on the bottom of the grate for kindling, two small old logs on top, and wadded up newspaper under the logs; then he lit a match. The yellow-and-blue flames began to rise and grow. Soon there was a roaring fire. The soft poplar made an occasional popping noise, spitting burning embers against the black chain mesh curtain covering the opening. He asked aloud, "How's Claire?"

Logan heard the water running as Beth cleaned the plates in the sink. "She's good, I guess. I was hoping she was coming home for Christmas, but apparently she has a new boyfriend in Boston and she's going to stay there for the holidays. But I guess . . ." She stopped when she saw him standing in the doorway.

He heard the hurt in her voice and walked to her. "Let it go, Beth," he said softly, trying to console her. "Life changes." He turned to leave, then stopped and said, "Hey, what about me? I'm here aren't I?" He faked sounding hurt.

She quickly moved in front of him, smiling. She wrapped the dish towel around his neck, pulling him close, then closer. "You will always be my very best friend, and that will never change," she said with a laugh. Then she did what felt natural; she kissed him. Her lips missed their target and landed on his lips. At that moment, something happened. Something changed. Something . . . They both stood in awkward silence, looking at each other.

Stepping back, she coughed, saying, "I think that as the fireman in the family you need to check on the fireplace. I'll be right in. Just let me finish up in here."

When she was done, she joined him. Just as when they were kids, they sat cross-legged next to each other on the old sofa in front of the fireplace, feeling the growing warmth from the glow of the embers. Watching the roaring blue-green flames from the burning waxed pinecones, they heard the embers pop against the metal mesh screen in front of the fireplace and saw them fall to the red brick inside.

"Brings back memories," they both said at the same time, then laughed. They were so much alike, finishing each other's sentences like an old married couple.

"I can't tell you how good it is to have you home," she said, leaning her head on the sofa. "It hasn't been the same. First Dad, then Mom, gone from my life. Then you. Then Claire moved to Boston."

"I'm only a phone call away," he said with a hearty laugh.

"I know that," she said, holding tight to his hand. "It's just not the same." She did not know if it was the wine or the fire or the wonderful evening with her best friend, but she was feeling . . . different. Happy.

She giggled. "If I tell you something . . . you promise you won't get a big head?"

"I promise."

"Or laugh?"

"Promise."

She sat up and looked at him tentatively. "When you and your family first moved in next door, I had the biggest crush on you. I thought you looked like a Hollywood movie star. I would look out my window and secretly watch you work in the yard, mowing the lawn with your shirt off and stacking the firewood by the side of the house."

"Really?" he said, surprised. He looked at her. "From the bedroom window upstairs? The corner window?"

She threw a pillow at him. "You knew I was watching you all along, didn't you? Logan Mitchell! Oomph!"

"Yes? And?"

"Well . . . then you moved into the apartment over the garage out back. And you became part of the family . . . my brother, so to speak," she said, and leaned in closer to him with her hand touching his shoulder. Resting there.

He resisted the urge to reach for it, to hold it. *What is going on?* he thought to himself. *Watch it. She's not only engaged but also your best friend. She's a friend you never want to lose. Or hurt. So cool it. What do I do?*

She inched closer and in a soft whisper said, "Logan, did I ever tell you that I have always wanted to—"

The phone rang on the table behind them, bringing them both back to reality.

Out of breath and with her head spinning, Beth stood, then waited for a moment before she answered the ringing phone. "Hello?"

"Dr. Harding? Beth? Hi, it's Drake. Sorry to bother you but . . . we have a problem."

"What's wrong?"

"Well, we just got a fire rescue call," Drake continued. "It must be a new ambulance team because they ignored the no-admittance directive we sent them and want to bring her here since it's closer, and they're on their way to us. What do you want me to do?"

She held the phone in her hand, gripping it tighter and thinking back to her conversation with Logan. Then she took in a deep breath. "Admit her," she said without hesitation, "and any others until you hear further from me. If anybody has a problem with that, have them talk to me."

She looked at Logan still sitting on the sofa. He gave her a thumbs-up and his movie star smile.

Drake breathed a sigh of relief that was obvious even over the phone line. "Good. That's what I told them to do."

"Admit all those we would normally admit. This nonsense stops now. I'll take the heat from Sidney. Thanks for calling, Drake."

"That's good, because I just got an alert from admissions, and we have more on the way. And the ER is full of flu victims."

"All hands on deck again tomorrow," she told him. "Including the desk supervisors. Let them see how it is to really work in a hospital. We just have to tell them to keep out of the way of the staff. See you tomorrow. Good night."

"Good night, Dr. Harding."

She looked at her watch. It was getting late, and he was still working. He was a good worker. Maybe between the two of them they could do something to save the hospital. After hanging up the phone, she smiled. Then she remembered Logan.

When she turned around, she saw he was curled up on the sofa in front of the fire, sound asleep. She covered him with a blanket, closed off the fireplace, and turned out the lights. She stopped on the steps leading upstairs to her bedroom and, standing in the dark watching him, she whispered, "Welcome home, Logan."

CHAPTER ELEVEN

"Jingle bells, jingle bells, jingle all the way," the little girl sang out from the backseat. "Come on, Mommy, Daddy. You know the words. Can't we sing it together?"

The man looked at his wife sitting next to him. The snow and the cold made it feel like Christmas, but singing those songs just brought back sad memories. He looked at her, sitting there unconsciously rubbing her stomach in large, gentle circles. The look in her eyes told him everything. He did not want to leave, but he had to. It was the only way. He had to find him and bring him home.

He shook his head, saying sadly, "I have to go. I must find him and bring him back. He doesn't know." He looked at his wife, then smiled. "I want him home for his twenty-fifth birthday next month."

The little girl began to sing again in the backseat.

His wife smiled, joining in. "Jingle bells, jingle bells . . ."

He finally gave in. "Jingle all the way. Oh what fun it is . . ."

The little girl saw them look at each other, and then she smiled. That was a good sign. "What time is the Christmas hayride, Mom?"

"It starts at seven, Lisa."

"Great! I can't wait. Jingle bells, jingle bells," she began again. "I want to come sit up front with you two. I want to be up front where the grown-ups sit," said the little ten-year-old girl, unbuckling herself from her safety belt.

"No," said her father. "Lisa, stay back there. Sit down," he said, turning around to caution her. "Lisa! Don't come up here. Stay. Put your seat belt back on! No!"

He did not see the deer on the road until it was too late. He swerved to miss it, and the car slid sideways on the snow-covered road, crashing through the guardrail and sailing over the icy riverbank. It flipped over into the swollen waters of the swiftly moving Baker River. The car floated upside down and drifted quickly with the current, drowning out the screams. Within minutes, it began to sink beneath the surface. It was soon out of sight.

CHAPTER TWELVE

Two hours after hanging up the phone with his boss, Drake Corrigan was finally finished for the day. He grabbed his coat, slid on an old pair of shoes he called his "snowshoes," and drove his old snow-covered SUV to the apartment building he had been staying at since his arrival in River Dale. He was glad his workday was over. *Good to be home,* he thought as he skipped up the steps to his second-floor apartment. Taking long strides, he carefully balanced his Chinese take-out dinner in one hand and his bulging briefcase in the other.

It had not been a good day for him . . . or his special project. It was another day filled with disappointment, one of many. How was he going to make his copper project a success? How was he going to convince the board of its merits? He had come all the way from England to work with Doc Sarah, and together they had made great strides. With her reputation and what they had achieved, he had thought their success was assured. They were so close to making history, and now she was gone—and with her, any hopes of his project succeeding. He missed her enthusiasm, her sense of humor, and her support. Beth was a good substitute, but it was not the same.

Drake slipped off his overcoat, suit jacket, shoes, and socks. After undoing his tie, he emptied the contents of the take-out box into a bowl and placed it in the microwave. He thought about opening a beer but decided instead to first have some of the spiced eggnog left over from the recent office party.

His small two-bedroom apartment was sparsely furnished with only a sofa, a dining table with two chairs, and a dresser and bed for each bedroom. Inside one room, his clothes closet was nearly empty, filled only with three suits, one sport coat, and two pairs of shoes that lay on the floor. However, the apartment was full of medical research books. Lots of books. Books on the table, on the floor, in the hallway, in the kitchen, books everywhere—even in the bathroom. His favorite book was the thick black-and-gold reference book titled *The Epidemiology of Hospital-Borne Infections,* by Dr. Drake Corrigan, third edition.

While waiting for his dinner to reheat, he tasted the spiked eggnog. The sweetness, mixed with the dark rum, quenched his thirst, but after the day he had experienced, he wanted something stronger. Much stronger. He reached for the bottle of Jameson Irish Whiskey underneath the kitchen sink and poured a healthy portion into the tall glass of eggnog. *Ah, that's more like it,* he thought to himself.

He sat on the floor in front of the television, leaning against the sofa as he ate his dinner and drank his eggnog. *Delicious.* He ate Chinese food from nearby Wong Song's Restaurant nearly every night. He watched a late-night talk show without the sound and laughed at how funny it seemed.

Drake glanced at the growing pile of employment offer letters on the table. Soon he would have to make a choice. The most interesting ones he put at the top of the pile—beginning with the one from The Royal London Hospital. He reached for it again and reread it.

> Dear Dr. Corrigan:
> We are pleased to extend to you an offer of employment to head our research facility of infectious diseases. The Royal London Hospital is world renowned in its research and applied sciences . . .

The letter droned on. It would take him home again, back to his own safe environment—research. He took another sip of his eggnog. Then he added more whiskey. Another offer letter was from the Isle of Man Research Institute. *Interesting.* A third was from the Madame Curie Foundation in Paris, the premier research institute for infectious diseases. The money they offered was not only flattering but also almost unbelievable. Beth had given him a glowing recommendation.

As his nimble fingers worked the chopsticks, moving the pork fried rice from his bowl to his mouth, his eyes kept returning to the blue presentation folder he had made that day and to the black one he had made earlier that summer for the state hospital board.

It was good report, a very good report. Even though she let him do his thing, Doc Harding suggested it might have been too technical, but he knew better. Drake finished the glass of eggnog and poured yet another. *Pretty good stuff,* he thought, adding even more Jameson.

He balanced the bowl of Chinese food on his knees as he read the report.

"*. . . the research and analysis of all particular operations both inborne and sub-borne of all HAI should be carefully ascertained by identifying risks inherent in targets for preventive health care . . .*"

Hmmm, he thought to himself.

He read on. "*. . . with the collection and study of all data received from operational and preventive designs and with the dissemination of all facts and data interpretation the study analysis should carefully require . . .*"

"Yes, this was perfect," he said aloud. Then he stopped. *Who could not understand this?* He thought, *Where are the numbers I remember adding? The analysis? The structure?*

He slowly read more. "*. . . the use of this methodology contained in units for research and in hospital settings cannot be overstated and the outstanding issues confronted in the day to day operations of all normalistic . . .*"

Oh no! No wonder he was not getting through to the state or local hospital boards. As he read further he finally had to admit Beth was right—the report was too technical. Both Doc Sarah and Beth had supported him all the way, but he had let them down. He had not made a strong enough case to the state board in Concord.

The only thing they understood was numbers. Money. Savings. That was what they all wanted. One percent readmission rate—that was all they needed to know. One percent and how they got to that magic number. It was also people's lives. Bureaucrats. They spent all their time in their ivory towers and never ventured out into the real world. He finished yet another glass of eggnog and picked up the report but could read no further.

What he had thought at the time was a clear and concise report now looked like a medical dictionary. No wonder they had made so little progress with the state. He continued to thumb through the report, slowly shaking his head with every passing page. *They have to see it for themselves to make an informed decision,* he thought as he tilted his glass and finished the last of the eggnog. *Bottoms up!*

A white business card fell from the report onto the carpet. He reached for it, reading, trying to focus. The card read, AMANDA PELLETIER—DIRECTOR—STATE HOSPITAL OVERSIGHT BOARD. She was one of the few who had seemed sympathetic at the meeting.

She should come down here and see for herself—see the real world. Yes, that's what she should do. Maybe she's just waiting for a personal invitation? He reached for his cell phone and dialed the personal office number listed on her card. He heard her voice—office voice mail. "Hello, this is Amanda Pelletier, director of the Hospital Oversight Board. I am away from my desk at the moment, but if you leave your name, number, and a brief message, I will be happy to get back to you as soon as I can."

He glanced at his watch and the empty glass of eggnog, then took in a deep breath. "Ms. Pelletier, hi, this is Dr. Corrigan from River Dale General Hospital. Dr. Harding and myself made a presentation this past summer there at the state capital, but we never heard any response back from you or anyone else on the board."

He paused. *Tell her what you want. Don't pussyfoot around, Drake.*

"Perhaps you would like to leave your ivory tower in Concord and come see the real world here in River Dale. See what we're doing here. I think you'd be amazed. And our numbers? One percent! Yes, that's our number here, a one percent readmission rate, and I would have to say it's the best in the state if not the country. Come here and see for yourself. You have an open invitation to visit us. Thank you. Looking forward to hearing back from you. Merry Christmas. Goodbye."

He finished his call wearing a huge self-satisfied grin, but then a state of fear gripped him and his eyes widened. "Oh my God! What have I done? What was I thinking? Oh no! What's Beth going to think? No. I can't believe I did that!"

CHAPTER THIRTEEN

"Hey, you!" the officer shouted, his loud voice piercing the darkness as his flashlight homed in on the lone figure asleep on the floor of the empty house. "This is the Glen View police! What the hell are you doing here? This is private property. Just because the owners are wintering in Florida doesn't give you the right to come in here and sleep. That's trespassing."

At the sound of the officer's voice, the young man awoke with a start from a deep, alcohol-induced stupor. He tried to clear his head. The figure in ragged clothes moved as the police officer and his flashlight came closer.

"Sorry, Officer," came the groggy reply. "I was just leavin'."

"You betcha you're leaving. And none too soon. You're going to jail. You just hold up there." The intense beacon from the flashlight moved from left to right as the officer came closer. His gun remained in his holster, but his hand was at the ready by his side. The red-and-blue flashing lights from his police cruiser bounced off the walls, the ceiling, and the white sheets, which covered the furniture in the bedroom.

"Stay right where you are! Don't move," ordered the officer, walking closer as he called for backup on his two-way radio. "Backup needed at 62 Elm Lake Road—West Glen View. Have a trespasser here. Code ten."

His foot kicked a half-eaten can of food across the floor, where it rolled away under the bed.

"What's your name?" he asked, still walking toward him.

"Stephen."

"Stephen? Stephen what? Hey, wait," he said, shining the light on his face. "I know you. You're that Collins kid, right? The country singer? Yeah."

Twenty-four years old and they still call me a kid, he thought to himself, still trying to clear his head and wake up. Must be the small frame or the baby face.

The officer moved closer to grab him but lost his footing as he slipped on a pool of spilled liquor on the hardwood floor and fell. The only light in the room came tumbling to the ground and crashed onto the old hardwood floor, spinning around in a circle. It made surreal shadows on the paneled walls of the vacant master bedroom.

Stephen saw his chance. With one leap, he was up and running. He sprinted for the door.

The officer yelled at him as he ran. "Stop!" he commanded.

Stephen ran down the stairs to the first floor, jumping three steps at a time, then out the back door, nearly slipping on the sidewalk coated with a light layer of snow. He ran as fast as he could, almost falling into the pool—empty but for a shallow layer of leaves and snow—at the back of the old mansion. He ran past the police car in the driveway, the large emblem on the door nearly hidden by the freshly fallen snow. The squawk box inside belched with voices responding to the officer's call for backup. He ran to the street and did not look back. He kept running. And running. Still trying to clear his head, he put more distance between him and the police.

At a stoplight on the main road, he saw his chance. A truck loaded with Christmas trees had stopped for the traffic light. He quickly hoisted himself up onto the rear of the truck and hid among the piles of freshly cut pines. He shivered in the cold as another police car quickly sped by, lights flashing and siren blaring. He lay there, safe only for the moment. The old truck lurched forward and rumbled across the railroad tracks before turning right onto the river road, driving over the old wooden bridge. He could feel the bump of each age-old timber as the truck crossed to the other side.

It was a jarring thirty-minute ride into town in the back of the old truck. The distinctive smell of the pine needles was all around him and brought such sweet memories of years gone by. Christmas. He lifted his head in time to see the truck pass the welcoming sign along the side of the road:

WELCOME TO RIVER DALE
POPULATION 3,809

When the truck finally stopped at the Christmas tree lot just outside of town, Stephen jumped off and started walking toward the edge of town. Try as he might to get away from his past, he was always drawn back to the small village by the river. Time to go home. It had taken him a long time to get here, but now he was home. What would they say? How would they greet him? His guilt was overwhelming; he knew it was all his fault. Soon he was drawn to a flashing green-and-white sign that read, CHUCKIE'S BAR AND GRILLE—RIVER DALE ALE.

The tavern inside was like all the other bars he had been in with its dark corners, old tables, and dirty glasses. The smell and haze of cigarette smoke lingered in the air. In the past, it had comforted him, but now it seemed to haunt his very being.

He took a seat at the end of the bar, a habit from his travels on the road. From that vantage point he could see whoever came in and, if needed, make a quick exit through the rear door, should the police arrive. He unfurled some rumpled bills from his pocket. They tumbled onto the bar top. Maybe enough for two drinks.

A half-smoked cigarette caught his attention in a nearby ashtray. His hand went to reach for it until he heard a gruff voice ask, "Whatdya have, buddy?" The barkeep wore a stained white shirt with an apron rolled up and tied under his protruding belly. It was covered in food stains, evidence of the menu served in the bar over the past week.

"Vodka." Then, rummaging through his pile of crumpled bills, counting them, he said, "Double."

Looking down at his hands, he saw they were black and covered in coal dirt from the truck bed he had slept in a few nights earlier. He studied them as if it were the first time he had ever really seen them, as if they belonged to someone else. Cuts and scrapes covered the backs and palms of his hands, and dirt packed under his once-manicured nails and a large open wound, something he must have gotten . . . somewhere.

"Where's your washroom?" he asked the bartender.

The barkeep eyed him carefully, surveying him before saying, "Back behind you. Second door on the left. Can't miss it." Then, with a hint of sarcasm, he added, "It's the one marked *Gentlemen.*"

Stephen stood, then paused for a minute to look around the bar. It was like all the other bars he had been in, drank in, sang in, and played his guitar in, just to have a place to stay . . . and a drink. They were all the same, but this one was in River Dale, home. Once he had it all—the condo in Nashville, the recording contract, the fast car, and lots of friends. Then he lost it. One careless act. All his fault. His *life* was a country song.

The bartender scooped up the pile of crumpled bills and set the glass of vodka on the bar.

Stephen eyed the drink. He studied the glass as rivulets of condensation ran down the outside to the stained coaster beneath it. Inside the glass was his oasis, his savior, his friend, his companion . . . his devil. He was tempted to finish it off in one large gulp, so nobody would steal it or drink it while he was in the bathroom. His hand shook as he reached for it. The television at the other end of the bar broke in with a news alert showing a TV reporter standing by the river in the snow.

"Good evening, ladies and gentlemen, this is Howard Nears of WKRD at the site of a one-car accident at the White River Junction, just outside River Dale. Apparently, a car plunged into the river earlier tonight with three passengers. The local residents, all members of the Collins family, were on their way to River Dale to the hayride festival celebrating the town's holiday festivities. A passing motorist said the driver swerved to avoid hitting a deer and plunged into the river."

The television camera panned to the side of the road, where a crane was hoisting a gold four-door SUV from the churning river waters.

Stephen stood in shock as he watched.

"All three occupants were pulled from the car and rushed to River Dale General Hospital, where they are listed in serious condition. This is Howard Nears, WKRD, River Dale."

The bartender pointed his remote at the TV to change the channel, looking for college football results. The stranger's glass of vodka was still there, but the young, weathered-looking customer was gone. The bartender felt a blast of chill wind, then noticed the front entrance door slowly swinging shut.

CHAPTER FOURTEEN

Johnny Ray Mason was one of the newest firefighters with the River Dale Fire Department, having joined less than a month before. His mother had been the principal of River Dale High School for three years before she passed away. He had been in Iraq with the army at the time, but he had rushed home for her burial. After her funeral, Johnny Ray left the military, returned to the quiet of the small town of River Dale, and promptly joined the local fire department.

He was tall, with broad shoulders, unruly red hair, and an easy smile. He was more like a fun-loving kid than a battle-hardened veteran. Everybody loved Johnny Ray. As the newest hire, he got to do all the jobs everybody else hated—including washing the dishes every day he was on rotation.

The night before, his best friend had kidded him about his cooking ability. "Hey, JR, you can do a lot, but I got to tell you, one thing you can't do is cook. This spaghetti is the pits. It's still hard."

"They call it al dente, Bo," Johnny Ray had chided his Polish colleague. "Man, haven't you ever had pasta before?"

"Yeah, I have. Just never had it like this before. My mom used to make it when I was living at home, but it was always so soft." Bo was always kidding him about his cooking. Johnny Ray and Bo Bruzinski had always been the best of friends, as kids going to school together in the nearby town of Winston. They had served in the army together, with his pal Bo getting out six months before he did. Bo was the one who had spoken up for the quiet veteran when he had applied at the River Dale Fire Department. They bunked again as roommates when Johnny Ray came home to stay.

A loud blast from the horn of the massive diesel fire truck brought him back to reality. His crew chief, Carl, at the front yelled, "Mason, hop aboard. We need you. Fire at the old Tucker printing warehouse on the east side. Get suited up. Come on, let's go. We're on the clock. Let's move."

Johnny Ray suited up, and then with three quick steps and one gigantic leap, he was on the truck's platform with the rest of the crew. Within three minutes they were on their way. He was ready as he said his traditional prayer to Saint Florian, patron saint of firefighters, but he knew that sooner or later he had to place his trust and hopes in the thousands of dollars of firefighting gear the city had bought to protect him.

"Mason, let's go. Look alive there, gents," bellowed Carl.

"Grab your hooks, men, and let's move out," Johnny Ray shouted as they arrived on-site. They started unrolling the hoses and went to work. Carl was approached by a man in a tan overcoat and a dark suit and tie. He was carefully trying to keep his oxfords dry, walking around the pools of muddy slush, but to no avail.

The men watched him approach their group as he stepped among the puddles.

"You the owner?" Carl asked bluntly. All he wanted was a yes or no.

"Yes, sir, name's Jack Damon," he said as he turned back to survey the damage being caused by the growing fire. They could see flames rising through the windows. "What happened to the sprinklers? They should have gone off?" Damon asked in amazement.

"When was the last time you had them inspected?"

"Well, my property management company is supposed to have it done every year, but I don't know when it was done last."

Carl shook his head. "What's in the warehouse? Any explosives? Flammables?"

"Old newsprint and a lot of paper stock."

"No liquids? No flammables, Mr. Damon? I didn't see the roster on the wall for contents that you're supposed to post. That's the law, and besides, it really helps knowing what we're dealing with in situations like this. We need to know if we have an explosive situation here or not." Carl glanced at his men as they got ready to approach the fire.

"I don't think so, but the management company just sublet it. You'd have to ask them."

Frustrated, Carl stepped toward him. "I'm asking you, sir. It's your building, so it's your responsibility. I don't have time to see if they've complied with the posting requirements. Get them on the phone and ask them. You're the owner; it's your job to know what's going on in your properties," he said almost in disgust.

"Listen, the last time I was in there, two weeks ago, I didn't see any flammables being stored there. All right? That's all I know. Okay?"

Carl turned to Johnny Ray and gave him the thumbs-up signal. That was what he was waiting for as he rushed to the roof of the building.

Time to put out a fire, thought Johnny Ray.

Dark-green smoke was pouring out under the doors. That was bad, very bad. Dark-green and black smoke meant the fire was just starting and had not burned off the combustible materials yet—that made it more dangerous.

Once on the roof, Johnny Ray quickly went to vent the rooftop with an ax. With one mighty swing it crashed through the rubber-clad roof. It was then that the blast erupted.

CHAPTER FIFTEEN

Beth lay in bed, reveling in the warmth of his breath on her neck as a barrage of kisses blanketed her. She had never wanted to admit it—not even to herself—but she had missed him. Wanted him. She wanted to grasp him tight in her arms, to hold him and feel him and his prickly whiskers . . . Whiskers? She opened her eyes and was confronted by the outstretched tongue of her favorite feline—Felix. Certainly not who she had expected to see. He purred, reminding her he was hungry. He was not used to waiting for his breakfast.

"Good morning," she whispered to her feline friend.

Beth finally stretched out her long, aching limbs, slowly twirling her neck in a circle to release the late-night kinks. It was just after seven o'clock, and daylight was breaking outside. She heard a car door slam. From her bed she separated the upstairs curtains and saw Logan's rental car pulling out of the driveway. *He's leaving early?* She let the drapes slowly fall back into place. She was alone. Felix purred again and then gently rubbed the side of her face before hopping off the bed to make his way downstairs and wait for his breakfast.

Usually she was out jogging along Riverside Drive by dawn and seated at her desk at the hospital before seven. But not today; this was a different kind of day. Today she would review her latest admissions and do something she had not done in a while—make her rounds of patients with her staff.

She stretched again and quickly slid her feet out from underneath her mother's down comforter, the one she and Claire had bought for her in Oregon so many years ago. It smelled of her. "I miss you, Mom," she said aloud in the quiet coldness of her mother's bed, in her mother's bedroom, in her mother's house. Her mother was all around her. It felt comfortable, but maybe the Realtor was right; maybe it was time to sell the family homestead and return to Chicago.

Maybe now was time to go back to Chicago—for good. Maybe everyone else was right, and she should close down the hospital—but it had meant so much to her mother. The mere thought of it was . . . She could not let it go.

The Realtor said the holidays were a good time to sell in New Hampshire. Yes, maybe there were too many memories here. *The hell with it, I like my memories. I'll just wait it out here and see what happens.*

Her feet searched the cold wooden floor for her dalmatian bedroom slippers until she found them and felt the cool warmth of the fluffy cotton lining. Absentmindedly, she smoothed the comforter with her hand, the way her mother used to. It brought back even more memories. Everything she did in this house brought back memories.

She threw back the covers and felt the cold December air grab her before she slipped off the slippers and quickly returned to the warmth beneath the covers. She had fond childhood memories of snuggling in bed next to her mother, who would chase the boogeyman away. Her mom would then tell her about all the famous women in the world, including her favorite, Madame Curie, the Nobel Prize winner. And she told her about Amelia Earhart, the famous aviation pioneer. Or the smart female doctor who truly made a difference in the world. She smiled to herself. *I love you, Mom. Dad. Time to get up. Things to do. Brrrrrrrrrrrrrrrr.*

It was still cold in the room as she grabbed her robe from the foot of the bed and her slippers and nearly ran to the bathroom. She closed the bathroom door, put on the hot water inside the shower, and soon watched the plumes of steam slowly seep into the rest of the room, warming it.

She hung her robe on the back of the door and glanced at herself in the full-length mirror. *Not bad for someone my age,* she mused. She stood taller on her toes, and her breasts jutted forward. *Not bad at all.* She tried to keep herself in shape by jogging along Riverside Drive every morning, and she also loved using the workout equipment at the hospital. It all seemed to be working in her favor—for now, anyway. Before pulling back the shower curtain, she glanced at her engagement ring and then stepped inside.

The shower felt good, and she luxuriated in the only time she had all to herself. She let the hot water rinse off the soap as it cascaded down her back, caressing her, soothing her pains and opening her drawn pores. *A long, hot shower. I should do this more often,* she thought. *Only so much time.*

Stepping from the shower, she toweled off and then grabbed the robe from the door. She slipped on her slippers and began to dry her hair. Walking down the steps, she could smell the overwhelming aroma of heavenly hazelnut coffee mingling with the strong scent of the fresh-cut pine garlands she had hung throughout the house. Her mother had loved fresh-cut garlands; it was another Christmastime tradition in the Harding household.

On the table was a sprig of holly placed on top of a Christmas card from Logan.

Beth—
Left early. Off to work. One day on, then two days off.
Back tomorrow. Dinner at Henley's tomorrow night? My treat.
Nice last night.
Sorry I fell asleep.
Logan

She smiled and then opened the cabinet door. As she withdrew her favorite coffee mug, she glanced through the kitchen window and saw the deck covered in a fresh coat of newly fallen snow. She loved snow. It was not Christmas without snow.

Beth sat in the kitchen lost in memories until a familiar scent filled her nose as she ate her toasted English muffin and marmalade. It was the scent of flowers—a strong scent of roses, jasmine, lilac, and musk. When she looked down, she realized she had grabbed her mother's robe by mistake from the back of the bathroom door. Pressing the soft cotton chenille deep into her face, she took in a long, deep breath. She had bought it for her years ago for Mother's Day, and now she would never part with it. It smelled of White Shoulders perfume intermingled with the unmistakable scent of Helene Curtis hair spray. Such memories.

She could still feel the warm, loving arms of her mother wrap around her as she sat in the kitchen. *Perfect.* The robe was white with large embroidered hearts, each the size of a palm print, in various colors randomly scattered about the fabric. Her mother had loved it, and even though it was covered in cocoa stains down the front, Beth refused to wash it. Instead, she wanted to leave it just the way it was, preferring to smell it at times when she missed her mother the most.

Why did she have to leave? There was so much more Beth had wanted to learn from her. *How did she manage to stay married to Dad for so long? What was the secret to her calmness? How did she handle the hospital board so well?* And, of course, baking. Only her mother could make apple crisp so sweet, so soft, and so cinnamony. And the best pineapple upside-down cake. Her mother knew people; she understood them. It was a gift.

When her mother had been diagnosed, Beth had come home from Chicago to be with her in River Dale. She had stayed by her side until the very end. A tear crept to her eye, and it was then she noticed a cabinet door ajar on the other side of the kitchen. She smiled. It was an odd habit of her mother; she never seemed to want to close a drawer or a cabinet door. She was always so tidy and fastidious, but for some reason she would leave doors and drawers open throughout the house. Beth would always follow behind her and close them. *It must have been Logan,* she mused.

She finished her coffee. *Time to get dressed and ready for work. A big day ahead.*

CHAPTER SIXTEEN

Young Mayerle Matthews sat in the chair, quiet and still . . . not making a sound. This was her chair. This is where she had sat every day for the last three days, four hours a day, smiling and waiting. Her bangs were cut straight across her forehead, framing her face and making her look even younger than her twenty-two years. She sat with both feet on the floor, knees together, her hands folded on her lap as she waited. She would occasionally smooth the wrinkles from her red-and-white-striped nurse's aide dress. Then she waited. *Maybe today is the day,* she thought.

Mayerle missed being with the newborns; she called them her little angels. She missed holding them, cuddling them in her arms, and singing softly to comfort them. Two had no one else to comfort them. Especially the one everyone called a problem child. She smiled to herself, thinking back. Then she heard him crying, screaming for her among the rows of other babies. It broke her heart, but she had to sit. That was what they had told her to do.

She turned her head sideways and saw them in the head nurse's office talking with their hands. Then she heard him scream again. They called him James, the noisy one. If only she could . . . Then she heard him again. Crying, screaming. He wanted her. She wanted to get up, to go to him. She had to do something, but she had been told by Nurse

Abrams to sit in the chair. And she always did as she was told. She did not want to make the new temporary nursing supervisor unhappy.

Mayerle heard her mother in the office talking, and she was sure they were talking about her. Maybe her mother could persuade them to let her walk among her angels again and hold them, comfort them just the way she always did. She saw her mother's red face as she stood before the desk of Nurse Abrams, the nursing supervisor. She could not hear what they were saying; they were too far away.

"I still don't know why you won't let my daughter just do her job. She went through all the volunteer training the hospital requires, the specialty training, and all the classes she needed to become a 'comforter.' She's never been late, she's conscientious, she's never been a problem with discipline, and"—she was nearly in tears defending her daughter—"it'll break her heart if she can't work with the little babies. She's good; she's very good with them. Ask anyone."

"I can certainly attest to that. Mayerle is very good with—" Agnes, Mayerle's longtime supervisor, halted her defense when her new boss raised a hand to silence her.

"I understand your love of this volunteer, Agnes," Nurse Abrams began stiffly, "but sometimes the hospital has other things to consider."

"Such as?" Mayerle's mother asked.

"Liability issues for one thing, Mrs. Matthews. Should any of these babies, in their tender newborn condition, develop an infection as a result of coming into contact with this volunteer, the consequences . . . Well, you can only imagine."

Agnes raised her voice in her defense. "Mayerle adheres to all the hygienic cleansing protocols and dress code procedures established in this hospital, better than most of the paid staff, including . . ." She wisely chose not to finish her sentence. The raised eyebrow told her that she might have gone too far.

"The hospital will be closing in a little over a week, and the board has directed me to—"

"Even more reason to let my daughter just do her job. She loves it. And it's only for a week or so."

"Well, there are other considerations here that must be taken into account—" began the new manager.

Mrs. Matthews knew where this conversation was going. "Wait just a minute." She paused to once again fight the fight she had fought for years. She took in a deep breath to help calm her nerves. "Yes, my daughter is special. She was born that way. Mayerle loves those little babies and does a good job of providing comfort to them. She has done this work for three years—prior to your arrival—with no problems or issues. Now to imply that she is unqualified to do this job, well . . ." She stopped to compose herself. "Then maybe we need to be having this conversation in the legal office with my attorney and Dr. Harding in attendance." She stood and grabbed her coat and purse.

"Wait. Sit down, please, Mrs. Matthews."

Once she was seated, Nurse Abrams looked to Agnes and asked, "You accept full responsibility for overseeing this volunteer?"

"Yes, ma'am, I do . . . as always."

"All right then, under those circumstances the volunteer will be reinstated immediately. Thank you for coming in, Mrs. Matthews," she said with a thin grin. "It has been a pleasure meeting you." She extended her hand.

"Thank you for your time, Ms. Abrams," Mrs. Matthews said, shaking her hand. "This meeting has been a very enlightening one." She started to walk away, then stopped, turning to face Nurse Abrams once again as she began to put on her coat. "By the way, that volunteer as you call her, has a name. Her name is Mayerle, and if I ever hear of you showing my daughter any further disrespect, I will take it directly to Dr. Harding . . . in a heartbeat. I hope I have made myself perfectly clear, Ms. Abrams. Good day and . . . Merry Christmas." She spun away and was overjoyed to see the look on her daughter's face as Agnes gave her the good news.

Mayerle smiled and waved excitedly as her mother gave her the thumbs-up. Today was going to be a good day after all.

CHAPTER SEVENTEEN

Rory Daniels was puzzled after talking to the CEO's administrative assistant. The new CEO wanted to meet with him for lunch. *Why just me? Why lunch? Why not the rest of the sales and marketing team? Why the executive dining room and not the conference room?* He had heard all the rumors about what a tough CEO he was at other companies, cutting staff and budgets. *Am I going to be fired? Great, just what I need to hear at Christmastime.*

The elevator quickly and quietly whisked Rory from his office on the twelfth floor to the ease and comfort of the private executive dining room on the ninety-third floor. He checked his tie and hair in the mirror hanging on the back wall of the elevator. His suit was Italian, his shoes English, and his silk tie French. He was ready. When he exited the elevator, a new uniformed security guard stood blocking his way. "Name please?" he asked, showing no emotion.

"Rory, Rory Daniels. I'm here for a meeting with Mr. Clarke." He looked around, then asked after surveying the room, "Where's Gary?" Gary had worked in the sales and marketing dining room until the month before, when he was promoted to the executive dining room.

"He doesn't work here anymore," he said without looking up from his clipboard, then nodded his approval, pointing to a man at the end of the hallway. He stepped aside to let Rory pass.

Rory worked on the project team that would be launching yet another new line of antibiotics that Ascot Pharmaceuticals was introducing in the next quarter. Usually this kind of presentation was done in the sales conference room on the sixth floor with the heads of sales, marketing, and advertising. But as one of fifteen assistant vice presidents of sales and marketing to be meeting privately, one-on-one with the new CEO, he had the feeling that it was a going to be a turning point in his career. He was meeting with John Clarke.

He passed a small sign on the wall that read:

QUIET PLEASE!
ABSOLUTELY NO CELL PHONES ALLOWED IN THE EXECUTIVE DINING ROOM.
PLEASE SILENCE THEM NOW.

"Good morning, sir," said the middle-aged man in a black-and-white waiter's tuxedo at the dining podium. "Mr. Clarke is waiting for you. Please follow me."

The plush brown wool carpet felt soft under Rory's feet as he walked down the hallway. He could tell it was new carpet as the thick threads stuck to the sides of his shoes, making them look like they had a small brown beard.

The private dining room was nearly empty. It was for the use of the top executives at Ascot. Two men and a woman were having a heated discussion at one of the tables near the front of the room. They quieted as he and the greeter passed before resuming their discussion.

The executive dining room contained floor-to-ceiling glass on the one outside wall and dark-wood paneling on the interior walls. Expensive artwork hung on the walls. As an art lover, Rory appreciated the eclectic collection as he walked by, seeing modern works of art by Kandinsky, Pollock, Rothko, and Warhol.

Through the oversize glass wall, he could see for miles and miles. He could see the tall buildings that dotted the city skyline and the expansiveness of Lake Michigan and beyond. It was all overwhelming. He had marveled at the view on the one other occasion he had been here, but Rory did not know which sight he liked more. He decided it was the artwork. John Clarke sat at the corner table alone, waiting.

As Rory approached, he noticed that the CEO was impeccably dressed. He was wearing a custom-tailored wool suit, high-buffed leather oxfords, an expensive-looking silk tie, and a starched white cotton shirt.

Clarke rose to greet him, shaking his hand. "Good morning, Rory. So glad you could join me for a quiet lunch and a discussion . . . regarding your future."

Rory gulped. *I knew it. But why? I thought my performance was recognized as an asset for the company. My division is one of the top five performers in the company, and I've been making a lot of money in bonuses. Where is that card from the executive recruiter I met at the vendor party last week? How much severance will they give me? Will they give me outplacement assistance? Car? No car! All of it down the drain. Where is my résumé filed? What about—*

"Please have a seat." The new CEO politely directed him to the chair across from his. He smiled at Rory but cast a disapproving glance at the three loud employees seated at the nearby table. The maître d' nodded; he understood that look, as it was one he had seen many times in the past. Rory noticed him stop at the other table. The three loud talkers glanced in his direction, and soon the group was scurrying out of the dining room. They were now all alone.

"Martini?" Clarke asked Rory.

"Ah . . . yes, if you're having one . . . sir." He usually made it a practice not to drink while at work. But today he was having lunch with the top boss. He would just go with the flow and follow his lead, curious as to the purpose of the meeting. *What's going on? What does he want from me?*

"What would you like?"

"The same as you're having."

"Jason," he said aloud, raising two fingers—another signal that apparently Jason was all too familiar with in his position. "The usual, two."

"Yes, sir. Right away."

Clarke unfolded the black cloth napkin onto his lap and said, "Wonderful view, is it not?"

"Yes, sir, it is." He could see all Chicago, now at his feet. "And I love the artwork."

"Yes, so do I. But they're only copies, mind you. The originals are worth far too much money to be displayed openly here on the walls, as I'm sure you're well aware. They're stored in a private art vault for safe keeping. A good investment for the company and its shareholders."

"Yes, sir, of course. But I love the city view as well; it's breathtaking."

"We'll have to see about getting you a view like this . . . in your new office, to go along with your promotion."

What? He almost blurted out the word but managed to keep his surprise to himself. He swallowed hard as his head began to reel at what he had just heard. *Promoted?*

John Clarke had been hired as the CEO a few months earlier to replace the former one, who had been fired for poor performance. Clarke, who had joined them from a high-powered consulting firm in New York, had a reputation for team building, and the newspapers called him a ruthless business genius.

"Rory, I am building a team, and from what I've seen, I think your future holds great promise at this company."

"Thank you, sir. I enjoy working here and—"

"Yes, yes, yes," he said, interrupting. "You're engaged to be married correct? To Dr. Harding's daughter?"

"Yes, sir."

"Have you set a date yet?"

"No, sir."

"Hmmm."

It was nothing Clarke said, but Rory got the distinct feeling of displeasure emanating from his newfound mentor. *Listen to him, Rory—don't talk. Just listen.*

"Marriage is a great institution, Daniels. I should know; I've been married four times. Here at Ascot, I feel teamwork is very important, and marriage is at the heart of that team. But I digress. Let me ask you something . . . Who are our customers?"

"Patients, of course."

"No. That's what I used to think as well."

Jason brought the martinis and carefully set down nearly overflowing frosted glasses in front of them. Three olives on a toothpick floated in the center of each.

Rory smiled to himself. He finally felt part of a team.

"Thank you, Jason," Clarke said politely. Turning to his newest protégé, he said, "Cheers, Rory." Their glasses clinked together, and they each took a sip. It was harsh tasting, like kerosene, and it burned as it went down his throat. It tasted like straight vodka—cold, straight vodka. He preferred a cold beer when he was out with his friends.

"Where was I? Ah yes, our customers. Lesson number one: the government is our customer, Daniels. The federal government funds Medicare, Medicaid, insurance premiums, veterans' health care, and everything else to do with medicine in this country—they pay for it all. Billions upon billions of dollars. The money may be doled out by the state, city, or county, but it all comes from the feds. Over eighty-six percent. Never forget that."

Rory took another sip. "Yes, sir."

"Lesson number two: the federal government spends over thirty-five percent of this country's entire budget on health care. Now they are finally starting to get wise as to how they can push hospitals to save money. They can't just keep slashing the funds they give the hospitals, and they also can't have people dying on the streets. The government has been desperately searching for ways to save money. Are you with me so far?"

"Yes, sir," he said and swallowed hard, then took another sip of his drink.

Clarke leaned in closer and whispered, "Do you know what they finally figured out?"

Rory moved in, merely inches from his face. "No, sir."

"Hospitals make their own revenue streams by readmitting patients to the hospital for days on end as a result of something the hospitals themselves caused. Botched surgeries. Infections. You name it. They get to bill the government to pay for their own mistakes. Great moneymakers—the biggest. They control it all. Nationwide, fourteen to eighteen percent of all hospital admissions are a direct result of hospital error, including staph infections, MRSA, CRE, and the like. Big moneymakers. Infections are the biggest reason by far." He leaned back and then mused aloud, "I wish I could figure out how to do that here. Make our own business and have the government pay you for it." He laughed at the thought.

Clarke sipped his drink. "When patients are readmitted, hospitals use a lot of antibiotics. Well, the feds have finally figured it out and will soon penalize hospitals for readmissions over a certain level. Currently ten percent. We just have to make sure that level is still high enough for us to make money. Got it?"

Rory was having a hard time following his logic. He took another drink from his glass. Clarke again raised two fingers to Jason for refills, which arrived promptly with their Cobb salads.

Leaning back again, Clarke observed, "Ascot Pharmaceuticals is the largest manufacturer of antibiotics in the world. We research them, we develop them, we manufacture them, and we buy companies who compete with us—we do anything and everything we have to do to stay competitive. I didn't take this job to be put out of business by some bureaucrat, which is what will happen if the hospitals ever figure out how to fix their problems and stop infections. Got it?"

Rory was slowly beginning to understand, or maybe the martinis were causing him to think like his boss or make him think he understood. "Yes, got it," he said with a slight slur. He was not used to this much heavy drinking, especially so early in the day. He began to eat the salad to have some food in his stomach, trying to clear his head. They ate for a few minutes in silence.

"Your fiancée, Elizabeth Harding, is in River Dale? Dr. Sarah Harding's daughter?"

"Yes, sir."

"I heard her and her mother speak at a health-care symposium in Denver a while back. That was a few years before her mother passed away. I was very impressed. They are both well respected in their field." He coughed and then took another drink, nearly downing his entire martini.

"I met her mother only once," said Rory.

"Well, let me tell you, both of them—very impressive. And Elizabeth . . . well, she's quite the looker, if you don't mind me saying so."

"Yes, sir, I certainly think so." *Where is all this going?*

"I saw a memo cross my desk the other day from Human Resources. They tell me that weeks ago we made a job offer for her to join us here at Ascot. But she hasn't responded yet, is that correct?"

"Yes, sir. However, she's still working at closing the River Dale General Hospital and will be for the next few—"

"I told them to send her another offer of more money. Do you think another fifty thousand would help her make up her mind?"

Another fifty grand? Whew. Why? He took a sip from his martini. His head and mind were reeling. "Well, yes, sir, at least it would help me make up my mind if I were offered that kind of . . ."

Clarke stopped eating, and his eyes narrowed. "Daniels, let's get one thing straight: Dr. Elizabeth Harding is not you, far from it. She has so much more . . ." He stopped himself, and then a thin smile pursed his lips before he continued. "Let's just say I want her on board . . . badly. I want her on our side helping us push our new family class of Rimdex antibiotics. If we do this right, they will be blockbusters, multi-billion-dollar sellers to the government and to the hospital market. We're pulling out all the stops. Do you hear me? And I think Dr. Harding, with her antibiotic research experience in pediatrics at the Curie Institute in Paris, is the key to working with the hospital boards and the government agencies. She is well respected by all parties. I want her married to this company, so to speak. Do I make myself clear?"

"Yes, sir, perfectly," said a now-confident Rory, who then turned and motioned to Jason as he held up two fingers.

Clarke raised an eyebrow, stopped eating, and said in a monotone, "Don't you have work to do, Daniels, flights to catch?" He then softened, saying, "They say New Hampshire is quite enchanting at this time of year. Christmastime in New England?"

"Yes, sir, you got it," he said. He got up quickly from the table and began to walk away, but he paused when the CEO spoke again.

"Oh, and Daniels . . . set a date for the wedding. You're a good salesman . . . make it happen. Be quick about it. I've got my eye on you." He raised his hand to order another drink. "Merry Christmas."

"Yes, sir, right away." Once safely inside the elevator, Rory looked down at his hands and saw that they were shaking uncontrollably. Then suddenly they stopped trembling. He straightened his tie and ran his fingers through his hair; now he was ready. Time to make things happen.

CHAPTER EIGHTEEN

"Morning, Dr. Harding," said Carlita, her administrative assistant.

"Good morning," Beth said, sounding more chipper than usual as she walked into her office.

"Right," Carlita responded, handing her a coffee mug and a pile of messages.

"What?" Beth stopped and looked at her assistant.

"Nothing."

"What, Carlita?"

"Logan Mitchell called. Said he would call you back. It seems to me that when Logan Mitchell is in town, your voice just seems so much softer . . . happier, so to speak. That's all." She spun around in her chair and returned to her computer.

"I don't know what you're talking about," Beth replied. She started to walk away, then stopped. "Oh, by the way, I'm making Monday rounds today. Have the attending physicians ready and waiting for me. Twenty minutes. All hands on deck today and the rest of the week. Have a nice day."

"Yes, Doctor. All hands on deck," she said with a smile.

Twenty minutes later, Beth slipped on her white jacket, pocketed her pager, and draped her stethoscope around her neck. She was ready, nervous, and excited . . . but ready.

When Beth left her office, she was received by a small group of white-coated doctors as she took the first clipboard and began a brisk walk. The group hurried to catch up with her.

"First patient. Room 205. Dr. Monroe, I see she's one of yours? Talk to me, Doctor."

A smallish young man walked up beside her, flipping the chart. "Ah, yes. A Jane Doe. An older woman; she was admitted last night. She was disoriented, bruised, and forgetful when she was first admitted. But I think she's fine now." He lowered his voice and said with a grin, "I think she's just old."

"Old?" Beth responded. She stared at him for a minute before asking, "She's a Jane Doe?"

"Yes, Dr. Harding. She didn't have an ID, and she seems, well . . . to be a little forgetful," he responded, following Beth into the patient's room.

"Good morning, ma'am. I'm Dr. Harding, the hospital administrator. But you can call me Beth."

"Ah, the big cheese. I must be somebody special to rate this kind of service," she said with a huge smile as she sat up in bed to greet them.

"You *are* special, but we're also a little shorthanded now with the holidays and all, so I'm just filling in and helping out for some folks here."

"Oh, I see."

"Let me ask you, how are you feeling today?"

"I was a little dizzy when I first came in, but now I feel all right."

"Are they treating you okay?" Beth asked with a smile as she began her examination.

"Oh, yes, they're wonderful here. You run a good hospital."

"Thank you." Beth paused for moment and sat down on the bed. "Can you do me a favor?"

"Sure."

"Since you're so new here, can you tell me your name?"

"Sure can. It's Sweetie."

"Sweetie?" Beth responded, stifling a laugh. "Are you sure?"

"Yes, I am," she said assuredly. Then she whispered, "At least that's what everybody calls me here."

Beth chuckled. "Okay. Sweetie it is, then. I'm going to have Dr. Monroe take a closer look at that lump on the back of your head. And then we'll run a test, just to make sure we're not dealing with any nasty concussions . . . if that's okay with you?"

"Fine. I like Dr. Monroe." The old woman nodded, then leaned in close to whisper. "It does hurt when I touch it like this." She tapped her head.

Beth leaned in even closer. "Well, you know what they say, don't you?"

"What?"

Beth made a funny hurt face and patted the top of her head while saying, "Doc, it hurts when I do this. Then don't do that."

They both laughed.

"I have another question for you . . . Sweetie. Do you know what year this is?"

"Why, yes, of course I know what year it is . . . it's . . . it's . . . 1962."

"And do you know who the president of the United States is currently?"

"Everybody knows that—it's that good-lookin' Irishman—Jack Kennedy."

Beth looked at Dr. Monroe, raising an eyebrow before returning her attention to her new patient. "You just lay back, get comfortable, and enjoy the personalized service. We'll take good care of you."

She returned the clipboard to the other physician. "Dr. Monroe. I think you know what you have to do now. And contact my office so Carlita can call the authorities to let them know we have someone here who may have been reported missing. I'm sure her family is worried sick."

"Yes, Dr. Harding. I'll get right on it. I'll also do an amnesia workup." He was gone down the hallway, and they could hear him shouting, "Nurse! Nurse!"

"Next," she said as she continued her rounds. They walked down the hallway toward Room 208.

A clipboard was quickly passed to her.

"Dr. Stone . . . Alicia. I see this one is yours. Tell me what we have here."

"Rather complicated, Dr. Harding," she responded.

"How so?"

"We have an auto accident here with both parents suffering from head injuries and in comas upstairs. Still running tests on them. The daughter was pretty banged up and is in this room. She was in the back-seat of the car, not wearing a seat belt, and she suffered a fractured arm, a slight concussion, and a broken leg. However, she could be released in a few days."

"What's the complication, Doctor?"

"She's a minor, and we would have to notify child services, because there is no family or guardian available. It's Christmas and all, and to be alone on the holiday, well . . . And if either or both of them die, then . . ." Her voice trailed off.

"Hmmm. I see. Let's look in on the little girl first. However, if you ask me, I think some other tests seem to be in order, just to make doubly sure she's okay. Check for any hidden injuries, if you know what I mean. That might take a few extra days and give us some time to sort this out—maybe find other family members."

"Yes, Doctor," she said with an understanding smile.

As they entered the room, the group of doctors could hear laughter coming from inside.

"Sounds like a party? Who's having a party in here?" Beth asked jokingly.

"My brother came back; look, my brother's here. He's Stephen Collins, the singer," said the little girl proudly.

"Welcome, Stephen," Beth said, shaking his hand. He looked as if he needed a shave, a shower, and definitely a change into some fresh clothes.

"He's come all the way from California. He sings a couple of songs on the radio, and he wants to sleep here in my room to keep me company. It's okay, isn't it? Isn't it, Doctor? Please? Please say it's okay. I don't want to be alone." She shook her head, then grabbed her pillow and clutched it tight. "I want my mommy. I want my daddy."

"All in good time, all right?" Beth's words seemed to quiet the little girl. Then she looked at the brother and said aloud to both of them, "I'm sure your brother would like to clean up first after his long trip. Maybe change into some more comfortable clothes?"

Stephen looked at his clothes and recognized the subtle hint from the white-coated doctor. "I haven't been home yet. I came here as soon as I heard the news about the accident. I haven't seen my family in six months, and . . ." He stopped for a minute, not sure of what to say.

He continued. "She's afraid of the dark, and sometimes I read a story or sing to her to help her sleep. I thought I would just sleep here in the chair or on the sofa to keep her company. I'll stay out of everybody's way, I promise. She's deathly afraid of the dark—the boogeyman. And with Mom and Dad in a—"

"I can have someone sit with her while you go home and change and—"

He made a disagreeable face. "I have no car, and I really—"

"Tell you what. Go see my assistant, Carlita Lopez, in Administration and tell her I sent you. Tell her to take care of you. I think we may have some donated clothes that should fit you until you can go home and get some things. Okay? Tomorrow, if you like, I can have someone drive you home to pick up what you may need."

"Thanks, Doctor. I really appreciate it."

She whispered to him. "I'm glad you're here. Makes my life so much easier. We're on our way to look in on your parents. I'll come back and let you know their condition after I finish my assessment. But first, let's see how your little sister is doing." To the girl she said, "What's your name?"

"Lisa."

"What a great name. My name is Dr. Harding, but you can call me Beth. It's really Elizabeth, but everybody calls me Beth."

"Really?"

"Yes, or you can call me Doc if you like. How's that?"

The little girl beamed.

"How are you feeling?"

"Okay, but my leg still hurts when I try to walk on it, even with a cast. And I get a little dizzy when I sit up too fast."

Beth turned to look at Alicia. "Really? We'll just have Dr. Stone take a further look at that, if that's okay with you."

"Sure. I like Dr. Stone. She's great."

"Well, that's good to hear," Beth said. "You take care of yourself now, Lisa."

"You bet, Doc."

Beth walked past the young singer on her way out the door. "Thank you," he said with a weak grin.

"Take care, Mr. Collins."

Beth and her entourage filled the elevator and alighted upstairs. "Dr. Stone, I believe these next two patients are also yours."

The dark-haired, intense doctor approached the room ahead of them and read aloud from their charts. "Two adults, a male and a female, both approximately—"

"Relax, Alicia," said Beth. "Just tell me what you know about these two. You doctors are no longer interns; I'm just helping out, making my administrative rounds with you today, that's all. Okay?"

"Sure, Dr. Harding," she said, then breathed a sigh of relief before continuing. "These are the parents of the young girl and her brother we just left downstairs. They were all involved in the auto accident when the car flipped over and went into the river. Both parents have head injuries. Physically they check out fine, but we won't know anything more until they come out of their comas. But they seem to be showing signs of improvement based upon some of the tests we have been running on them."

Beth pulled their charts and reviewed them. A nurse handing them the latest test results interrupted them saying, "No change, Dr. Stone."

"I think you had better let the family downstairs know that right now it's just a waiting game to see when they wake up," Beth said.

"Yes, Dr. Harding. Right away."

Beth turned to watch the two patients lying side by side, their monitors and breathing apparatuses almost synchronized. Pulses fine. Breathing fine. *Come on, you two, wake up. Wake up. You have people counting on you. You have so much to live for,* she shouted to herself. She watched intently as their chests rose and fell together to the beeps of the machines. It was only a matter of time. Her thoughts were interrupted by the buzzing of her pager. It was Drake. She went to the nurses' station and, using the house phone, called him in his office.

"What's up, Drake?"

"The staff is ready to work with the movers, and they want to know where to start."

"I'll be right there." She turned to the doctors. "We'll finish our rounds later."

She passed the nurses' station in a rush and did not see the small group milling about. The white-haired man in charge of the group smiled at her as she walked by.

Taking the elevator to the second floor, which overlooked the lobby, she could hear the din of people in the entrance hall area as the doors opened.

Vince, her chief of maintenance and building operations, was waiting for her in the anteroom of her office. He and his helpers were ready. "Mornin', ma'am," he said slowly. "Where do you want us to start?"

She breathed deep. "Walk with me, Vince." She went to the railing, which overlooked the lobby below, and turned to him, saying, "Tell me what you see."

He leaned on the railing, looking to the right and then to the left. He had seen it a thousand times before, having worked at the hospital for more than twenty-eight years. "Well, ma'am, I see a lot of people comin' and goin', and I can see it's snowing outside. Same thing I been seeing at this place for almost thirty years."

She moved close to him along the railing. "Now tell me what you don't see, Vince."

"Don't know what you mean, ma'am."

She stood tall and folded her arms. "Vince, this is Christmastime. In my walk through the building this morning I didn't see any decorations anywhere."

"But, ma'am, the board sent out a memo and said not to put up any decorations this year. I think they wanted to save some money."

"But we already have the decorations paid for, so I don't understand what the board was thinking. We must have both misunderstood. Besides, I think people like decorations and love this time of year. It makes them feel good. And that's good for us. Let's go out with a bang. What do you say? Get the Christmas decorations out of storage, all of them, and let's make this place look special." She had that gleam in her eye that he had seen in her mother's eyes many times over the years.

They began their walk back to her office. Beth stopped at Carlita's desk when Vince asked, "Are you sure, ma'am?"

"Yes, I am. Absolutely. Let's get this place in the Christmas spirit."

"Yes, ma'am," he said with childish enthusiasm. "Whatever you say." His eyes sparkled and danced.

"What about the move?"

She winked at him. "Don't worry about that, Vince, just put up the decorations. Merry Christmas."

He smiled a broad grin. "Yes, ma'am. Come on, boys—we got work to do," he said to his waiting crew.

Beth watched them hustle off on their new assignment.

"What are you up to?" Carlita asked slowly, seeing the mischievous look in Beth's eye. Carlita was a single mother from Cuba with two kids, and she knew Beth well. She was wise beyond her years but still young at heart.

"Merry Christmas," Beth said as she turned to leave. "And Carlita, let's hear some Christmas music in this place." Then under her breath she said, "Let Ron French and the rest of the board be damned." *But am I doing the right thing?* she wondered, walking into her office. She froze. Every drawer and cabinet door in her office was wide-open. The smile grew on her lips. *Thanks for the support, Mom.*

When she turned around, he was standing there, waiting.

Logan.

CHAPTER NINETEEN

They stood in a small group off to the side of the nurses' station. The white-haired man in the white jacket looked at them and smiled. "Good morning, ladies and gentlemen, I'm Larry," he said, pointing to the name tag on his jacket, which he proudly wore—**LARRY OF RIVER DALE**.

"As you know, the hospital is overloaded with patients, and our administrator has asked for all hands on deck. That's a navy term meaning that everybody pitches in, including administrative personnel and volunteers. Therefore, I'll be assigning each of you to two-person teams to work together today and travel to various departments around the hospital, strictly as observers. Help out only when you're asked, but please do not interfere with day-to-day operations here at the hospital. Does everyone understand what I'm saying?"

They all nodded. A woman in the rear giggled and whispered to the man next to her, "He looks like somebody I feel I should know, but I just can't place it."

The man laughed and started to say something, but Larry interrupted him. "Would you care to share your amusing comment with the rest of the group"—he leaned in closer to read her name tag—"Maria?"

"Ah . . . no thank you, Larry. It's not that important."

"I thought so." His face grew somber. "Maria, we take our work very seriously here on the wards, as you will see. Even for those of you who are working with us for a few days from other areas. In many cases we are dealing with life and death. Please keep that in mind as you work in these departments. Now everyone gather around me for your department assignments for today, please."

The man next to Maria leaned in closer and whispered, "I agree with you."

She laughed.

"I'm Michael," he said, shaking her hand. "Are you also from River Dale?"

"Yes. I live—"

"Okay, okay, enough jabbering," Larry said, interrupting him. "Maria. Today, I'm going to put you and your friend Michael together as a team. Make your way to the Admissions Department and see if you can help out there. And remember, stay out of the way of the professionals."

"Yes, sir," they said in unison, and made their way downstairs to Admissions.

The Admissions Department was a mad and chaotic scene. Some people were asking for directions to different hospital wards, others were looking for patients' rooms, and even more waited their turn to be seen by a doctor. Maria looked around. People with the flu were on couches, waiting for appointments. She saw so much coughing and sneezing that she instinctively put her hand over her mouth to protect herself from all the germs. It appeared the whole world had the flu, and they had all descended on the local hospital.

"Can you believe this place? I feel like I need to take another shower," she said, gasping and taking a step backward away from the crowd.

"No, I can't," he said, watching the scene before him.

After a few minutes, she took in a deep breath and said, "Well, here it goes. All or nothing." Maria cautiously headed for the crowd, looking to see where she could help while still staying out of the way. She held a tissue over her mouth and nose with her right hand and another in reserve in her left hand. Michael walked behind her and then laughed quietly at her to himself. He could not believe it; a germophobe working in a hospital. He smiled, then coughed as he moved faster to catch up with her.

CHAPTER TWENTY

"Hiya, Logan," Beth said with a smile, looking surprised to see him. "What are you doing here? I thought you had to be at the station house today."

"I do. I have to relieve Carl at ten o'clock. But when I got to the station, they told me to have this form signed by the hospital medical director, a Dr. Crosby. Clark said it has something to do with insurance and compliance issues."

"What is it?"

"A physical release form saying I'm fit and able to perform my firefighter duties as needed," he said with a chuckle. "I had an annual routine scan done the week before I left California. I think they need to have the workup results forwarded here, that's all. Sounds like a big deal for somebody who'll just be filling in. What will they think of next? I also stopped by to check in on the Colonel. And I just found out that Johnny Ray was admitted last night."

"Johnny Ray Mason?"

"Yeah."

"Johnny Ray? I didn't notice his name on my admissions list this morning. How is he?"

"He's in really bad shape with some pretty severe burns. Doesn't look good. He's all bandaged up, including his face, arms, and hands."

"What happened?"

"An arson fire at a print warehouse down near the river. The police think they found the guy who set it, but they're not sure yet."

She shook her head. "I'll look in on him later."

"Yeah, that'd be great. Hey listen, I gotta go. I need to get this signed. I promised Carl I would check in early for roll call so he could spend some time with his family—Christmas shopping."

"Well, Crosby may want to see the scan results from California or do a quick physical on you before he signs it. He's a real stickler. Either way, it shouldn't take long, especially since you're here early before it gets crazy hectic."

He hugged her and placed a soft kiss on her cheek. "I'll see ya tomorrow." He turned to walk away, then stopped and faced her. "I tried to call you earlier to have some coffee. Did you get my note? Are you up for dinner tomorrow night? Henley's?"

"Yeah, sure. That'd be great. See you tomorrow."

"See ya," he said as he walked away, waving his hand high above his head without looking around.

She watched him leave, noticing his self-assured swagger. With what had happened to the Colonel and now Johnny Ray, for some reason she wanted to run to him and tell him to be careful. *Be safe. Don't take any chances.* She watched him disappear around the corner—he was gone.

CHAPTER
TWENTY-ONE

Logan drove down the river road, and as he drove, he noticed that the roads were getting slicker and more dangerous as the temperature dropped and ice and snow accumulated. The Baker River was churning with white, frothy waves crashing on the rocks below. Shorter days and colder temperatures signaled that old man winter was taking hold.

He pulled into the parking lot at the station and made his way inside.

"You're a man of your word," said Carl, obviously happy to see him. "Follow me. I can finish up my paperwork now that you're here. Come on into the office. Fletch and the other guys went down to the market to pick up some things to fix for lunch and dinner tonight. They'll be back soon. Your share of the cost is eight bucks. Just give it to Fletch." They walked down the hallway. "I heard you were at the hospital. How are the Colonel and Johnny Ray?"

"The Colonel's the same. Johnny Ray is in pretty bad shape. Bandages everywhere—face arms, legs, and hands."

"I'm going to stop by quick on my way home when I leave here." Carl motioned to him. "Follow me. You're in for a treat tonight, my friend; I think Fletch is making his world-famous paella for the crew. He makes it with saffron rice, shrimp, sausage, calamari, and tomato sauce. I think he also uses some mushrooms, peppers, and lots of seasoning."

"I'm hungry already just listenin' to you."

They stopped in front of the door with a sign that read, CHIEF.

"Make yourself at home."

Logan slowly walked around the office, saying, "Carl, I still don't feel comfortable with all of this, if you know what I mean. I think maybe you should be the—"

"Whoa, not me. Besides, this is what the Colonel would have wanted if he was here and had a say in things. Besides, you're the only one who has the experience running a fire station. So you're the new acting fire chief . . . temporarily."

"But it's been years since I've worked a desk," Logan pleaded.

"Doesn't matter. Between Margie and Clark they'll handle all the administrative paperwork for you. Just follow their lead. Piece of cake."

"Says you," Logan replied with a chuckle.

"Roll call soon, then two hours of training, then lunch—the best part of the day."

Logan smiled as he thought that most firefighters liked the camaraderie and the fellowship of the men and women they worked with. They put their lives on the line every time the big trucks rolled out of the station house. They also liked their routine, at least any time they could actually adhere to one. Roll call. Training. Lunch. Inventory. Equipment check. Dinner. Training. However, alarm calls had a way of changing things.

"Attention, everybody," Carl said to the assembled group. "I want you all to meet Logan Mitchell. He's going to be filling in for a while as the Colonel takes a vacation in the hospital."

They all chuckled.

"We talked him into working with Clark and handling the administrative paperwork and taking it off the chief's desk. In a weak moment, he accepted our offer. So give him a hearty RFD welcome."

The men cheered and gave out whoops and catcalls. Logan realized what had happened. Nobody wanted to handle the mountains of paperwork that came with the job of chief, and now he was stuck with it.

Logan saw a familiar face in the crowd.

"Hey, good to see you again," Fletch said, shaking his hand.

"Yeah. What have I gotten myself into?" Logan asked.

Fletch laughed. "You'll do just fine. It comes with the territory."

Logan took roll call, and they did an inventory of all the equipment to make sure everything was in working order. They did a communications check, then checked the generators on the pumper trucks. Finally, he called on the men to wash the pumper trucks inside the truck bay. A daily ritual.

Logan signed in as watch commander and then settled into the Colonel's chair. It felt funny sitting there, as if he was usurping his authority. Pictures cluttered the old man's desk. He still had the picture of the two of them in Fallujah, Iraq. He picked it up and smiled a bittersweet smile. They had lost a lot of good men in the desert. Looking up, he saw a tall, skinny kid at the door.

"Excuse me, Chief. I'm Clark, Clark Parker. I'm on light desk duty and handling the admin details and paperwork while Sue Diller is out on maternity leave."

"Come on in, Clark. Have a seat," Logan said, pointing to a side chair. "First off, I'm not the chief. I'm filling in, just like you, okay?"

"Yes, Chief. Got it . . . sir."

"Second, it's been years since I ran a station house, so I'll take all the help I can get. Okay?"

"Yes, sir."

Logan looked at him sitting there, taking in his short dark hair, starched white shirt and tie, and eager grin. His gig line was as straight as an arrow.

"Army?" Logan asked.

"Yes, sir. How could you tell?"

"Lucky guess. And your gig line's straight." He looked down at the place where Clark's belt, shirt, and pants met in the center. Yep, straight and correct, all meeting in a straight line—the army way—the only way. That was what every soldier was taught.

"Well, I got an early discharge. Wounded in Afghanistan. Applied to the Winston Fire Department, but they turned me down. The Colonel took a chance on me and sent me to the fire academy in Boston. However, I've been out on administrative leave for the last sixty days . . . back injury . . . light desk duty."

Logan liked the kid. "Okay, show me what you got."

Clark handed the temporary chief an action item list for the week, including a list of fire inspections that needed to be handled for fire permits by the end of the year.

"Also, the chief was supposed to attend the annual laying of the wreath at the heroes' memorial that honors local fallen firefighters, police, and veterans. He usually attends to represent the firefighters."

"When is that?"

"Saturday night, Christmas Eve. Sir."

"I'll make it my business to be there, to stand in for him. "

"Even though it's held on Christmas Eve, a lot of the guys come, out of respect, and bring their families. Kind of an annual tradition."

"I remember. What else?"

"There's a federal requirement that municipal fire departments, police departments, and emergency services all be equipped with the new P-25 communications gear."

"Yeah? And—"

"Well, it has to be initiated by the end of this week or the feds won't pay for it."

"How much money are we talking about for River Dale?

"It's a grant of about four hundred thousand dollars for all services."

"Whew . . . wow." Logan whistled softly. "And if we don't do it now, the feds won't help pay for it, right?"

"Right."

"That's a lot of money. So what's the next step?"

"Well, to show compliance, the city or municipality must attend a presentation of the new equipment. Those in attendance must include yourself—the fire rescue chief—the head of the police department, and at least two city officials. The mayor, an alderman, a council board member, you know . . . someone like that. Mr. French is attending, after strong pressure from the board. Royce is going, too; he can keep you company."

"I see. When is this shindig?"

"Wednesday."

"Where?"

"Boston."

"Boston?"

"The chief arranged all the details a while back, including transportation to and from the presentation."

"Maybe Carl should go. Or you. I'm just a substitute here."

"Yes, sir, I understand. It's just that . . . it's Christmastime, and it's his day off and . . . I just thought—"

"Okay. Okay, I'll go." It would be good to catch up with Royce; it had been a long time since they had sat and talked. "Set it up."

"Already done, sir."

"What else?"

Clark handed him an employment application. Logan glanced at it, nodding his head after reading aloud, "Kelly Macdonald. Originally from Winston, New Hampshire, thirty-two years old, army combat brigade, EMT certified, five years at the Seattle Fire Department. Okay, looks good. So what's the question?"

"Well, sir . . . she's a girl."

His eyes grew wide. "So? She's well qualified. I've had plenty of women work for me in my unit as smoke jumpers out west and on my watch at the station house in Arizona. Good firefighters—they never give up. Some of the best. What's the beef?"

"Well, sir . . . the chief interviewed her and signed off on her hiring, pending completion of a physical exam. That paperwork came in this morning. She passed. All I need now is your signature, and I can call her to make her an offer of employment. Sir."

Logan lifted the pen from his desk and quickly signed the offer letter. "Do it. And Clark . . . I'm counting on you to personally make her feel welcome and part of our team. We need more female firefighters in our business. They bring a different perspective . . . a breath of fresh air. You got it? Don't forget, the Colonel took a chance on you when you applied here."

"Yes, sir." Clark stood at attention, then handed him a sheet of paper.

"What's this?"

"My request to return to full active duty, sir. My release is signed by my doctor . . . there on the second page. My sixty days of light duty time is over today, sir. I just need your signature to go back to . . ." His voice trailed off as he watched Logan hold his future in his hands. He could not take his eyes off the silver pen Logan was twirling between his fingers.

Logan smiled, then signed the papers—in triplicate. "Okay, Clark, you're back on active duty. Merry Christmas. Check with Margie to see when you start rotation."

"Yes, sir," he nearly shouted with a huge grin and ran out the door. Logan heard a loud yelp from the hallway. *That's one happy firefighter,* he thought to himself. *Time to take a look around.* He passed the fitness room and saw some of the men working out—pumping iron and running on the treadmill.

Making his way to the wash bay, he saw another group of men just starting to wash the trucks, a never-ending task. "All these trucks have to last us a very long time," Logan said as he joined in to help wash the heavy-duty pumper.

"Yeah, like, forever," chimed in Yancy. The fire department was on the bottom of the list to receive extra funds when it came time to do budgets. But they were the first to be called any time there was a problem and people did not know who else to call. The Colonel called them the unsung heroes.

When Logan looked up, he was happy to see Clark pitching in, part of the active-duty roster again, helping wash the big truck. He had to smile, seeing him joking around with his fellow firefighters, all of whom were happy to have him back on the truck. Clark began to sing Christmas carols, and they all joined in.

Everybody knew what had to be done, and they all worked together to complete the tasks assigned to them from the Colonel's checklist.

Logan suddenly realized he was hungry.

As if on cue, Yancy appeared in the doorway as they finished drying the truck to start a thorough safety check on all equipment. He also brought a weather report for anyone who was interested. "Hey, everybody, it's snowing again."

"It's always snowing here in New Hampshire. What's to eat?" hollered an impatient Fletch, sounding grumpy . . . and hungry.

"Burgers and potato chips for lunch. Spaghetti and homemade meatballs for dinner, along with string beans and potatoes."

Logan was working next to Fletch and heard him say, "I was going to do paella for dinner tonight, but he volunteered to do a spaghetti dinner, his specialty, so . . ." He shrugged. "His burgers and meatballs aren't bad. He uses cumin-seasoned ground beef, ground veal, and ground pork. All three mixed together. It's actually pretty good." The more he talked about recipes, it sounded to Logan like Fletch fancied himself a gourmet cook. "His pasta is a little overdone, but there is a constant running battle over how to make pasta here."

Never changes, thought Logan. Every fire station he had ever worked at, there was always some good-natured kidding about the best way to prepare pasta. Some always thought it was too stiff. Or too soft. Or too salty. Thing was, it did not really matter to a group of hungry firefighters. It only mattered that there be large quantities of whatever was prepared. When they finished eating dinner, it was customary to box up the huge amounts of leftover food and deliver it to a needy family in town.

Yancy headed up the stairs to make lunch. An hour later, it was ready. Logan heard his stomach growl; he was hungry, and he had to admit that it felt good to be working again with a group of fellow firefighters. He loved being a smoke jumper, high in the mountain forests, but he had missed the camaraderie of the fire station and working with his band of brothers.

They grabbed plates and helped themselves to burgers, chips, and sodas before settling in at the long dining table. It smelled delicious. He took his first bite; it tasted even better than he had expected. Fletch was right.

"Logan, so tell us, what's it like working as a smoke jumper?" Yancy asked from the far end of the table. He had a questioning look on his square face and sported a three-day growth of beard.

"The best," Logan said, trying to talk with a mouthful of burger. He swallowed before continuing. "Just like working here, you never know when you're going to get a call and—"

"RFD 17, RFD 17. Please respond to a car fire at 6912 Plymouth Road at Brighton Lane."

Before the announcement was even finished, six firefighters hit the pole to speed their way downstairs. At the bottom of the flight pole, they suited up in their waiting gear. They quickly boarded their truck as the massive garage bay doors slowly lifted out of their way, being rushed by the blaring sirens. Logan, sitting in the passenger seat, looked at his watch. Total time from alert to start to roll was less than three minutes. *Very good.* The Colonel had trained them well. The adrenaline was rushing through their veins; they never knew what they would find when they got to a site.

Luncheon burgers were left behind. They had work to do. The snow and sleet pelted their vehicle as cars and trucks moved to the side of the road to make room for them to pass. Time was of the essence. People's lives were all that mattered.

Two hours later, they backed the truck into the bay and returned to their now-cold burgers. Fortunately, no one had been injured in the car fire. The car had been left running in the garage to let it warm up, and a rag underneath it had caught fire and ignited the blaze. They got there just in time to keep the house from catching fire.

"Microwave time," said Logan, picking up his cold burger and watery soda. "Then we get to clean the truck, again." Salt from the icy roads on a fire truck was a killer to the precision vehicle. It had to be cleaned quickly.

"RFD 17, RFD 17. Please respond. Apparent heart attack on Henderson Street near Maple Avenue. See the man on-site."

Without so much as a word of complaint, the men, most trained as EMTs, dressed again quickly and headed back outside into the cold, not knowing what they would find until they reached the site. They slid down the pole, suited up, and soon were off to where they were needed.

"Really glad you guys could make it," said a River Dale uniformed police officer as the rescue vehicle pulled up.

"What do you have?" Fletch asked as he grabbed his equipment and quickly made his way toward the car in the middle of the road. Another officer was directing traffic, while a third was comforting an older woman crying on the side of the road.

"Seventy-eight-year-old male named Jake Pillory, of South Winston, was sitting in his car at the stop sign here at the corner, and his wife said all of a sudden he just slumped over onto the steering wheel. Unresponsive. She says he does have a history of heart attacks."

"Thanks," said Fletch, rushing with Logan just behind him. Fletch knelt down close to the man in the front seat. "Jake? Jake can you hear me?" They both heard a low moan. "Jake, just take it easy, partner. You're going to be just fine."

The old man's eyes flickered. "*Ahh . . . Ahh . . .* Mildred?" he moaned aloud, his voice barely audible.

"She's right here, but let me get you comfortable first, okay?" Fletch looked at Logan. "Stretcher."

Within minutes, they had him stabilized and comfortable on a gurney, an oxygen mask securely over his mouth and heart monitors affixed to his chest. They loaded him into a waiting rescue truck to transport him to the hospital.

Two hours later, they sat down once again to finish their soggy lunch. This time they made it through the meal. *Hopefully dinner will be slower,* thought Logan. Hot spaghetti and meatballs. He could taste it already.

That afternoon he and Fletch went to do a permit inspection of a building under construction just off the highway. They also did a pre-plan inspection that would be scanned into the computer. This would make it available to everyone in the county should they ever have to respond to a future fire in the building. The building passed inspection.

At eight o'clock, the meal was ready and so were they. This time they got halfway through when they heard the inevitable: "RFD 17, RFD 17. Please respond. Overturned truck on Route 4, the river road, near the Baker Bridge. Nonhazardous cargo. Please respond."

The same drill was repeated, and once again they were out the door in less than three minutes. The truck's cargo was maple syrup—sixty thousand gallons of dark, sticky, gooey maple syrup. When they used the hose to clean the roadside, they had to pressure wash it four times. For extra traction, they added a layer of sand from the truck. The sand got heavier and heavier. The water turned to an icy slush as it streamed into the nearby river. *Sweetwater,* thought Logan. *Now I gotta file an environmental report because it's going into the river.*

They had only one other call that night—a flooded basement at a home just south of town. Logan turned off the water and called a plumber after making sure the elderly woman had a place to stay for the night. *All in a day's work,* thought Logan.

CHAPTER

TWENTY-TWO

Logan was happy to see his replacement at nine thirty the next morning. "It's all yours," he said with a smile as he turned over his nightly activity log. "See you Thursday."

As he was leaving he said goodbye to Margie. "See you Thursday, Marge."

"See ya," Margie replied. Then she seemed to remember something and said, "Hey, Logan . . ."

"Yeah?"

"Join me for a minute in my office, will ya?"

"Sure. What's up?"

"I'm takin' over some of the administrative paperwork for Clark, now that he's back on rotation. I still need your NH 809 form."

He gave her a puzzled look.

"You know, your physical papers? Just for my files . . . for the insurance company. I gotta have it since you're on the payroll now."

"Gotcha. I was just at the hospital seeing the doctor yesterday."

"Right . . . I guess it takes a while to get from the hospital to here, that's all."

"You know that Doc Harding over at the hospital runs a tight ship," he said with a broad grin. "I'm sure it'll be here soon. I'm going to stop by the hospital later on and check in on the Colonel. I'll ask about it. See ya later." He turned to walk away.

She looked up at him and asked, "Why don't you tell her?"

He turned with a bewildered look on his face. "Tell who what?"

"For somebody as handsome and intelligent as you are, sometimes you're just plain dumb."

"What do you mean?"

"Do I have to spell it out for you?"

"I guess so," he responded.

She stood up and walked closer to him to make sure she was not overheard.

"I know that maybe I shouldn't get involved, but . . ."

"Margie, has that ever stopped you before?" he joked.

"I'm serious, Logan. I've known the two of you kids since you were youngsters. It's obvious to anyone with a set of eyeballs that you and Doc Harding are crazy about each other . . . obvious to everybody except the two of you." She drew a deep breath.

"Now you're going to leave here soon, go back to California, and never tell her—and both of you are going to be miserable for the rest of your lives. Just walk up and tell her how much you care for her. She won't bite." She raised her eyebrows in a mischievous fashion. "You didn't see her after you left, after the funeral. She was moping around like a lost puppy."

"Margie, dear heart, she had just lost her mother. And you know how close she was to her mom."

"I know, but that was just one part of it. But if that's the way you want it, you just go ahead and be miserable. She loves you, though she herself might not even know it . . . yet. There now, somebody has said it aloud. And you're both just too blind to see it."

"I think you're making way too much of all of this. Besides, Marge, she's engaged to another guy. Have you forgotten about him?"

"No," she said flatly.

"I'm not going to break up the two of them." He relaxed and whispered sincerely, "Regardless of my feelings for her. I only want what's best for Beth. That's it, believe me."

"Believe what you want; I'm outta this. But if you don't do this, you'll regret it the rest of your life. He's not right for her. I never met the man, but I know it deep down in my heart." She looked at him and could tell she was not going to change his stubborn mind. "Men. Hmmph." She spun around and went back to her computer.

Logan was tired and hungry as he headed home that morning. When he pulled into the driveway, Beth's car was still there. Rubbing his face, he could feel the stubble. He needed a shave. He never felt like a human being until he shaved. *All I want to do is shave, shower, then sleep and sleep some more,* he thought as he walked toward the garage. Jet lag was finally catching up with him. He looked up and glanced at the snow-covered kitchen window. No one there. He trudged through the snow, his boots soaking wet from the ice and slush.

He heard the back door creak open and a familiar voice say, "Morning."

"Morning, Doc," he said with a smile and a wave as he passed the porch. He stopped to look at her.

"You up for some ham and eggs? Coffee? I just brewed a fresh pot."

Doc Sarah always said that a way to a man's heart was through his stomach. It might not have been anatomically correct, but she did have a point.

"You bet. Best offer I've had all day." It began to snow again as he walked inside, sat down, and pulled off his work boots.

Looking in the living room, he saw the Christmas tree sparkling in the corner. Some wrapped presents were scattered about the floor. He heard the radio playing Christmas carols. The house smelled of holly and fresh pine. Christmas in New Hampshire.

He could not help but notice how professional Beth looked in her dark-navy business suit. The skirt clung softly to her, outlining the curved contours of her body. She poured him coffee, and his eyes could not stop following her around the room as he talked about his first night in the station.

"I miss being on the line as a smoke jumper, but I had forgotten how much I enjoyed working in a station. It was great. It's a good group of guys. And you'll appreciate this: I hired our first female firefighter yesterday. I think she'll be a great addition."

"Good for you. Who'd you hire?"

"A gal with about five years of firefighting experience. Her name is Kelly something. The Colonel interviewed her, and I just signed the final paperwork to hire her." Then he continued to tell her about his day at the firehouse.

She laughed a deep, sincere laugh as he told her about hosing down an icy road filled with thick maple syrup.

"It's not funny," he said. "Sixty thousand gallons of Grade B maple syrup. That stuff was six to eight inches deep in some places and sticky as all get-out. My boots kept getting stuck in the stuff."

That only caused her to laugh harder.

"Yancy slipped and fell in it." Now he began to grin. "He was covered head to toe in the sticky goop. When we finally got back to the station house, it took me over an hour to clean all the gunk from my boots. Look at 'em," he said, pointing to the boots on the floor. "Go ahead, smell 'em. They still smell like brown sugar pancakes," he told her, trying to be serious as he ate his breakfast. Then he, too, began to laugh as he visualized the humor of his exploits from the night before.

He looked at the clock on the wall. "What are you doing home? Who's running the hospital?"

"I'm working from home this morning, but I gotta leave soon," she said, sipping her coffee. "Besides, I thought you might want some company and a nice breakfast after a long day at the office." She smiled.

He leaned back in his chair and said softly, "Sure did."

They talked for another two hours.

"Are we still on for tonight? Yule Log ceremony? Dinner?" she asked.

"Absolutely. I just need to catch some z's and then shower and shave later. We can go to the memorial log ceremony and then have a nice dinner at Henley's."

"Great. I'll make a reservation for us tonight. You look tired. Why don't you get some sleep?"

"Yeah, I will. You know, I worked three days straight as a smoke jumper at the Los Lobos fire and don't remember feeling this tired."

A worried look crossed her face but was gone in an instant.

"How's the Colonel doing?" he asked, pouring them each some coffee.

"He's about the same. All his vitals are stable; we're just waiting for him to wake up. But the longer he's in a coma, the worse it is for him."

"I'm going to stop by and see him later on. What's on your calendar for the rest of today?"

"Well, I'm going to finish my rounds of seeing patients from yesterday. And then I think I have to come face-to-face with the reality of closing the hospital. I try not to think about it, but without the two million dollars for the equipment, we're out of compliance and . . . we're breaking the law." She glanced at her watch and took a gulp of coffee.

Her phone beeped, signaling a text message. "Gotta go." She kissed him on the forehead and said goodbye. "Looking forward to tonight," she said sweetly, her hand trailing across his shoulder as she left.

I wish she wouldn't do that, he thought.

❊

Beth backed the car from the driveway and headed for work. The hospital was closing, and she did not know where she was going to work or what was going to happen to her. Rory? What about Logan? California? For now, it was time to enjoy Christmas. Her favorite song was playing on the radio as she drove to the hospital, "The Little Drummer Boy." As he began to beat his drum she tapped her fingers in time on the steering wheel.

She drove alongside the river and noticed the water was higher and churning rough and white over the rocks in the shallows. It was a fast-moving river, great for fly-fishing in the spring and summer. She watched it roll along beside her as she traveled. Over the last week, a lot of snow and rain had fallen into the river . . . and maple syrup. A smile came to her face when she imagined Logan being stuck in the thick, gooey stuff in the middle of the road. Sticky. Sweet. *Ugh!* She laughed aloud.

"Oh, Logan, you goofball," she said, laughing to herself. She needed to loosen him up. He had sounded so serious when he told her about the experience.

Tonight is dinner. What should I wear? Do I need to go to the mall in Winston to buy something special? What about—

Her cell phone rang and interrupted her thoughts. She hit the "Answer" button on the steering wheel. "Hello?"

"Hi, sis. It's me, Claire."

"Hey. It's good to hear from you. How ya doing?"

"Good. You sound chipper."

"Just my regular self."

"I just wanted to call and say how bad I feel about not coming home for Christmas, but you know that—"

"Claire, it's okay. Really. However, you'll miss seeing Logan."

"Really? He's in town? So that's why you sound so peppy?"

"No. He has nothing to do with it. He's only in for a couple of days or so. Came in to visit the Colonel and say hi to everyone here."

"I'd love to see him," Claire said. "Where's he stayin'?"

"In his old room . . . over the garage. Of course."

"Really?" Claire observed with a mischievous tone.

"Really."

Claire was always trying to play matchmaker between her and Logan. It seemed to her that the whole world was trying to push her toward Logan.

"Cut it out, Claire. Don't forget, I'm engaged."

"What's Rory think about all this? I mean the hunky Logan stayin' under the same roof as you . . ." She faked a pining voice and said, "Single, lonely, all vulnerable, and . . ." She laughed.

There was a long pause, and then Beth coughed nervously. "Claire, stop. He's out back in his room over the garage. And, if you must know . . . I haven't told Rory anything, but it's no big deal. It only makes sense that Logan would come home for Christmas. Logan's just a friend, almost like a brother to me . . . and to you. And if I did tell Rory, I know he wouldn't mind one bit." That was only partially true. She talked so much about Logan that she felt that Rory was becoming slightly jealous. He would have to get over it. "So what's up?"

"Hey, I can't talk long." Claire's voice lowered. "He's due home at any time and—"

"Who?"

"Roger."

Beth heard it in her voice. Fear. "What's wrong, Claire? You don't sound like yourself." She pulled her SUV to the side of the road. "What's going on?"

"We just had a fight, that's all. He's a really sweet guy, but some-times . . . he just flies off the handle."

Beth was silent for a moment before she said, "Claire, you're a big girl. You're twenty-four years old and have your own life, but I have to ask you . . . Did he . . . hit you?" She was trying her best not to sound alarmed.

There was a heavy pause of several seconds, then a short response. "No."

Silence.

"No, he didn't hit me. He was just upset about some things, and we had a big fight. I think he's going through a rough patch. I just needed somebody to talk to, that's all . . . and I wanted to say how sorry I am about not coming home for Christmas."

"Tell me about Roger," Beth asked, not wanting to change the subject.

"He needs a job and . . . money. I think I hear somebody at the front door. He's home. I gotta go. I'll be fine. Love ya. Merry Christmas. Bye."

"Claire, wait, call me later and we can—"

Click. The phone went dead. Her sister had never had much luck picking the right guy, but now it seemed like it was only getting worse. *I'll call her tonight. I don't want to wait for her to call me.* She turned off the radio; her Christmas spirits were dampened, and she was worried about her sister. There was something her kid sister was not telling her. A knot began to grow in her stomach.

Beth strode into the hospital lobby and was amazed at the transformation. It lifted her spirits. Christmas trees and decorations were everywhere. Fresh-cut wreaths dotted the hallways; multicolored ornaments were strung about the railings and the steps. Much of the hospital staff sported red or green Christmas elf hats. Above the door at the gift store, someone had hung some sprigs of fresh mistletoe. *Vince, no doubt,* she thought to herself. The place was cheerful; she had made the right decision. She might get fired for her right decision, lose her bonus, and forfeit a possible job in Winston. *All the fresh-cut wreaths will be a hit to my budget, but it was worth it. I will be gone soon anyway. But where?*

"Merry Christmas," she whispered.

CHAPTER
TWENTY-THREE

"Afternoon, Dr. Harding. Merry Christmas," said Carlita as Beth strode past her and into her office.

Carlita was wearing silver Christmas bell earrings that rang when she moved her head from side to side. A fresh pine wreath with gold and silver ornaments hung on her office door.

"Good afternoon, Carli," she said. "Merry Christmas. Beautiful day, isn't it?"

"Yes, indeed. I must say, we're getting a lot of compliments about all the Christmas decorations and the Christmas music on the intercom system. A lot of compliments. Good job there, Doc. But from what I hear, it may cost you your job."

"So? I'll be out of a job in a week anyway. Carlita, have the doctors meet me here. I want to do rounds today with the staff."

"Okay. Sure thing." She paused, then lowered her voice to say, "Drake is waiting in your office to see you. Been here over an hour, and he looks really stressed."

"Got it. Ten minutes, then I'll be ready for rounds. I'm leaving early to do some shopping."

"Really?" she said, sounding surprised. "Coming in late, leaving early—something must be going on. Any hints? Tall? Dark? Handsome? By the name of—"

"Nothing like that at all. I'm going to the Yule Log festivities tonight and then dinner at Henley's. I just need to pick up something to wear."

"Oh, nothing to wear? Hmmm. Are you going by yourself?"

"Well . . . no . . . not by myself . . . I'm going with . . ." She took in a deep breath and said, "Carlita, round up the doctors, please. Gotta go. I don't want to keep Drake waiting any longer."

Drake stood as she walked in and said, "Beth, we need to talk. Do you have ten minutes? It's important."

It sounded ominous. She glanced at him; he looked nervous and anxious. "Sure. Anytime, you know that," she responded, closing the door to her office. "What's up?"

He did not speak at first, trying to remember the words he had been rehearsing. "I've been doing a lot of thinking, about the different presentations we made . . . or rather that I made for our project. And I was all wrong. I'm not a salesman," he blurted out. "And when I looked through the folders with all the information, I realized . . . I let you down . . . and I'm sorry. I didn't present a clear and compelling case."

"Drake, sit down," she said, sitting down next to him. "First of all, one person was not responsible; it was a team effort, both of us. Team effort, remember? Okay? Besides, it doesn't really matter anymore. I thought I could prolong the life of the hospital, but at some point, you have to know when to let it go." She sounded resigned to her fate. "I plan to institute closedown procedures next week, right after Christmas."

She started to stand and he said, "Wait, there's more." He pulled out a folded sheet of stationery from inside his suit jacket pocket. She read it. It was his resignation.

"And?" She held it up in the air with a puzzled look on her face. "What's the rest of the story?" she asked as she sat back down on the sofa.

"I wanted to resign so you could tell them it was all my fault."

"Tell who? What was all your fault? Drake, start from the beginning. Please."

"I was reading through the presentation materials and realized how convoluted and difficult they were to understand. I was drinking rum eggnog and . . . whiskey. Well, I got a little carried away. A card fell on the ground. It was from Amanda Pelletier, director of the Hospital Oversight Board. We made the presentation to her this past summer, and well . . . I . . . called her and left a message on her voice mail."

Beth smiled, imagining Drake tipsy and making a phone call in that condition. "Go on," she said cautiously.

"I told her that if she wanted to see the real hospital world she should leave her ivory tower and come down here and see our program in real life. At least that's what I remember saying . . . I think."

"Don't worry about it, Drake," Beth said in an effort to reassure him.

"Well, her office called this morning. She's coming here to visit on Friday."

Beth laughed. "Don't worry about it. Anything else?"

"Yeah, wait—it gets better. She's coming here with Michael McKerney."

"The governor?" Beth said with alarm creeping into her voice.

"Apparently he's a close friend and an old army buddy of the Colonel. When he found out he was in the hospital . . . well, he wanted to visit him. So they're both coming here to see him, and while they're here they want another presentation on our special copper project."

"Now you can start worrying and preparing. And I think you need to take another look at your proposal. You need to make it easier for everyone to understand. It must be clear and concise. The governor's a very powerful and influential person both here in this state and nation-ally. He can help or hurt our careers tremendously. He sits on a lot of national boards. Bring Carlita into the loop, and she'll help you get anything you need, and I mean anything. Laptop, whiteboard, admin support . . . anything."

Carlita's voice came over the intercom. "Dr. Harding, the physi-cians are here, waiting for you."

"Be right with them," she said to her assistant as she hurried to put on her white clinical jacket. "Drake, start working on that presentation, and see what we can salvage to make it stronger. Then let's you and me huddle later and discuss it. And Drake . . . everything is going to work out fine. What can they do—fire us?" They both laughed nervously.

The group was milling about outside her office door. "Let's roll," she said as she addressed the group. "Let's start in the maternity ward today."

It was her favorite place in the whole hospital. After walking through the first-floor natal security, her face brightened as she saw young Mayerle cuddling a baby.

"Good morning, Dr. Harding. How are you today?"

"Fantastic, Mayerle. How are you?"

"Great."

"Who do you have there?"

"His name is James, Dr. Harding. At least that's what I call him. He's the abandoned one. He cries all the time unless he's cuddled. I think he just needs a little more love than all the others, that's all," she said with the sweetest of smiles.

"Good job, Mayerle. Keep up the good work."

Nurse Abrams came up quickly to the group.

"Good morning, Nurse Abrams. I see that everything is fine here. No problems?"

"No problems at all, Dr. Harding. None at all."

"Good. That's what I like to hear. Good day, Nurse," Beth said. Then she turned to the young woman and said, "Bye, Mayerle. See you soon."

"Bye, Dr. Harding," she said with her kind smile. It was obvious she loved doing what she was trained for, caring for the babies.

"Who's next?" she asked as they walked away.

Dr. Benjamin Waters raised his hand as they resumed their fast-paced walk. "Third floor, Room 300. Patient's name is Nancy Davis. She's a twelve-year-old cancer patient."

Dr. Harding suddenly stopped walking, and she took in a deep breath before continuing. Not many things upset her, but a child cancer patient was one of those things. "Proceed," she whispered.

"She was receiving treatment at the Children's Cancer Clinic in Nashville. But they found there was nothing more they could do for her. So they sent her home. She is receiving her final chemo treatments here, and we're trying to provide her with whatever she needs until—"

Alicia chimed in. "We are trying to keep her as comfortable as possible."

"I see."

They walked down the hallway and soon entered Room 300.

"Good morning," Beth said as she entered. She was immediately greeted by two anxious parents and a smiling twelve-year-old. It broke her heart to see the sweet eyes of the little girl. So young but so—

"Wow," the young girl exclaimed. "I must really be moving up in the world. A whole flock of doctors. And the handsome one is back, too," she said, nodding toward Ben, who was obviously her favorite doctor. Ben smiled.

"My name is Dr. Harding. How are we doing today?"

"I'm doing fine, now that Dr. Ben is here," she said, flirting girlishly.

"I see. Is this something I should be concerned about?" joked Beth, trying to sound stern as her part of the conspiracy.

"No, I know he's already taken," the girl said with a fake pout. "He's married with two kids . . . but I still like to see him. He's just so cute," she said with a mischievous twinkle in her eye.

Beth sat down on the bed beside her. "I agree," she said with a smile. "Who's this?" she asked, pointing to a teddy bear on the bed.

"That's Leo. He's my best friend. The nurses at the children's hospital in Tennessee gave him to me. He's missing one eye."

"He's still very cute."

The little girl managed a weak grin; it was obvious she was tiring. "Thanks, Doc."

"Nancy, is there anything I can get you?"

The little girl looked at her with imploring, shallow blue eyes and then touched her bald head. She looked out the window, imagining days gone by. "I used to have such long blonde hair, and I would brush it every night . . . just like my mom always said—fifty strokes. I don't need a soft hairbrush anymore, but I would still love to have one."

Her mother chimed in, "Nance, I can bring one from home for you . . . if that's what you want?"

"That'd be great, Mom." Then turning back to Beth, she whispered, "If it's not too much to ask, I would love to have some raspberry frozen yogurt. Like we used to have when I was little. If you can get that for me, that would be wonderful."

She nodded to Ben. "I think we can manage that," she said. "I'll see what we can do. I have to go now, but if you need anything, anything at all, you just tell them Dr. Beth said it was okay. All right?"

"You're the best, Dr. Beth. Thanks for everything."

She rubbed the little girl's small, fragile hand and said, "Hey that's why they pay me the big bucks." She smiled. "Bye for now, Nancy. I'll come back to look in on you a little later. If that's okay?"

"I would like that," she said as she cuddled her teddy bear.

"See ya later."

Beth firmly believed that humor could help heal her patients—or if not heal them, then make their journeys that much less difficult. That was what her mother had always trained her to do.

The doctors walked out in silence as they made their way to the next patient's room. "Dr. Stone, I believe the next patient is yours?" Beth finally said.

"Yes, ma'am," she said. "John Mason, twenty-eight years old, firefighter. Severe burns across most of his body sustained during a building fire. We're trying to keep him comfortable, but all of his signs say . . . well . . . it doesn't appear hopeful."

Dr. Harding turned to the young doctor. "I know you're new in town, but the whole world calls this patient Johnny Ray Mason; everybody except for his own doctor." She stopped, and her voice softened. "There are many facets of medicine, Dr. Stone. You need to learn them all." Beth spun around and walked inside the room . . . slowly.

She could see the silhouette of a lone figure in the hospital bed in the corner of the room. His face, hands, and arms were bandaged. The room was quiet and dark. "Open the drapes," she said quietly. "Give us all some light."

Beth walked to his bedside and reached for his wrist, the only area not bandaged. "Hi, Johnny Ray, it's me, Beth Harding. How ya doin'?" She touched him. His head moved slightly. It was obvious he was in pain.

Her voice and tone softly shifted, and she whispered close to his ear, "Hey, when are you getting out of here? We miss havin' you around." The monitor at the bedside jumped in response. She stood there in the corner, with the light streaming inside, and held his hand, whispering things the rest of the group could not hear.

On the monitor they could see his pulse rate becoming stronger.

Before she finally turned to leave, while still holding his hand, she said, "Don't go away now, you hear me? I'll be back to check in on you from time to time. So long, Johnny Ray. And don't you give these cute nurses a hard time. You hear me? Bye for now."

She was quiet as she left him. It was time to check on the Colonel. After a few minutes reviewing his stats on her laptop, she could see there had been no change in his condition. "Hang in there, Colonel, old friend," she whispered.

When she reached the second floor, she found Stephen Collins reclining on the sofa next to his sister's wheelchair. They were sitting patiently in the ICU waiting room. She could tell the little girl had been crying. *I need to find them something to do to keep them occupied,* Beth thought. *And fast.*

Two men rushed past her, toward the girl and her brother. She recognized one of them immediately—Howard Nears from the local television station, WKRD.

"Excuse me!" She called out to them, but they kept on walking. "Excuse me," she said more forcefully. "You can't be in here. This is a hospital."

He spun around and tried to turn on the charm. "Oh, if it isn't the wonderful and talented Dr. Harding. You were next on my list to interview, and I just thought while I was here that—"

"You can't be in here. You have to leave now, or I'll call security and have you escorted out."

He leaned in closer to her and whispered, "Doc, this is major news. Christmas week and here in River Dale we have multiple fires, an arsonist, firemen in the hospital, and a local family in a coma as a result of an auto accident. That's local news anywhere in the country, but here in sleepy River Dale, where nothing ever happens, it's national news."

"You mean the kind of news reporting that gets national attention and promotes the career of an enterprising reporter from a small local station to the big networks? That kind of news?"

"Exactly. So glad you see it my way, Doc."

As he started to turn away, she said, "Leave now, or I'll call security."

"But, Doc—"

"Now," she said firmly. "You can wait outside if you like, but I have a hospital to run."

"Yeah, sure, for the next couple of days," he muttered under his breath to his cameraman. "Come on, Gerry, let's go outside. Let's get some shots from the emergency room. We can do our feed from there."

She watched them leave and, once the elevator door closed behind them, she turned her attention to Stephen and Lisa.

"Hi, guys," she said to them. He looked different cleaned up. Clean shaven, clean hands. Handsome. Well dressed.

"Hey, Dr. Harding," said Stephen. "I went home this morning to clean up and change clothes. Any word on my mom and dad? I know it can't be good for them to be in a coma for this long."

"You're right, but all we can do now is sit and wait . . . and pray."

"I gave blood this morning. I just wish there was something else we could do."

Beth leaped at the opportunity. "Well, if you really want to do something to help . . . No, I'm sorry. I can't ask you that. You're so busy, but this waiting must be driving you crazy."

"What, Doc? We'll do anything. I hate this this sitting around, waiting . . ."

"Well, if you really want to help out, every year we have employees from the various hospital wards and local schools sing Christmas carols to all the ambulatory patients in the cafeteria. Then they go to the other floors to sing to those who are bedridden. This year our regular volunteer choir director is out on maternity leave, so the choir program has really fallen apart. They could use some help and direction." She saw the spark of interest in his eyes.

She continued knowingly. "I understand you like to compose songs and sing and . . . I thought if you wanted to give some pointers to our group . . . well, it really does cheer up all the patients this time of the year."

He knew immediately what she was asking and why. "Sure, Dr. Harding. We'd be happy to, right, Lisa? Want to go sing in a choir? It'll help take our mind off things here. We won't be far away."

"I'll go anywhere with you, Stevie. Let's go."

He pushed her wheelchair down the hallway, and as he left, he mouthed the words, "Thank you."

After they were gone, Beth went into their parents' room and checked their charts from the computer. Not good. She closed her eyes and silently prayed, *Oh please, Lord, help us help them.* Medicine could only go so far, her mother always said.

Once back in her office, she thought about all the patients she had visited that day; then she closed the door and silently began to cry.

I should have the board and county council make the rounds with me. Let them see the hurt and suffering and the good we do here.

She glanced at her watch and stopped by Room 205.

"Hiya, Sweetie," she said, walking into the woman's room.

"What a nice surprise," the old woman said with a smile, looking up from her magazine. "Well if it isn't Dr. Big Cheese."

"Yes," Beth said with a grin. "How are you feeling?" she asked, sitting down in the chair beside Sweetie's bed.

"I'm fine. But from the looks of it, I have a sneaking suspicion that I'm doing much better than you."

"What makes you say that?"

The woman patted Beth's hand. "Dearie, I may be old, I may be forgetful, and I can't even remember my own name, but I can still tell when someone is down in the dumps. And, Doc, you look like you could use some cheering up."

"You're right. It hasn't been the best of days. But I'm trying."

"What you really need is to have someone you can go home to and sit and talk to. A shoulder to cry on. Someone you can sit in front of a fire with, share a glass of wine with, and make tender, passionate love to on a cold, snowy night. That's what you need. You don't want to be taking home medical reports to read in bed every night for the rest of your life . . . now do you?"

"No . . . I don't."

"Do you have someone special?"

Beth had to think for a minute before saying, "Yes, I do." She paused while still holding Sweetie's hand and asked, "How did you get so wise?"

"I don't know. Ask me again when I can remember my own name, and I may be able to give you a better answer." They both laughed. "Now go out and find that special someone and hold him tight and never let him go."

Beth went back to her office and finished her paperwork. Then, true to her word, she made her way back in to check on all the patients she had visited during the day before going to Winston to shop for some new clothes.

Driving home after a successful trip, she remembered what the old woman had told her. She realized what she needed now was someone she could share her day with, the good as well as the bad. It was all building up inside her. She needed someone who would listen to her. Someone who would understand.

Logan.

CHAPTER TWENTY-FOUR

Logan knocked on the back door and waited for her to answer. His new shirt and sweater felt scratchy on his neck and arms. *Suck it up, Logan. You want to look nice for tonight, now don't you?* He moved his finger around the shirt collar to stretch it, but it did not help. Then he noticed he had shaving cream on his new pants; when he went to brush it off, he heard the door open.

"Hey, I thought that was you. You should have come inside. It's cold out here."

She was right about that. It was cold, and it had started to snow again. "I didn't want to barge inside, just in case you were getting dressed or . . . something like that."

"Oh, Logan, you're so gallant and so old-fashioned. One of the things I love the most about you." Beth went back inside and soon pulled on her coat and wrapped a long scarf around her neck. "I'm ready to go if you are."

"Yep, I sure am."

She closed the door and, grabbing his arm, pulled him close. "I found the Christmas card you left on the table. It was very sweet. Thank you."

"You're welcome. I'm a sucker for Hallmark cards. I guess I'm just an old-fashioned kind of guy," he said with a laugh. He looked at her. She was a vision. She looked so beautiful, so fresh. She was wearing a long red skirt, high leather boots, and a formfitting navy sweater. On her jacket lapel was a sprig of mistletoe.

He kidded her as they walked to the car. "Remember when we were kids and we'd take our sleds up to the end of the yard and ride down the hill?"

Turning to look fondly at the backyard, she said, "Yeah, and then we would come back here and, when the snow was fresh and deep, we would fall backward and flap our arms and legs to make snow angels. Then at night, we would look up at the sky and see all the stars. The Big Dipper. Orion's Belt. I remember sometimes, on rare occasions, we could see the northern lights from here, and we would make a wish."

She paused for a minute and then whispered, "My wish was always the same." She was getting misty-eyed. "Now look at the backyard. Look at mom's favorite rosebushes all covered in white snow . . . waiting for springtime. Makes you sad to see."

They both stood together looking at the garden in the backyard. "Yeah," he said. Without thinking, he put his arm around her shoulders and held her close. It just felt like the natural thing to do. She was his best friend.

She sighed, patted his hand, and said, "I guess we'd better be going. We don't want to be late for the Yule Log ceremony."

"No," he said quietly, "I guess not. Let's go."

Logan held open the car door for her, and they drove together toward town. After a few minutes, he turned on the radio and found some Christmas music. He began to sing along. "Jingle bells, jingle bells, jingle all the way."

She joined in the singing. Another memory. When the song was over she asked him, "So how was your day?"

"Fine. I slept late after you left, then stopped by the hospital to look in on Johnny Ray and the Colonel. I went by your office, and Carlita said you were out. Then I went into Winston to get some things." He instinctively touched his shirt collar.

"Me, too. And I spoke to Claire today."

"Sister Claire?" he joked.

"Yeah, the one and only. She called me from Boston. I must say, she has the worst taste in boyfriends. This one sounds controlling, and I got a little concerned after talking to her. But the spooky part was, she sounded . . . scared.

Logan's voice changed. He became serious. "Why do you say that?"

"I don't know. Maybe it was her tone. He walked in while we were talking, and she rushed to get off the phone. I just didn't get warm cozies from our conversation, you know what I mean?"

"Yeah, I do." He drove in silence, and then his face beamed. "Hey, listen, I'm going to be in Boston tomorrow for a fire and communications demonstration."

"You are?" she said, sounding disappointed.

"Yeah. I have some free time after the program set aside for sightseeing in the city and some shopping. I can break away and stop by to see her. If you want?"

"Could you?" she asked, now sounding excited and relieved at the same time. "That would be great. I'll let her know you're coming by to see her. Make sure she's going to be home. As a nurse she has a real crazy schedule. But if you could, that would be wonderful. Thanks, Logan." She leaned over to hug him and kiss him on the cheek. "I know I can always count on you to come through."

She thought about what she had just said and realized it was true. She could always count on him, no matter what. That was Logan. Dependable Logan. Sweet Logan. He would be leaving soon, and it might be years before she would see him again. *Years*, the word sounded harsh. The thought of that made her sad. She looked out the side window.

He glanced over at her and remarked, "Hey, cheer up. I'm sure everything is fine. Claire can take care of herself, believe me. She's not going to let some guy she just met steamroller over her, that's for sure."

Logan looked to the tree line beyond the meadow alongside the road. He saw something running in the snowy field. "Look, Beth! See?" he pointed in that direction. "Remember the old New England wives' tale? Two foxes a runnin'—more storms a comin'. Remember? More snow must be on the way."

"Yeah," Beth said softly, distracted as they pulled into the parking lot off the main square and rushed to find a seat for the ceremony. The square, the streets, and the stores were all dark. In the center of the square was a fire pit with a large grate containing two charred logs.

The Yule Log ceremony was one of the oldest Christmas traditions in New England, dating back some two hundred years, and could be traced back further to similar ceremonies in Europe. It was one of Logan's—and Beth's—favorite traditions.

The mayor walked to the stone mound in the center of the square and held up his hand for silence. "Today is the winter solstice and a night to remember those who are near and dear to us and cannot be with us tonight. We begin the Christmas season with the lighting of the logs from last year's ceremony. Pause to reflect on those loved ones who are not here with us." As he talked, he poured a pungent brown liquid onto the logs and then tossed a match onto it. It burst into flames.

He next took a small log, doused it with spiced red wine, and threw it onto the fire. When he was finished, one of the women from the local church group handed him a glass of traditional cherry wine to drink. The next woman handed him a small cup filled with sand with a small lit candle in the center. The procession of townsfolk behind him followed in line.

Townspeople picked their own logs and added wine to them before throwing them on the growing bonfire. Others took items from one of the baskets on the sidewalk to toss onto the fire. One basket contained corn stalks and sprigs of holly. Another was filled with pieces of unleavened bread and a small container of walnuts soaked in brandy. The last basket was smaller and contained slices of oranges and apples. They represented sustenance, the warmth of family, the Christmas holidays, and good harvest.

Beth and Logan made their way to the fire. They each picked up a log, then dunked it into the bucket of wine. "Goodly be thy memories," the pastor said with a solemn smile as they passed by.

They paused before tossing the logs onto the fire, remembering loved ones who were no longer with them. Logan handed her a candle and a glass of cherry wine.

They felt the growing warmth of the fire as the flames reached high into the night sky. The burning mixture of the wine, brandy, oranges, and corn stalks filled the air. The flames sizzled when the logs hit the now-roaring bonfire, and the aroma was unmistakable. It was intoxicating. It was an aroma Logan never forgot, and it always brought back so many memories.

Logan and Beth stood next to each other, each holding a candle in one hand and a glass of wine in the other. When the last person had fed the roaring fire, it began to pop, with red-hot cinders landing on the nearby sidewalk. The crowd began to sing a traditional English Christmas carol by Robert Herrick called "Ceremonies for Christmas." Beth smiled, and they both joined in, holding hands in the spirit of the holiday night.

> Come, bring with a noise,
> My merry, merry boys,
> The Christmas Log to the firing;
> While my good Dame, she
> Bids ye all be free;
> And drink to your heart's desiring.

With the last year's brand
Light the new block, and
For good success in his spending,
On your Psaltries play,
That sweet luck may
Come while the log is a-tinding.

Next the crowd began a rousing rendition of "Silent Night," followed by "Jingle Bells," "The Little Drummer Boy," and other favorites.

Soon the church bells rang loud from the white steeple high above the crowd. Everyone turned to face the church and the majestic Christmas tree in the square. With the signal given, the multicolored lights on the town's Christmas tree were lit to a chorus of oohs and aahs. The lights were barely visible under the coating of snow, flickering in an almost surreal vision. Slowly, the lights of the village came back on inside the shops, the streetlights, and around the square. The Christmas spirit was alive in the small hamlet of River Dale.

Fireworks from the hill behind the church lit up the night sky, bursting over them in multicolor, another Christmas tradition. They stood together arm in arm watching the huge, spectacular bursts open in the December sky. The finale seemed to last forever.

"Wonderful!" said Logan with a huge smile on his face as they walked away from the ceremony.

"Yes, it was," Beth said.

"That is one of the things I always miss being away from here," he said.

"One of the things?" she queried. "What else?"

"I miss fly-fishing in the river in springtime. I miss the valleys covered in spring flowers. Biking along the river road. In summer, I miss the array of sunflowers in the open fields, as if they're smiling at everyone as you drive by."

She had a look of dejection on her face.

"And I miss . . . seeing you every day." *Where's your brain, Logan? No! She's engaged to be married, you dope.* He hastened to add, "And I miss seeing the Colonel and everybody else in town."

"Oh," was all she could muster in response.

"Hungry?" he asked, changing the subject.

"Famished."

"Me, too. Let's go eat."

They passed Richmond's, the small clothing store on the main square, with its Christmas lights flickering in the windows. They slowed in front of the bakery on their way to Henley's Restaurant and, as always, old Mrs. Schmidt was still inside, waiting on customers. The aroma of freshly baked chocolate chip cookies was inviting.

"I can almost taste those cookies," Beth said. "Maybe we can stop later and get some? What do you say?"

"Sounds good to me."

CHAPTER
TWENTY-FIVE

Henley's Restaurant was a River Dale institution, serving great local and regional specialties and drawing a large following from the surrounding towns. The bar was directly ahead of them as they entered, with a podium off to the left of the foyer, where a young hostess greeted them.

"Good evening, Dr. Harding," said the young girl with a boisterous smile. "Remember me? Monica? From the nurses' training clinic this summer?"

A flicker of recognition slowly dawned on Beth's face. "Ah yes, Monica Sullivan. I remember you. How are you?"

"Very good. I got into nursing school starting next semester. I can hardly wait," she said with another huge smile. She picked up two menus and said, "Follow me, please." She made her way through the crowded restaurant.

Over her shoulder, she said, "It can get kinda noisy in here when they open up the dance floor and the music starts. Follow me. I reserved a small booth for the two of you back here in the corner, just as you requested."

Henley's was divided into two distinct parts. The room off to the left of the entrance was the bar area that served a smaller menu filled with tapas, chicken wings, fresh oysters, small seafood plates, and happy hour specials to a large and often raucous crowd. The main restaurant to the right of the bar served a full menu and featured white tablecloths and candles in the center of the tables. The candles were more practical than romantic, since the low lighting made it otherwise difficult to read the menus.

"Perfect," they both said in unison.

There was a small, empty dance floor off to the left, just steps away. In Henley's, country music was usually the tune of choice, but since it was Christmastime the DJ was featuring many of the old standards and new renditions of Christmas classics for the holidays.

In the far corner of the room, beyond the dance floor, stood a tall memorial Christmas tree. The blue spruce was so tall, it crouched just beneath the ceiling of the restaurant. Hanging from it were many different brightly colored ornaments—red, green, blue, and white. Each had its own special meaning. A large American flag hung prominently on the back wall.

"Your server tonight will be Jonathan. Enjoy," Monica said after handing them their menus.

Their server was a college student home for the holidays. "Hi, I'm Jonathan. Would you like to hear the specials for tonight?"

"Yes," they said, looking at the menu.

"Tonight we're featuring a fourteen-ounce venison steak that's been marinated in Worcestershire sauce, red wine, cognac, allspice, cloves, limes, and oranges for ten days. After that we rub it with our special spices and slow sear it over a hickory wood fire grill to keep it nice and juicy. Very tender, and it is absolutely out of this world," he said enthusiastically. "It's served with garlic and olive oil smashed potatoes with a side of fresh green beans. Next we have—"

"Whoa, no need to go any further for me. I'll have the venison," Logan said.

"Ditto for me," chimed in Beth.

"That's an easy one for me. What can I get you two to drink, red wine? Water? Beer? Soda?"

"Make mine a glass of merlot," said Beth.

"Gimme a glass of River Dale Pale Ale, and bring us an order of chicken wings to share. I've missed those," said Logan.

"You guys are too easy," he said, grabbing the menus from the table. "Would you care to donate to the Christmas tree memorial? It's for the kids' campaign, Toys for Kids. For a five-dollar donation, we hang a memorial ornament on the tree for you. A white ornament is for a family, a green one for POWs, a red one for the House of Ruth, and a blue one for special intentions for those loved ones who aren't with us for the holidays. Would you like to donate?"

Logan gave him a twenty-dollar bill. "Tell them to put up two blue ones for me, for Mom and Dad, and two green ones, for friends." He turned to Beth.

"Two white ones and two blue ones for me, please," she said, reaching for her purse.

Logan fished in his wallet and gave the waiter another twenty dollars. She touched his hand. "Thanks, Logan."

"I appreciate it, folks. And the kids thank you as well. Be right back with the beer and wine, along with your appetizer."

They sat across from each other as people walked by and said hello and merry Christmas to both of them. Some of them were friends Logan had not seen in years, and those individuals were disappointed when he said he was only in town for the holidays. "Stay longer next time," was a familiar refrain.

"This is like old home week," he said with a smile before turning back to Beth and asking, "So how was the rest of your day?"

"I called Claire again tonight before we left home."

"And?"

"She sounded okay, but I think he was right beside her because I could hear whispers in the background. He seems so controlling. I'm just a little afraid, that's all. You know, being big sister and all."

"I understand. I'll check in on her tomorrow when I'm in Boston and give you a full report when I get back."

The waiter brought their drinks and appetizer order. Spicy chicken wings. "Here, try this," he told them.

They each picked one up and took a bite.

"Hot and spicy!" Logan nearly shouted as he waved his hand over his mouth in an attempt to cool it down. He hoisted his beer glass in the air. "I forgot how spicy they are."

Beth could not stop laughing. "You've just gone soft, that's all, Logan. Too much California livin'. Besides, I thought you liked things hot."

"Ha ha ha. Very funny," he said with a chuckle.

Just as they finished their chicken wings, young Jonathan brought them their steaks. They were huge and sizzling hot. Beth and Logan listened to the steaks crackle on the plates.

"Time to eat," Logan finally said.

"I don't know whether to eat it or ride it home," Beth joked, picking up her knife and fork to slice into the juicy, tender steak. She took one bite and proclaimed loudly, "Oh my God! This venison steak is the best I've ever had in my life, ever." She was obviously enjoying herself.

Logan cut his steak and, after tasting the first piece, said, "Wow! This tastes like nothing I have ever had before."

They continued to talk as they slowly consumed their wonderful meal.

In making conversation Beth told him, "I found out today from my chief of staff—you remember Drake, the Brit?—that he had called someone in the governor's office when he was a little tipsy and invited them to visit the real world here in River Dale. Now they're coming to hear a presentation on a special project we did here. Unfortunately, it's the same presentation we made to them a few months ago."

Logan looked puzzled. "You're closing the hospital soon, so what does it matter?"

"The governor and Amanda, his director of the state hospital board, are very influential nationwide. It can make or break a career. I don't think Drake knew what he was putting into motion when he made the phone call."

"You'll manage, I'm sure of it," Logan said. "I have the utmost confidence in you. What else is bothering you?" He continued to eat his steak as they talked.

She smiled. "For me, today was a day of revelations. I discovered that I really missed the day-to-day doctoring, the tending to patients. I miss the interactions. I comforted a little girl whose mother and father are in comas; we don't know if they will ever wake up. And a young cancer patient who . . ." She coughed, then stopped. "I looked in on the Colonel and on Johnny Ray. It's so horrible to see them in pain."

"I know. I feel the same way."

"And then I looked in on an elderly woman who lost her memory and is trying to put on a brave front, trying to show everyone she's not afraid to be alone in her own world. Then she's giving me advice. Telling me to find someone that I can . . ." She paused, smiled, and took a sip from her glass of wine.

Logan set his fork down and listened to every word she said. Not judging her, not directing her, merely listening.

"And I keep trying to put it out of my mind . . . but I have to face the reality of closing the hospital, the place that my mother worked so hard to build. For a small hospital, she was doing innovative work. She had papers published in *JAMA*. She was, right to the end, trying to save the world one patient at a time. She had some very innovative ideas and practices. Then I ask myself, what do I do now? Should I return to Chicago? Or do I open up a private practice as a pediatrician? On the other hand, do I go back to school? Or do I look for another administrative job? Or take the job at Ascot Pharmaceuticals?"

Looking at her and breaking his silence, Logan asked, "What job is that?"

"Marketing consultant. I'd be working for the same firm Rory works for in Chicago. It's more money than I make now, but it involves a lot of travel. And it's with a pharmaceutical company, a whole new field for me." She paused to reflect, managing a weak smile. "I just don't know, but I tell you . . . it's been great to be able to think aloud and at least talk about it with somebody. Thanks, Logan," she said, placing her hand on his.

"That's what friends are for, to be there through thick and thin."

She was still holding his hand in the center of the table when their waiter reappeared.

"Can I interest you folks in some coffee and dessert? Great homemade pies. Baker River Mud Pie. The best in town. Or some homemade apple pie. Or cherry pie?" Jonathan asked.

"Split it?" they both said at the same time, then laughed.

"Sold," Logan said. "But which one? Maybe the mud pie or . . . They all sound so good. I don't know."

Beth smiled as she saw another familiar face. "Well, look who it is? Drake. Hiya, Drake," Beth said as he passed by on his way out the door. "I thought you only ate Chinese food," she joked.

Drake watched as she slowly removed her hand from Logan's. "Hi, Dr. Harding. Yeah, my one great vice, I love Chinese food. But some neighbors in my apartment building had a little get-together and invited me along. Nice folks. Fun." He waved at a young dark-haired woman in the crowd by the bar. "Very nice."

"Oh, Drake, I want you to meet an old friend of mine. Logan Mitchell, Drake Corrigan. Drake is from England and is my right-hand manager at the hospital. Don't know what I would do without him."

"She would manage just fine, Logan; don't believe a word she says."

They shook hands, and Logan said, "Nice to meet you, Drake. I've heard your name mentioned on numerous occasions. Would you care to join us?"

"No, thank you. I had best be going. I have a lot of paperwork and research to review before my presentation Friday. Good to meet you, Logan. Good night, Dr. Harding." He made his way through the crowded restaurant toward the door.

"He seems nice," said Logan.

"Very nice. I could not run the hospital without him." They both chuckled, then looked at each other in awkward silence until Jonathan returned to take their dessert order. "So did you decide which pie you wanted to order?"

"Apple," they both said.

The DJ turned up the volume on the music and said, "And now for a changeup, something to dance to—an old rock-and-roll classic. Come on, everybody, let's fill the dance floor. Come on up. Grab your partner and join the fun."

"Jonathan, can you come back in a few minutes?" Beth asked.

"Sure."

She looked at Logan and asked, "Wanna dance?"

"I don't really dance that well."

"So what? Most people out on the dance floor don't, either. Just look confident, and you'll do fine. Move your feet and wave your arms," she said with a laugh. "Come on. I feel like dancing . . . *pleeeease*," she pleaded.

"Okay, okay, if you want to dance, but I warn you that I—"

She grabbed him by the arm and pulled him from his seat, out onto the dance floor. "It only matters that you have fun when you dance," she shouted over the blaring music.

The beat was loud and wild, but he soon began to enjoy it. *This isn't so tough to do,* he smugly thought to himself. He could tell Beth was having a ball. They danced to another song, then another, and soon he was getting into the groove of a regular beat. *Hmmm, not bad*, he thought. He watched her move and smile—that wonderful smile.

"Now for a slow song for the lovers out there," said the DJ.

The music started, and they both stood there, looking awkward in the middle of the dance floor. "May I have the pleasure of this dance, my dear?" he finally asked her in his most chivalrous manner, bowing from the waist, extending his hand to her.

"I would be honored, sir," she said in reply, faking a curtsy and then laughing.

Their hands intertwined ever so lightly, they began to sway to the melody. Logan held her close as they danced to the slow song. The DJ dimmed the lights.

Beth snuggled closer to him, her body next to his, her heart beating faster and faster. She swayed with him, in tune with his body. Cheek to cheek, chest to chest. She felt the strength in his arms and the coarseness of his hands after all the years of working with axes, chain saws, and shovels—the tools of a firefighter. But the way he held her now, how he held her, his touch was ever so gentle. But that was Logan; that was always Logan, the gentle warrior. She placed her head on his chest, slowly moving to the music.

Closer.

Something was different. *This is Logan . . . my Logan. My best friend. What's going on here? I don't understand.* Even though she had known him most of her life, she struggled to admit to herself that her feelings for him had been changing. But soon he would be gone. She knew now what she had to do. She had to tell him before it was too late, before he left. She had to tell him how she felt. Carlita was right. *Tell him*, she thought.

There were only two other couples on the dance floor swaying to the rhythms of the slow music as the snow began to fall outside.

✳

Logan had never been this close to her before in his whole life. Holding her like this, he was in heaven. He could feel her chest against his, and he felt her heart beating. Or was it his heart that was beating so loud? *It doesn't matter,* he thought. The scent of her sweet perfume was intoxicating. *This was not a good idea, but I can't let her go.* When he took her in his arms, he commanded her body. She was now his. *Let it go, Logan—admit it. Finally tell her. Tell her!*

He had dreamed his whole life of holding her in his arms like this, dreamed of this very moment—their bodies pressed close together, his cheek against hers. He never wanted to let her go, and he never wanted the song to end. *Tell her, Logan! Tell her now!*

"Beth," he whispered, "I have something I need to tell you. Something I should have told you a long time ago." Her hands and body felt so soft, so inviting, so—

"Excuse me," said a loud voice just as Logan felt a tap on his shoulder. "May I cut in? Can I have this dance?" They both turned around.

It was Rory, her fiancé.

CHAPTER
TWENTY-SIX

"Rory? What are you doing here?" Beth asked in amazement, taking a deep swallow while she was still entangled in Logan's arms.

"I thought I would come and surprise you. Obviously, I succeeded."

She stood there speechless, not knowing what to say to him as she reluctantly let go of Logan's hand.

"Don't I get a kiss or a hug, or something? It's been a while since we've seen each other."

"Oh yes, of course." She put her arms around him and kissed him on the cheek, while Logan stood beside them. "Oh, where are my manners? Rory, this is Logan Mitchell. Logan, I'd like you to meet Rory Daniels . . . my fiancé."

"Good to meet you, Logan. Thanks for keeping the Doc here company while I've been away." The music stopped and the crowd thinned, leaving just the three of them on the small dance floor.

"Join us, Rory. We were just going to have coffee and dessert."

"Great . . . I'm starved. I'd like something a little more substantial," he said. As they returned to their table, Rory's hand reached down to hers. "You guys can have dessert. I want a steak or something." He sat down next to Beth and placed his hand on her leg.

"So tell me, why didn't you call me? When did you get in?" she asked, sounding excited.

"I wanted to surprise you. And I thought of what you must be going through, closing the hospital and all . . . Well, I wanted to come here and give you some moral support. It's been a long time since we've seen each other. Thanksgiving. Besides, I've always wondered what it would be like to experience Christmas in New England. Everything here looks so wonderful."

Beth turned to Logan and explained. "Rory is originally from Los Angeles, and his family didn't really celebrate Christmas much."

"Well, welcome to New England. Do you ski?"

"No, not really. I'm not an outdoorsy kind of guy. What do you do, Brogan? For a living, I mean."

"Logan. His name is Logan, Rory, remember?" Beth said with a tense smile.

"Sorry, I was just so excited to see you it must have slipped my mind. Sorry, Logan."

"No problem. I work as a firefighter," he said proudly.

"That's right, I remember now. So you're one of those crazy guys who goes running into a burning building when everybody else in the world is running the other way?"

"Yep, that's me. Most recently, I've been out west fighting forest fires as a smoke jumper."

"Smoke jumper?"

"Yeah. They fly us in front of a forest fire, then we parachute to the fire and create a fire line to try to stop it from moving farther and growing."

"And what happens if you don't?"

Logan paused before he continued, trying not to show his irritation. "If we don't stop it . . . then we die. The goal is to stop the fire before that happens."

"Well, obviously you're successful. You're still here, aren't you?" Rory said with a chuckle.

"Yes," responded Logan, glancing at his watch.

"Here comes Jonathan, our waiter," said Beth.

Jonathan appeared with a smile. "You folks ready for your coffee and dessert? Homemade apple pie."

"Two coffees and we'll split a piece of apple pie," Logan replied. "And our friend here wants to order some dinner." Logan turned to Rory and said, "The venison special is outstanding."

"Isn't that deer? Ugh," Rory replied, peering over the menu that he had found on the table.

"It was wonderful. Try it—you'll like it," responded a gleeful Beth.

"I don't think so. I'll pass, thank you. Give me a bacon cheese-burger, rare, and fries, along with a beer. Chicago Ale."

"Sir, unfortunately, we don't carry that brand of beer here. But we do have thirty other kinds of microbrew beer."

"The River Dale Pale Ale is good. It's a local brew," Logan chimed in.

Rory ignored the recommendation. "Tell you what, just give me a Bud. Thanks."

He returned his attention to Logan. "Firefighter, huh? Tough job?"

Logan squirmed. "I never thought about it that way. It has to be done, and every firefighter I've ever known thinks of it more as a commitment than a job. Like a cop or schoolteacher. You'll never get rich being a fireman, that's for sure."

"Hmmm. One thing I could never understand. With all the improvements in housing codes and construction, greater use of sprinkler systems, and the huge decrease in fires, why has there never been a corresponding reduction in the number of firefighters?" He looked around for their waiter. "Also, it seems for every little thing that happens, people call the fire department. Then, when they respond, they bring out those huge trucks just for minor fender benders."

He turned to Beth sitting next to him. "In Chicago, we had a fire on our street, in a townhouse about three weeks ago, and this big fire truck came by and knocked the mirror off my BMW. Cost me over four hundred bucks to get it fixed. Can you believe it?"

"Were the people okay?" Logan whispered.

"What people?"

"Your neighbors. The ones with the fire."

"Yeah, I guess."

"Then the firefighters did their job. You see, as a firefighter in the national forests my job is not to protect property but to stop the fire from spreading. But firefighters in cities are charged with putting people first and property second. I kind of like the distinction."

"Here you go, sir. An ice-cold Bud," said Jonathan, setting Rory's beer down in front of him.

"Thanks."

Logan leaned forward and continued. "The way I see it, fighting fires is no longer a firefighter's primary mission. Most modern-day firefighters are trained as emergency medical technicians—EMTs. They're trained to respond to all sorts of emergencies. Not just fires. We handle suicides, train derailments, gas leaks, car accidents, water leaks, fires, heart attacks, building permit inspections, and a lot of other things. Because of where fire stations are located and the fact that we are on call twenty-four hours a day, we're usually the first responders."

"I see," Rory said as his burger and huge plate of french fries were quickly delivered.

Jonathan asked him before he left, "Sir, would you like to donate to the annual kids' campaign? For five dollars, we hang a Christmas tree ornament to honor the memory of a loved one. The money is then donated to a needy charities, House of Ruth, and a special children's fund."

Rory looked up at him while holding his burger in his hand. "No, I don't think so." Then after Jonathan left, he turned to Beth. "Everybody always has an angle to get more cash out of your pocket. Some type of scam. It's always something."

"Rory! That's a horrible thing to say," Beth said.

Logan explained to him. "I can assure you, it's not a scam. The money they collect goes to help out needy kids."

"Hmmm," mumbled Rory with a mouthful of food. "You were saying, about your view of firefighters?"

Logan was silent at first, then continued. "I've always said that it made sense that instead of having firefighters and ambulances plus redundant EMTs, to combine the operations into some sort of Urban Response Team capable of handling all kinds of situations. And it would save money. An easy transition but slowed by the tradition of having separate operations, separate budgets, and by the mere fact it's never been done until recently. They're trying it in Oregon, and it's saved lives, shortened response time, and saved a lot of money."

Rory seemed intrigued. "Hmmm, obviously you've given this a lot of thought, Logan. It makes a world of sense; why not present it to the powers to be?"

"I'm not a politician. I'm a firefighter. That's what I do. I'm a smoke jumper—and always will be."

Beth asked, sipping her coffee, "What if you had to give it up?"

He turned to look at her. "Well, I guess maybe I am getting a little old to be jumping out of an airplane, but as long as they'll have me, and my age isn't a danger to me or my coworkers, I guess I'll keep doing it." He paused for a moment then asked, "What do you do for a living, Rory?"

"Basically, I'm a salesman. Even though I have a master's degree in biology, I started out selling flavored water for a big multinational company in Atlanta, then shifted to selling plain water. Who'd figure that people would pay for something they can get right out of their tap at home for free? Then I worked in sales and marketing for two different cruise lines. Now I'm working for a pharmaceutical company, selling

the virtues of antibiotics. Good company, good job. It pays the bills."
He laughed, then said, "Oh my God, Beth, I almost forgot to tell you,
I got a promotion. And I got a raise, a big one. You're looking at Ascot
Pharmaceutical's newest vice president of brand development. And I
got a new corner office!"

"Oh, Rory, that's wonderful. I am so pleased for you. And so
proud . . . you deserve it." Her eyes beamed approval.

"There's more." He pulled an envelope from his suit jacket and
handed it to her. "I got you a better job offer, with a salary increase of
more than fifty thousand a year. I told them if they wanted to keep both
of us happy, that this is what it would take."

Beth opened the envelope, and her eyes never left the offer letter that she held in her hand. "Rory! Wow! I can't believe this," she
exclaimed as she reread the employment offer letter.

"They want you, Beth; they really do. You'll get your copy in the
mail in a few days. Slow because of the holidays, but I wanted to bring
this to you. Isn't it fantastic?"

"Oh, Rory," she said, "I don't know what to say."

"Just say yes. But there's more."

"More? More than this," she said, her eyes moving across the table
to watch an increasingly uncomfortable Logan.

"What is the one thing that you've been asking me for since we
got engaged?"

She looked at him and then at Logan. She was starting to feel
uncomfortable before she finally shook her head and shrugged. "What?"

"A wedding date. So, I was thinking, all your friends are here on the
East Coast, your family, your neighbors are all here. Let's get married
here. I passed a quaint little New England church in town with a simple
little white spire. We could have a small, intimate wedding here and
then have a really big one back in Chicago with all of our friends there.
What do you think?" Before she could respond, he added, "And the
hospital will be closing soon. We could get married on New Year's Eve."

"New Year's Eve?" she nearly shouted. "Wow, that's so soon."

Logan heard the nervousness in her voice.

"Well, if we do it, then we can take the married tax deduction for this year. I'll take care of all the details so you won't have to worry about a thing. I'll handle the license, flowers, a band, a hall, the works. Then we could take a nice honeymoon to the Caribbean. Relax on the beach. Drink piña coladas with little umbrellas and have a great time, just you and me. What do you say? This is what we've talked about for months. Right? Now you get your wish. Well, what do you say?"

Beth looked at Rory, then at Logan, then back at Rory.

"What do you say, Beth? Come on, go for it. This is what you've been asking for, isn't it?" Rory stopped for a minute, sneezed, then leaned away from her, asking, "You still want to get married . . . Don't you?"

"Yes, of course, of course. It's just that it's moving so fast. It'll be a tight time frame . . . but I guess we can do it." She hugged him tight, then said to Logan, "Isn't this exciting?"

"Yes, it is. I'm happy for you, Beth, really I am."

Rory sneezed again. "And since Logan is the only guy I know in town, maybe he'll consent to be my best man?"

Logan fidgeted. "Well, if I'm still here. I had planned to come here and see how the Colonel was doing and then . . . visit friends. I should be getting back to California soon. There's not much more for me here." He glanced at his watch and then said, "Speaking of which, I have an early-morning trip tomorrow. I'm off to Boston. Where are you staying, Rory?"

"I'm booked into the Holden Inn, just outside Winston. Small four-story boutique hotel. Very clean. Very nice. And no dust. Brand-new, just the way I like it."

"Rory, would you mind driving Beth home? I am up early tomorrow and . . ." Logan wiped his mouth with his napkin and stood.

"No problem, Brogan," said Rory, shaking his hand. "No problem at all."

"Good night, Beth." Logan turned and walked away.

"Thanks, *Logan*," she said as she watched him leave. "His name is Logan," she said, turning to Rory. "And you know it. He's my brother, and you acted like a real jerk. He means a lot to me."

"Brother? Yeah?" said Rory, as he popped the last of the french fries into his mouth. "I saw the way he held you on the dance floor. And the way he looks at you. The way I see it, I think that guy's crazy about you."

"You're the one who's crazy. He's just a friend. A very good friend. I've known him since we were little kids."

"Well, I got here just in time to save you . . . from family. Besides, I don't think he minds being called Brogan. He doesn't appear to be thin-skinned."

"No, he's not," she whispered. "But I don't like it, even if he's too much of a gentleman to say something to you. Don't do it again."

She continued to fume when he reached out and touched her arm. "Look, you're right. I'm sorry. I acted like a jerk. It's just that it's been a long day for me, that's all. Forgive me?"

"Yeah," she said. Then she quickly added, "Just don't let it happen again."

They finished their drinks, and Rory waved to their waiter for the bill.

"Oh, the gentleman who was with you took care of it. It's all paid for, sir."

CHAPTER
TWENTY-SEVEN

Logan left early the next morning for Boston, glancing up at Beth's window as he drove out of the driveway. *Still asleep. She's getting married. It was all over before it even started. Probably for the best. Why didn't you tell her? You should have said something, you big oaf.* But that was not his way, and he knew it. *But what does she see in him? He's so obnoxious. Beth is way too smart not to see what he's really like.*

A chartered bus drove them from River Dale City Hall to the Boston Fire Academy, picking up other participants along the way from other municipalities in New Hampshire and rural Massachusetts.

Logan grabbed a seat toward the rear of the bus by himself. He tried to stay away from Ron French, the finance person on the county and city councils who was seated at the front of the bus.

He knew he would want to talk about how the hospital shutdown was going. Or ask him about the cost of the P-25 radio system. He did not feel like talking about it now and would avoid him for as long as he could. Royce got on last and sat down at the front.

It was a long drive to Boston, and Logan had a lot of time to think about everything that had happened to him since his return home.

Beth was getting married, to some other guy. *She must love him, otherwise why would she do it? Rory will be home every night after work, and he'll come home alive. You never know with a firefighter. She won't ever have to worry about the knock at the door, a uniformed police officer standing there to bring her the bad news. Or waking up to the phone call in the middle of the night and hearing the dreaded words, "Ma'am, it's your husband. Come to the hospital, quickly. He's been injured." Yes, it's probably for the best.*

He enjoyed the work at the fire station, and he liked the camaraderie of working with fellow firefighters. Maybe it was time to find a job at a station house? He had many connections in California and Arizona. *Yeah, maybe that is the thing to do.*

Royce had been napping, and when he woke, he made his way to the back of the bus and sat down next to Logan. "Can't take these early-morning trips anymore without a nap," he said with a laugh.

Logan laughed with him, then asked, "Tell me again why they're having this training now, right before Christmas? It's a busy time at the station with Christmas tree fires and a lot going on in people's lives. You know, shopping, parties, the whole bit."

"I hear you, and I agree with you. I don't like it any more than you do, but this is the last training class for the year. The feds added it a month ago when they found out there were still a few communities that hadn't completed it. They require that all training be completed before the end of the year to qualify for federal funding. It's a lot of money for a small town like River Dale. Sorry. Hey, cheer up, it'll give you some time to wander around Boston." Then he got more serious, asking, "So what're your plans, Logan? Long term."

"Royce, I don't know," he said, sounding exasperated. "I forgot how much I love it here in New England. I forgot how much I love the day-to-day life at the station. And everything else."

"I know what you mean. That's why I came home. Sooner or later, everybody comes home, Logan," he said, sounding like an older brother.

"You know that the Colonel is scheduled to retire next year. He told me he wanted more time off and maybe to just volunteer on the weekends to help out at the station and travel during the summer. So I'm going to need a new chief soon."

Logan knew what he was asking. "Yeah? What about Carl? Fletch?"

"I talked to both of them already. Carl's going to Florida in two years; he has family there. And Fletch is debating leaving River Dale. Just think about it, that's all I'm asking. Think about it, please?"

"Okay. No promises, but I'll think about it. Just don't count on anything, okay?"

"Got it. Oh, I have a few things planned in Boston to show French the value of firefighters, so just go along, if you get my drift. And I may need your help with some of the training if that's okay with you?" He winked, and Logan got the message.

"Okay," Logan said with a large grin, looking at French at the front of the bus reading through folders.

His phone rang; it was Marge.

"Hey, Margie, what's goin' on?"

"I just came back from the hospital; I was visiting Johnny Ray and the Colonel. The hospital accounting people were there waiting for me, and they asked a lot of questions. According to them, Johnny Ray was certified as a full-time employee on the city certification list we sent to the state, but he was listed as a temporary contract employee on the city payroll. That means he has no benefits. Not good. Makes you wonder what else that finance weasel French is doing. He has to know about all this stuff—he signed everything. Just thought you'd want to know. Please tell Royce for me, will you? Gotta go, the hospital's on the other line. Enjoy Boston; I'll see ya tomorrow back at the station."

Logan was furious. It was one thing to put your life on the line, but another to be told you had to pay your own hospital bills if you got hurt. He was glad that he had avoided French so far on this trip.

He asked Royce if he knew anything about it.

"Not a thing," the mayor said. "The guy's a real jerk. Anything to save a nickel."

"Well, if the town doesn't come through for him, you're in for a big lawsuit. And, if it hits the media, forget about recruiting cops or firemen in River Dale."

"You're right. I'll have my staff look into it right away. As a matter of fact, I'm going to call my office right now to have them look into this."

Ron French was waiting for them as they got off the bus. "Logan, how long is this whole shindig supposed to take today?"

"It all depends," Logan said tersely and walked away.

"What time will we get back home?" French asked, running to catch up with him.

"According to the briefing schedule information I received from them, it's an hour-long demonstration on the efficiency, integration, and safety features of the new P-25 digital communications system. Then there is participation in a hands-on firefighting program for another hour or so. Then the wrap-up and lunch. You'll have the rest of the afternoon free for shopping or whatever."

"Yeah, that's what you firefighters love to do, take breaks and eat lunch and dinner. Easy job. Just hang out with your buddies." He shook his head. "I still think we could just use the old communication system. Sometimes I wonder if all this is worth it. Just to get money from the feds. We don't really need it; our budget is balanced."

Logan had had enough. "Yeah, balanced on the backs of civil servants, firefighters, and the police force. I just found out from the station house that young Johnny Ray Mason was classified as a full-time employee when you sent in our annual certification roster to the state. But now I hear from our office manager that he was classified as a temporary employee to save money and not entitled to benefits," Logan shouted; he was starting to show his anger.

French blustered and coughed. "Watch it, Logan."

Logan pointed his finger toward French's chest. "Yeah, I will. But that's the roster you, as the town's chief finance officer, signed and certified as legal and true. It's a legal document. You're the one legally liable for any errors. You had better change it, and I mean change it quick." *Calm down, Logan.*

"And you did it just to save the town a few bucks. Now Johnny Ray Mason doesn't have any health benefits while he's in the hospital. And when . . . or if . . . he gets out, he won't have any sick leave time to recover. This lawsuit is coming right to you. Really thoughtful. Great job, Ron." It felt good to tell the man off, but it would not change anything; Johnny Ray was still in for the fight of his life.

Logan turned and walked away, toward the tall warehouse building that housed the Boston Fire Academy, leaving Ron French behind him.

CHAPTER

TWENTY-EIGHT

Beth was at her desk at seven o'clock, reviewing files and contemplating the closure of the hospital. She knew her boss would be furious when he learned that the planned closing had been pushed back and that they had not started it or begun moving patients. She wanted to try one last appeal to save the hospital. *How can you just shove a sick patient out onto the street?*

Later that morning, Carlita stuck her head in the door and asked, "Want some fresh coffee? I just brewed a pot."

"Thanks, Carlita," Beth said, sounding as if she had just gotten out of bed.

"What's wrong, Doc? What's the letter you're holding?"

"My offer letter from Ascot Pharmaceuticals." She held it up for Carlita to read.

Carlita came forward, handed Beth a coffee cup, and read the letter. Then she whistled. "Whew, that's a lot of zeroes, Doc. So what's the problem?"

"Nothing I guess. Oh and by the way, I'm getting married . . . next week."

"What?" Carlita smiled, then sat down in the tall leather chair that Doc Sarah had always loved. "That's quick." She sipped her coffee and studied her boss, who had become a good friend. "I'm glad to see you finally came to your senses and are going to grab that man before he heads back to California. Good for you." She had the biggest grin on her face.

Beth did not answer at first, and the two of them sat there, both looking out the window, watching the snowfall. "It's going to be another beautiful Christmas here," Beth said. "I love it here at Christmastime." She sipped her coffee, then added, "I'm marrying Rory."

"What? Oh, yes, of course. What was I thinking?"

"We have so much stuff to do. He wants to get married on New Year's Eve . . ."

"Hmmm, for the tax deduction no doubt."

"Funny," she said. "Carli, I thought you'd be happy for me." She stopped. "Rory's been a real sweetheart about everything and has been calling me all morning about the church, the license, and the flowers. He wants to handle everything. I know I should be happy, but . . ."

"Well, you know how I feel about . . ." Carlita paused. "You're a smart girl, and I'm sure you'll figure it out. I better get going; I got a lot of work to do today." She turned to leave the office. "I'll see you later. Glad to see you're so happy that you finally got what you wanted. Oh by the way, Drake is out here."

"Send him right in."

He burst into her office. "Good news! I have been revising the presentation and feel really good about it."

"Great."

He beamed. "Did I overhear you say you're getting married next week?"

"Yep. Does the whole world know about it?"

"I thought you and he made a great pair. I could tell it just from the way you looked at him."

"Thank you, Drake. At least somebody appreciates him."

"You bet. I could tell by the way you were holding hands last night. I have to leave, but I'll be back later. Congratulations to you and Logan."

She started to say something but thought better of it as she watched him leave. He was a man on a mission. *Why does everybody think I should marry Logan? I need some fresh air.* "I'll be back," she said to Carlita, who merely waved without looking up from her computer.

It was almost noon, so Beth debated having lunch at the cafeteria. She slowed her steps when she heard singing coming from the conference room next to the café. It was unfamiliar music, but it was beautiful. Their voices sounded wonderful.

Christmas day is not so far away
Snowfall on the meadow on this day
The ways we want to care
The gifts we want to share
On this Christmas day

She slowly opened the door and peeked inside. Stephen Collins was at the front of the room, directing the employees in the choir. They sounded wonderful.

He noticed her at the back of the room. Beth listened to their heavenly voices until he told the choral group, "Okay, everybody, take a five-minute break. We'll pick up from where we left off."

He pushed his sister in her wheelchair toward Beth, and they seemed very excited to see her.

"Hi, Dr. Harding. Everything okay? Any word on my mom and dad?" Lisa asked anxiously.

"No change. I think I'll stop by and see them now. You'll be the first to know if there is any change, I promise you."

"Thanks Dr. Harding," Stephen said.

"Don't they sound great?" asked the little one.

"They sound wonderful."

"I hope you don't mind us using this room. They said it was empty for this afternoon," interjected Stephen. "The group wanted to practice as much as possible before the show on Saturday night." He looked at her. "And they're all on their lunch hour," he hastened to add.

"No problem at all. I just wasn't familiar with the song, that's all. It was beautiful."

He looked down, avoiding her eyes.

"It's new!" said Lisa. "Stevie wrote this one just for us. Doesn't it make Christmas so special?"

"Yes, it does." Beth could not help but smile. Turning her attention to Lisa's older brother, she said, "It was beautiful. I can't wait to hear the whole program on Saturday. Don't let me stop you; have a good practice session."

As she closed the door behind her, she heard the voices once again singing the glories of Christmas. She smiled, whispering to herself, "I love it here at Christmastime."

Putting off lunch a bit, she stopped by to see their parents.

Lucia, the attending nurse, approached her. "Good afternoon, Dr. Harding."

"Good afternoon. Any change?"

Lucia slowly shook her head, saying, "No. And it's not good. We don't know why they are lingering in a coma. Dr. Stone ran some other tests, which all came back in the normal range. She says we should know something more in the next day or two."

"Thank you, Lucia." Beth walked in to see them for herself.

It was quiet in their room, the silence punctuated only by the sound of the monitoring equipment. The drapes were drawn. Lying before her were the stricken parents. She checked their vitals and read their files. No change.

How can we close this place down and move everybody? Especially people in their condition. It just doesn't make sense. We'll try for one final appeal to keep the hospital open for another six months. By then . . .

She knew she did not have a lot of time as she watched the couple in their beds. *Come on, you two—wake up. You have a family here that loves you and is waiting for you. Please wake up.*

The machines labored to keep them breathing. Nothing had changed. Soon she would have to tell their kids what she feared. Decision time.

Lost deep in thought, she did not see Larry and the small group off to the side of the hallway as she walked away to lunch.

CHAPTER
TWENTY-NINE

"Okay, okay listen up, you two," said Larry, their temporary supervisor, still wearing his name tag—**LARRY OF RIVER DALE**—that now hung crookedly from his shirt pocket.

"Maria, today I am going to have you stationed in the emergency room. Michael, you can start out there as well, but then later I want you to work in the burn unit. Michael and Maria, I want you to keep away from Room 313, the couple in comas. There is nothing for you two to do there."

"We were just walking around and heard a commotion coming from their room. Someone was crying, and we thought we could help out," said Maria.

"I see. Just stay away. Also, Maria, please stay out of everyone's way, will you? We don't want to have a repeat of what happened in the admissions area. No more disruptions! Do you understand me?"

"Yes, sir," she said meekly. *It wasn't my fault the group of kids had wanted to play soccer at the front desk,* she thought, shooting a sideways glance at Michael. She liked him a lot. Maybe they would get a chance to talk again. She liked talking with him.

"Okay, off with you two. And behave. You're not back in school. We have serious work to do here. And stay away from the intensive care unit. Those folks at the ICU are very busy, and they need quiet for their patients. And remember, stay away from Room 313."

"Room 313?" Michael queried.

"Yes," said Larry, showing his obvious irritation, "the room with the couple from the car accident. Just stay away. Do you have that?"

"Yes," Michael replied. "Yes, we do"—he leaned in to read the name tag again—"*Larry Of River Dale*." And then they were off.

"How much longer do we have to do this?" Maria queried her newfound friend.

Michael stopped in the middle of the busy hallway and gave her a strange look. "He didn't tell you? You didn't have . . . a talk . . . with Larry?"

"No. About what? Come on, Michael, tell me what you know."

"Not now. I'll tell you later. Right now I got work to do."

"Okay. Promise you'll tell me?"

"Yes, I promise, unless Larry tells you first. Bye. I'll see you later." For some reason he wanted to kiss her goodbye as if he were going off to work, like an old married couple. He resisted the urge and waved instead, raising his hand over his head without looking back. He stopped, changed his mind, turned back to her, and took her by both arms. He planted a kiss on her surprised lips. "Goodbye, Maria. See you in the ER, just be a minute. Got a stop to make first."

She was shocked, and it must have shown on her face. A quiet "So long" was all she could manage to say. Maria watched him disappear down the hallway. It was as if they had known each other for a very long time. She liked Michael and wished she could spend more time with him, but now it was time to go back to work. The emergency room was full of activity, and soon she was rushing from one area to another. It was a very busy place.

A Christmas Flower

When things slowed down, she looked up from the stack of files and paperwork and saw Michael walking down the hallway hand in hand with a young boy. Later she saw him walking with his arm over the shoulder of an old man; it looked as if Michael was consoling him. She walked by them, but try as she might, she found she could not hear what they were talking about. She made a mental note to ask him about it later.

It was a very long day, and Maria sat down on a metal chair to take a break for a few minutes. Her eyelids must have closed briefly, because she did not see him arrive and was startled when she looked up to see him sitting two seats away from her. It was Larry, beckoning her.

"Maria? I think we need to talk. You need to understand some things. Please come with me," he said in his quiet, comforting voice. They began to walk together. "Let's go somewhere private," he said. "Perhaps the chapel. I'm sorry, maybe I wasn't clear before when I spoke to the group. Or perhaps you were not paying attention." He looked at her but decided not to say anything further about her inattention.

"Maria, I don't think you truly comprehend what your role is here. Come. Walk with me, please." Assuming the role of a father figure, he draped his arm over Maria's shoulder and whispered to her. By the time they reached the chapel, tears had begun to run down her cheeks.

171

CHAPTER THIRTY

The conference room at the Boston Fire Academy was on the outskirts of the city. The classroom was only half-full, many of the attendees in uniform. Royce, always the politician, shook hands with the many participants he knew, as if he were running for office again.

A short, stocky man wearing thin-rimmed gold glasses and a Boston fire captain's uniform took the podium at the front of the converted classroom.

"Good morning, ladies and gentlemen. My name is Captain Jack Roach; I am the regional liaison here in New England for the P-25 project with the Department of the Interior, the Department of Homeland Security, and the National Firefighters Agency. Welcome." He took a quick drink of water before continuing.

"Let me start by stating the obvious for many of the firefighters in this room. We have all been to fires where it has gone to multiple alarms. We would find trucks from many jurisdictions and ambulances from different counties and municipalities. There would also be emergency medical personnel responding—and most of these responders could not communicate with us or with one another. We all remember the Bridgeman Apartments fire. We had sixteen jurisdictions responding, and, as the building imploded, some of our men were trapped inside, unable to communicate with their command center. We lost three women and six men, all good firefighters, all with families. We don't want that to ever happen again. The new P-25 system will help ensure that it doesn't." There were murmurs of agreement in the room.

"Today we will walk everyone through the features and rationale behind the new digital radios, and then later we'll break down into smaller groups and fight a mock fire. This is for the benefit of nonfirefighter attendees who sometimes ask what exactly a firefighter does. We'll show you all later when everyone here will be fitted with bunker gear, air packs, and all the other equipment that firefighters wear to fight a fire." He looked around the room.

"Congress has mandated that all government radio operations be narrow-banded." He looked around the room and saw many confused faces. Logan listened as the captain explained why they needed to use the new radio bands and watched French fidget in his seat. Logan could tell he was bored.

"I'm sure you have a lot of questions concerning the functionality and compatibility of analog radios versus digital radios . . ." Logan heard him drone on about the complexities and other safety features with the new P-25. His mind wandered back to River Dale. Beth. She was getting married. He should have said something; he was too late again. He should have told her what he was feeling, should have kissed her—anything. She must still think of him as only her best friend. But he was torn, because he never wanted that to change. He valued her friendship far too much. *What a fool I was. Now I'm going to lose her. Stop thinking just about yourself. Keep your mouth shut, Logan. She has enough on her mind—the hospital closing, Claire, the wedding, and losing Doc Sarah. Cool it.*

Logan's thoughts continued to wander in circles around his dilemma. Somehow an hour passed, and the captain was wrapping up his presentation.

He concluded by saying, "And now if there are any questions, they can be directed to Hank Silverman."

Royce joined Logan at the back of the room and was soon followed by French.

"Well, now I finally get to see what this firefighting stuff is all about," commented French. "Then I'm going into Boston to buy some Christmas gifts for my wife. What else are they going to do after this?"

Logan told him. "They'll show you all the firefighter equipment, tell you something about it, and review the cost. You'll suit up and go through the simulation, and then you're done."

"How long will it take?"

"No more than a couple of hours. However, if you would rather pay for the P-25 out of the city funds, we can try another bond issue and pay for it ourselves. It's only about—"

"No, no, that's okay. I'll stick around."

Royce smiled, then turned to Logan. "I may need your help with the presentation later. Okay?"

"No problem."

Logan had to chuckle at French's discomfort as they made their way outside to the firehouse portion of the huge, warehouse-like building with training rooms and simulation areas. They walked through Building 1, with warehouse bays over sixteen feet high. Next door was Building 2, a six-story structure meant to look like an apartment building.

The attendees were broken down into Blue Group, Red Group, and White Group; each group would later be fighting a different kind of fire. Once in the training and dressing area, they were offered coffee, doughnuts, and bagels, then asked to take a seat.

Captain Roach stepped up to address the crowd. "Since this is the last training program of the year for the academy, and since we also have a few more attendees today due to the P-25 mandatory requirement by the feds, I'm running a little shorthanded. So, I'm going to ask a retired firefighter, Royce Wilson, and smoke jumper Logan Mitchell from California to volunteer to assist us in the training."

Royce approached the podium. "Thank you, Captain Roach. Happy to help out." He faced the group. "Everyone assigned to the Red Group, please follow Logan and me down the hallway. Then we'll make our way outside this building to Building 2."

They filed into a large locker room. It had a fire pole protruding from the floor below in the center of the room. Logan said to the group with a smile, "Don't worry; we won't be using the pole as we do in the fire stations to get down to the lower level because—"

"What's with those silly poles anyway? Is this a macho thing or something?" interrupted French.

"No, sir. It's very practical. In a fire, timing is everything. You can reach the truck in less than six seconds here using the pole versus forty seconds using the stairs. Firefighters must be dressed, at their positions on the truck, and out the door in less than six minutes. Timing is crucial if—"

"And if it takes you longer than that?"

Logan looked him in the eye and answered him in a subdued tone. "Then the fire wins . . . and people die. When you're at home and you turn on a faucet, you expect water to come out. When you flip on a light switch, you expect the lights to come on. When you call 911 because you have a fire or an emergency, you expect the fire department to show up quickly and save you. That's our job."

He glanced at Royce, who nodded in agreement.

"Many of you may not know, but anyone who wishes to be a firefighter must complete not only a job interview but also a physical examination. Then they must pass a lie detector test, a swimming exam, and an ethics test. Next they have to pass a medical knowledge test. That's just to get the job. Once hired, you have weeks, if not months, of ongoing daily training to prepare you for when the alarm sounds and you rush off into the night to fight a fire. That's the commitment a firefighter makes in order to do his or her job. It's not boasting, it's just the job we do, and we take it very seriously."

French appeared stunned by the explanation. "I never thought about all of that. I always just thought of it as . . ." His voice trailed off.

Royce moved beside Logan and patted him gently on the shoulder. "Thanks, Logan." Then he turned to the group and said, "Over the next hour, we'll be showing you the equipment we use and then talking about cost. Then we'll ask you to imagine that the alarm has just been sounded and you're on your way to fight a fire. Blue Group, in the other building, will be fighting a real fire using a pumper truck and actual fire hoses." He paused for a brief moment.

"Red Group, we will be fighting a controlled fire to simulate a blaze at an apartment building. Our mission is to quickly climb the stairs wearing full firefighting gear to rescue some people in the apartment building. Your gear includes a helmet, an oxygen mask and tank, fireproof gloves, and a fire-retardant suit that includes a coat, pants, and boots."

He walked to a table covered in equipment. As Logan picked up items one by one, Royce explained what each piece was and talked about the cost: $5,000–$10,000 total for each firefighter.

"And last but not least is your oxygen pack, ranging in cost from one thousand to five thousand dollars each. During a normal fire, this oxygen should last you twenty minutes, meaning you have no more than ten minutes to travel into the burning building, and then ten minutes to travel back to the truck to retrieve a new air pack before going back to the fire and starting the process all over again. The life expectancy of these packs is anywhere from seven to ten years, but many stations are still using older, outdated systems to save money. And sometimes, it cost lives."

Logan chimed in. "This is just the basic equipment that a firefighter needs to do his or her job. Firefighters will also have multiple personal items, such as five or six flashlights, survival belts, work harnesses, work shirts, and T-shirts."

"Why so many personal flashlights?" asked a short woman at the back of the room.

"When you go into a burning building, it's dark and smoky. You have a limited amount of oxygen, and there are no signs telling you where to go or how to get back. And unlike fairy tales, you can't leave a trail of crumbs on the floor to help you find your way out. So we leave our flashlights with our names and ladder unit numbers to create a trail out. In addition, when firefighters from other units follow you inside, they can see where you've been because your name and ladder unit number is listed on each flashlight. It's simple, but it works."

They spent the next ninety minutes learning about what they would each face, what they would have to do once the alarm sounded, and what each of their individual jobs would be. They listened intently, but Logan knew from experience that once the alarm sounded, much of their training would be forgotten.

On the other side of the room, Royce walked over to a full set of bunker gear laid out on a table, ready to be slipped on. "Now you will all be given a pair of boots in your size and told to pick up your bunker gear. You'll need to suit up as soon as the siren goes off. Or you can use this stuff that's already been prepared for anyone who wants to use it."

"What's the difference?" asked French.

Royce slowly turned to face French and said, "Not much, really. As a matter of fact, this is the same equipment that is in use today in many fire stations across the country. Including the stations in and around River Dale."

"And?" said an impatient French.

"Well," commented Royce as he walked to the equipment and pointed to each piece as he talked. "These River Dale air packs have exceeded their useful life . . . so they may only operate for ten or twelve minutes rather than the full twenty minutes that they're supposed to. You might find yourself stranded in a burning building . . . with little or no oxygen to get out."

He next pointed to the gray-and-yellow jackets. "These jackets need to be cleaned on a regular basis to make sure nothing is stuck to them, so they don't catch fire. Each time you clean them, some of the fire-retardant properties are diminished; the same can be said of the bunker pants, the boots, and the gloves. So, you may be able to make it into a building to fight a fire, but you may not make it back out . . . alive." He gave a Cheshire cat smile and said, "So you have your choice: old River Dale Fire Department's finest for you to fight an eight-hundred-degree fire or . . . brand-new equipment. Take your choice."

French was beginning to sweat. Royce had made his point.

"I'll take the newest stuff you got," French said quickly.

"I thought so. Pick up your equipment, then get ready to suit up." Royce made one last comment. "In a few minutes an alarm will sound, then a siren to simulate the fire alert. After you have suited up in your equipment, wait by the door. Before you leave, trained firefighters will come around the room to make sure you are properly fitted. Any questions?"

The uninitiated looked at one another in silence—a silence born of fear. French gulped but did not say anything. His eye began to twitch, and his hand shook.

Minutes later the alarm and siren rang with an earsplitting, high-pitched screech, repeating again and again as they rushed to suit up. Everyone in the room—including French, River Dale Police Chief Mark Richards, Logan, and Royce—quickly put on their gear.

"Twelve minutes," proclaimed Royce. "Too long. Six minutes over the maximum time allowed."

Logan could see that French was already uncomfortable wearing his gear and was having a difficult time breathing. Drops of perspiration beaded his forehead. His nostrils opened wide, then closed, then opened again even wider, as he gasped for oxygen.

"Follow me," said Logan as they made their way to their appointed site. They stopped in front and could see the fire and the smoke rising before them from the simulated six-story apartment building. The alarm and siren began again.

"Remember your training and what you were told," Logan shouted. "Stay close to your team leader. Your mission is to bring out the dummies representing people in the building, then put out the fire. Stay close to your team leaders. Red team—go!" Royce shouted to them through the communicator affixed to their oxygen masks.

Logan led the way. They ran inside the building, encumbered by the more than forty-five pounds of firefighter gear. They could hardly see anything other than what was directly in front of them.

It was hot inside the suit. It was smoky. It was noisy. Voices were garbled. Bursts of flame appeared on the left, then on the right. Green smoke, then black smoke. The equipment was heavy. Bulky and awkward. Hard to maneuver. Their masks and the thick, black smoke obscured everyone's vision. French could not see more than a few feet in front of him. His heart was pounding so loud he thought for sure everyone could hear it. The look on his face told everyone that he was already regretting his decision to take part in this exercise.

Logan moved directly behind French as they made their way into the old building. Water from the hoses and sprinklers snaked across the floor. French started to turn left and go the wrong way, venturing down a dead-end hallway. Logan grabbed his shoulder and pointed him in the right direction, mouthing the words, "Follow me. Stay close."

French understood even though his communications gear was not working properly.

They were the first to reach the room where the dummy rescue was to take place. Logan pointed to the dummy on the mattress, waiting for French to pick it up. It weighed over sixty pounds. French nearly fell backward but managed to right himself as he hoisted it onto his shoulders and headed for the door.

Hmmm, spunky fellow, thought Logan. *He might make a good fire-fighter after all.*

✳

They made their way to the hallway, back toward the entrance, as their teammates worked to put out the fire.

As they waited outside and changed into street gear again, French approached Logan and Royce. "Logan, thanks for saving my butt in there," he said, managing a weak grin. "It was very intense. My anxiety and adrenaline level was off the charts. I couldn't see anything or hear anything. I don't know how you guys do this day in and day out, every week . . . Thank you for your service."

"It's what we do. Every day."

French turned to walk away and said to Royce, "You can count on my support in the council meetings for any expenditure on fire equipment that you feel is necessary." He paused and smiled. "Within certain limitations, of course."

"Of course," said Royce.

Logan stopped him. "French, you'd make a good firefighter someday. That is, if you ever get tired of crunching numbers."

"Thanks, Logan. But after seeing this, I think I'll leave firefighting to you professionals. I'm skipping the lunch here and grabbing the shuttle van into Boston to sightsee and do some Christmas shopping. You guys coming?"

"You bet," they said in unison. They would rather shop and eat in Boston than do lunch at the fire academy.

Logan shouted to French. "Have them hold the shuttle. We'll grab our gear and be right there."

"Good job," said Royce. "You should run for office someday."

CHAPTER THIRTY-ONE

"You wanna do a late lunch in Boston?" Royce asked as they settled into the short bus ride to downtown Boston.

"No thanks. Rain check? I'm going to stop by and see Claire while I'm in town."

"Claire?"

"Claire Harding. She's working as a nurse at a hospital here in Boston, and I thought I would stop by and say hello while I was in town. Beth asked me to look in on her." He was quiet. "Besides, the last time I saw her was at Doc Sarah's funeral. Not the best of circumstances. I just wanted to say hello."

"Yeah. I heard the good doctor set a date for the wedding."

"Well, her fiancé did, and I think Beth just went along with the decision."

Royce leaned back and stretched his long limbs out into the aisle. "I always figured you and Beth to be the ones to get hitched, if you know what I mean."

"Yeah, but it's not meant to be . . . He seems like a nice enough kind of guy. I guess. I'm sure they'll be happy together."

"Yeah, I'm sure," said Royce, looking out the bus window as the stately redbrick townhomes of downtown Boston passed by. They could see the outlines of the tall buildings in the city skyline ahead.

"I'm going to jump off here. She's not far from Beacon Hill—just off Charles Street. It's a quick walk from here. See ya later, Royce." He signaled for the driver to stop, got off the small bus, and began walking.

Logan walked along the street through an older section of Boston with many restored buildings, including cafés, delis, and bookstores, scattered about the neighborhood. He had always loved Boston. He walked past the innumerable pubs and taverns, all sporting Christmas lights around their front doors and windows. The sound of Christmas music escaped from the open front doors of the quaint restored taverns as patrons made their way inside. Logan smiled; Boston was his kind of town.

When he passed a small heirloom and antique jewelry store, he peered through the window and decided to go inside. The store seemed as old as the city itself. The worn wooden floors creaked under his feet as he strolled through the shop. *Antique stores like this all seem to smell the same,* he thought, *and this one is no exception. Old lace, old wood, frail books, dried flowers, stale perfume, and the like.* Sweet and sour, he always liked to say.

"Merry Christmas. Good afternoon, sir," said a primly dressed woman with a pair of reading glasses perched high on top of her head. Her grayish-black hair was pulled tight behind her ears. "Is there anything in particular I can show you?" she asked, following him as he leaned over and began looking inside the shiny showcases that lined the wall. The long glass top in the main case was cracked but had been repaired with brown tape, which served to mark the crack's beginning and end.

"Just browsing, thank you. I'll know it when I see . . ." He stopped, and a slow smile grew on his face as he pointed at two pieces of jewelry inside, just beneath the crack in the glass. "I'd like to see those two, if I may."

"Yes, but of course." She reached inside the case and brought out a long jewelry tray covered in purple felt. In the center of the tray were two pieces of gold jewelry. His hand went to them, holding up both items.

"You have very good taste," she said as he held them both in his hand. "This is a three-part memento that was all meant to fit together. Unfortunately, I only have two of the pieces. However, I can give you a very good deal on the two. The third piece was lost or separated or just plain missing. They still make for a very nice gift even with just the two. Wouldn't you agree?"

He could not take his eyes off them. "Yes. It's perfect," he said. Then he looked at the price tag dangling from the bottom and whistled softly.

She smiled her prim smile.

Drawing in a deep breath, he told her, "They're worth it. I'll take both of them. Can you gift wrap them for me, please?"

"Of course, sir. I'll just be a minute." He knew that they would make a perfect gift. Once she was finished wrapping them, she tied brightly colored ribbon around the small boxes. He paid her and, after thanking her, glanced at his watch as he headed toward Claire's apartment. From his inside jacket pocket, he retrieved the note Beth had given him that included Claire's address, and he turned right onto Pinckney Street.

He walked up the steep hill, the snow and ice accumulation causing him to nearly slip and fall. Not far up ahead he saw the street sign he was looking for and turned right into a small alleyway. Checking for the numbers, he found it: 162 Cedar Lane Way. Opening the door into a small alcove, he read the list of names until he found the name he was looking for: C. HARDING / R. NELSON—APT. F.

A few seconds after he pushed the button, he heard her voice. "Logan? Is that you?" She squealed with delight. "Come on up. We're on the top floor."

The old wooden steps creaked as he made his way upstairs. One floor, then two, then three floors on a steep, narrow, and winding staircase. He looked up and saw her smiling face leaning over the top of the bannister, two stories above him.

"Come on, you slowpoke, only two more flights to go."

When he reached the landing, she threw her arms around his broad shoulders and gave him the biggest hug. She held him close. "Boy, is it good to see you. Wow! Come on in." She grabbed him by the arm and pulled him inside the small one-bedroom apartment.

Newspapers littered the floor; beer cans were piled on the glass cocktail table and scattered on the small rug underneath. Stacks of books were piled everywhere in the room. The pale-green drape was hanging crooked, allowing only some dusty light into the living room.

"Don't mind the mess," she said, dismissing the disarray. "Cleaning day isn't until Saturday." One thing he also noticed as he entered— he saw no Christmas decorations anywhere. No Christmas tree. No Christmas cards. No wreath. No nativity scene. No stockings. Nothing.

"Are you hungry? Want a soda? Glass of wine? Roger went out to buy some beer. He should be back soon." When she mentioned his name, a strained smile came over her face—but just for the briefest of moments. She swallowed. "He's so funny. You'll like him. But he's under a lot of stress now, not having a job and all. However, he'll find something soon, I'm sure of it. Come on in, sit down, and tell me everything. It is so good to see you. What's going on at home? How's California? How's the Colonel?" She peppered him with rapid-fire questions as they sat down on the old floral sofa with a blue plaid blanket slung over the back. A shower of dust spun into the air as they settled onto it.

Claire lowered her voice and said, "How do you feel about Beth's upcoming wedding?"

He leaned back. "I'm happy . . . if she's happy. If that's what she wants, then I'm happy for her." The words came out as if they were wrapped in barbed wire. Of course he wanted her to be happy, but . . .

Claire reached for his hand and held it in hers. She looked into his eyes and said, "Strange to be talking about it because I always thought that the two of you would be together some day. Even when we were younger. I think even Mom thought the same thing."

"Claire, she's my sister, just like you. That's a tough mountain to climb, for me to get over."

"Almost a sister," she corrected him.

"You know what I mean."

"Yes. But deep down inside, she really loves you—she always has. She just doesn't know it yet."

"Yes, but in a different sort of way."

"She's missed you, I know that. I can hear it in her voice anytime she mentions your name."

"Claire, even if that was true, what do we do? Think about it. I know I have. She belongs in a city running a hospital, and I belong in the hills, fighting forest fires, jumping out of airplanes. It would never work."

"Stranger things have happened, my friend. You never know until you try." She moved closer and squeezed his hand tighter, sharing the pain of his dilemma. She loved them both.

"Are you staying for the wedding?" she asked quietly.

"No. I don't know if I could take it—watching her walk down the aisle with someone else. I couldn't bear to see . . ."

The front door burst open, and in walked a tall, dark-haired man wearing a down vest jacket covered in snow. His beard was thicker in some parts, thinner in others; it looked more like he had just stopped shaving than intentionally grown a beard.

"Roger! You got home just in time," said Claire, pulling her hand away from Logan's.

"Obviously," he said without emotion.

Logan extended his hand to shake Roger's. "Hi, I'm Logan, Logan Mitchell," he said with a welcoming grin.

Roger just stood there, looking first at Logan, then at his out-stretched hand, and then at Claire. "I know who you are. Claire told me all about you and her sister growing up together. I guess that was pretty cozy, wasn't it, you and these two pretty girls hanging all over you. Hmmph, and it looks like nothing has changed."

Logan lowered his hand to his side and watched the man in front of him walk away. "Gotta put this beer in the fridge. You want one, Logan?"

"No, thanks. I need to get back to the fire academy soon. I just stopped by to—"

"Have a safe trip back to River Dale. Nice to meet you," Roger said, his voice echoing from the other room.

Logan hugged Claire and started to leave. "Oh, before I forget, I have something for you. A Christmas present."

A look of apprehension spread across her face.

"It's not much," he said as he handed her the small gift-wrapped box with its curling green spiral ribbon. She looked behind her as she ripped off the wrapping paper. Inside was the small piece of coin pendant dangling from a chain. "I saw this in an antique store . . . and I thought of you."

She placed it gently around her neck and closed its clasp. "It's beautiful, Logan," she whispered, touching it ever so gently. "You didn't need to do this."

"I know, but I wanted—"

"You still here?" asked Roger, walking into the room with a beer in his hand.

Claire sprang to his defense. "Roger. Logan is a longtime friend. He was giving me a Christmas present, that's all. Now be polite—he's a guest in our home."

"Yeah . . . we don't celebrate Christmas here," he said flatly.

"You don't?" responded a shocked and confused Logan. "Why not?"

"We just don't."

"But Claire does."

"So long, Logan. Claire, it's time to say goodbye to your old friend."

The look on her face was one of dread.

"Claire, I can stay for a while longer . . . if you like."

"I said so long, Logan," interjected Roger.

Claire looked him in the eyes, pleading, "Logan . . . maybe you had better leave. Tell Beth I love her and I'll call her."

"I'm not going anywhere until I know you're okay."

Roger began to walk toward the both of them. "I said . . ."

Logan slowly tightened his hand into a hard fist. Watching. Waiting. "Roger, I'd be very careful what you say from this point forward," he began in a slow, steady, even tone. "I'm not leaving here until I know that Claire is okay. And if I hear that you—"

"Logan . . . please . . . go. Please," she pleaded. "I'll be fine, really. Please go." She was almost in tears.

He relaxed his grip and pulled her close to whisper in her ear. "Call me if you ever need me. Okay?"

"Okay. Bye, Logan. Good to see you."

As he walked down the steps, he could hear the yelling behind him, and then . . . silence.

He felt helpless.

CHAPTER
THIRTY-TWO

"You wanted to see me, Dr. Harding?"

"Yes, Drake. Did you want to go over your presentation to the governor? As a dry run?"

"No, I think I'm fine. I've really smoothed out the rough parts, and I am as ready as I'll ever be. Really. Believe me, this one's a winner."

She hesitated and then said, "Well, if you're sure. I thought maybe we could just go through it a couple of times. Remember what happened the last time?"

"How can I forget? But no, thanks, this time is the charm. I feel really good about it," he said confidently.

"Okay good. Just thought I'd ask. We have a lot riding on this presentation." She stopped for a minute, then said, "I have a favor to ask."

"Sure, anything. What's up?"

"Well, Rory insists on doing all the arrangements for the wedding here, but he needs some signed documents from me. I signed them, but I don't know if I'll have the time to break away and get them back to him. So I thought, well maybe . . ."

"Oh . . ." Drake started to say something but had second thoughts. "I'd be happy to drop them off with him. Where's he staying?"

She handed him an envelope. "He's staying at the Holden Inn near Winston. Room 408. Drake, I really appreciate you doing this for me."

"No problem." Winston was not far—a forty-minute drive—and he felt he could use the time productively to practice his presentation in the car.

✳

Drake knocked on the door three times, then double-checked to make sure he had the right room. "Yep, 408. I could have sworn that was the number Beth told me," he said aloud to himself. *Maybe I should leave a note on his door telling Rory I left the envelope at the front desk?* As he searched his pockets for a pen and something to write on, the door swung open.

The man greeted him with a blank stare. "Hello? Can I help you?"

"Hi, I'm Drake Corrigan," he said, then waited for it to sink in. "I work at the hospital . . . with Beth."

"Oh, Beth. At the hospital. Right. I got it now. She called to say you were coming over. Please come in. I'm Rory Daniels."

The room had that new-car smell. It was a very large room, almost as large as Drake's apartment. It featured a sleeping area with a kitchenette, along with an office area and modern office desk that was now filled with files, notepads, and a laptop. The dark-green drapes were closed, and only a sliver of sunlight beamed through the slit of an opening between them.

"You have something for me?" Rory asked.

"Yes, I do." He reached inside his suit jacket pocket, retrieved the envelope, and handed it to him.

"Great," said Rory as he opened it and studied the contents. "Yep, everything is here. Thanks for bringing it over to me." He paused and looked like he wanted to say something more, then unconsciously shook his head. "I appreciate it." He stopped, then set the envelope on the cocktail table. "You're the Brit, right? From Great Britain?"

"Yes, indeed. That's probably where I'll return when they close the hospital here."

"Elizabeth has mentioned your name many times. You were hired by her mother, weren't you?"

"Yes, a real sharp lady. I miss her humor. Beth is a great boss, too, and an all-around great person. Down-to-earth. Much better than other bosses I've had in the past. You're a lucky fella." He leaned forward as if someone was listening and said, "I don't think she likes working as a hospital administrator."

Rory's face brightened as he interjected. "Well, in her new job—"

"I think she likes dealing with patients much more."

"Oh," Rory replied. Then he asked, "Has she been doing a lot of that lately?"

"Yes, doing more rounds now with other doctors. It's been tough, with the shortage of personnel. Much of the nursing staff has been forced to find other jobs. With the flu epidemic, well, everybody has been manning the floors, including some of the administrative staff. It's made matters even worse. We would have lost a lot more staff, but they have a tremendous loyalty to Dr. Harding. So many of them have stayed around, hoping for a miracle, I guess." He laughed nervously, then shrugged. "Including myself. I guess I better be getting back now. It was nice to meet you, Rory. I have to get ready. Beth and I are making a sales presentation to the governor and the head of the state health board Friday. I'm still going over it in my mind, rehearsing what I'm going to say."

"Hmmm. Want to run it by me? I do that kind of stuff all the time in my job. Have been for years."

"Really? You don't mind?"

"No. I can use a break, as a diversion. Want a soda or a beer?" he asked, opening the door to the minibar and grabbing a soda can from inside.

"No thanks. Bad for my digestion." Drake stood, nervous, in front of Rory and began his presentation.

"Thank you, ladies and gentlemen, for coming today. On behalf of Dr. Harding and myself, I want to share with you what we feel is a revolutionary and cost-effective way to lower the levels of hospital-acquired infections. As you know, effective January of last year, the federal government began cutting payments to hospitals that have the highest rates of hospital-acquired infections over a certain level. This includes potentially avoidable complications such as blood clots after surgery, hip fractures, and sepsis infections. This will impact over eight hundred hospitals nationwide."

He nodded to Rory, who gave him a thumbs-up. He went on. "The new Government Care Program reduces reimbursement to hospitals for treating complications they themselves have created. Furthermore, infections still remain a grave threat to patients, occurring during twelve of every one hundred stays, according to federal estimates.

"The current nationwide readmission rate is twelve to sixteen per-cent, and River Dale General Hospital has historically fallen right in the middle of that range at fourteen percent. However, you will be pleased to know that after implementing our copper-clad pilot program in the ICU, where all touch surfaces were covered in copper, the readmission rate for that unit is down to"—he paused—"one percent."

"Wow!" said Rory under his breath. "That's impressive."

Drake looked at Rory and smiled, seeing he had his rapt attention. "Thanks. I'll take that can of soda now if you don't mind."

"Sure." Rory went to the fridge, pulled out another can, and glanced outside through the drapes. "Some kind of commotion going on out there. Probably Santa coming to town for the kiddies," Rory said, handing him the soda. "Go on. This sales presentation is right up my alley. And I must tell you, I'm very intrigued."

"Thanks, Rory." Drake continued his program after taking a sip. He cleared his throat. "Readmission rate is an even more pressing matter because the federal government is withholding a year's worth of payments to over eight hundred hospitals nationwide. This includes payments to some of the most prestigious teaching hospitals in the country. It affects any institution that exceeds the readmission threshold of ten percent. And to make matters worse, next year, starting in January, a second round of penalty cuts will take effect costing millions more . . . unless something is done. I would like to share with you what we have done at River Dale General Hospital, but first some history and background." Drake began to talk about the history of infectious diseases, causes, and remedies. He felt very comfortable with the subject matter, having written multiple books on the subject.

". . . the research and analysis of all particular operations both inborne and sub-borne of all HAI should be carefully ascertained by identifying risks inherent in . . ." He droned on. ". . . with the collection and study of all data received from operational and preventive designs and with the dissemination of all facts and data interpretation the study analysis should carefully require . . ." His grin faded when he noticed the blank stare on Rory's face.

Rory held up his hand and shook his head. "Time out! Stop, stop, stop," he pleaded. "Drake. You had me in the palm of your hand at the beginning, then you meandered into all that murky technical stuff. You lost me. It got way too technical."

Drake could see the look of frustration on Rory's face.

"Anytime you are making a sales presentation, you should always be asking yourself, 'What's in it for them?' Do they want to make money, save money, save time, save lives? What's important—I mean *really* important—to them, to your audience? These guys want to continue to get the federal money from Washington. And from what you're saying, copper will help them get what they want." He could tell from the look on Drake's face that he did not understand a word he was saying.

"Tell you what; you got time to grab a bite? I never had lunch. However, I think I know what your problem is. And I think I can help."

"Sure," Drake said his face brightening with a smile. "If you don't mind. Do you really think you can help?"

"I know I can. Come on. Tell you what, let me buy you lunch. Bring your stuff." He grabbed his jacket and cell phone from the counter, and they headed for the door. "I know I can help you with your presentation. I also must tell you, I'm absolutely fascinated with the material you presented and can't wait to hear the rest of your—"

He turned the knob on the hotel room door and was confronted with thick, black smoke. He closed the door and quickly called 911. He shouted, "Help! Please, send the fire department! Hurry!" The hallway fire alarm began ringing, alerting guests to the danger.

Within minutes a fire rescue team was leading them to safety. The two of them, along with other hotel guests, stood in the parking lot wrapped in fire department blankets, drinking hot coffee, and trying to keep warm. They watched the hook and ladder truck move back and forth, spraying high-pressure hoses onto the building. The main damage seemed to be on the first floor, and Rory wondered about all his things from his room.

"Wow, that's a lot of smoke," Rory said. "It's up my nose. I can still smell it. I can imagine what my clothes will smell like when I get back inside." He began to sneeze uncontrollably.

"I don't think they'll let you back inside there for a couple of days."

Taking another sip from his foam coffee cup, Rory said, "No answer at Beth's office or cell phone, or at the travel agent who booked the room. Beth already has a house and way too much dust from her remodeling. I guess I'm going to need a new hotel."

Drake looked at him. Rory had been very helpful and giving of his expertise with the presentation. And he was Beth's fiancé. "Tell you what, I have a spare bedroom at my place. You're welcome to stay with me if you want. At least until you find something more suitable."

"Really? You don't mind?"

"No, but only on one condition. You must get some different clothes . . . that don't smell like smoke."

Rory sniffed his jacket and sweater, then made a face. "Whew! I see what you mean. One question, I'm really hyperallergic to dust and I just wondered, is your—"

"I have no pets and no dust."

"Great. You got a deal. Thanks."

"We can stop at the River Dale General Store for clothes and stuff if you like. They sell everything, and it's on the way to my place."

As they stood there watching the Winston firefighters do their job, Rory took another sip from his coffee cup and said, "Tell me more about this copper project stuff."

CHAPTER
THIRTY-THREE

The hospital was quiet as Beth packed up her briefcase and decided to call it a day. Just then her office phone rang. "Hello. This is Dr. Harding," she responded.

"Hiya. It's Logan." His voice sounded tired. "I'm on my way home from Boston. We need to talk. I'll be home in about an hour."

She slumped back down into her large leather chair. "It's that bad? Is Claire okay? Is she safe?"

"Yes, but I can't really talk here. Not really private and very noisy. I'm with a lot of people on the bus, but yeah, she's okay. I'll tell you all about it when I see you at home."

"Are you hungry?"

"Famished."

"I'll pick up something, and we can both eat when you get home. I better call Rory and see what he's doing for dinner. I've been so busy, I only talked with him briefly this morning."

Logan did not respond, though she thought she heard a grumble of some kind.

"I'm just going to make some quick rounds of the hospital before I leave, but I'll be home before you are."

"Okay, Beth. See you then. I love . . ." There was a pause, and Beth held her breath waiting for him to finish the sentence. The word *you* almost slipped from his lips, but he caught himself and said, "Pizza."

"Sounds good. Pizza and some red wine?"

"Perfect."

After hanging up with Logan she sat back in her desk chair, then glanced at her watch; time to go.

Her cell phone rang. It was Rory.

"Hello," she said. "I was just thinking about you. Do you want to join Logan and me for some pizza? We can go over the wedding plans you've made so far, or do you want to go to—"

"I got burned out of my hotel today."

"What?" she shouted. She began to pace back and forth across the room.

"I was at the hotel, and Drake had dropped off the documents you signed. We were going over his presentation, and when we took a break, we found the hallway was filled with smoke. It was terrible. And making matters worse, only half of the sprinklers worked—and those were only on the first floor. I tried to reach you but only got your voice mail. Didn't you get my message?"

She glanced at her cell phone—no messages. "No, I didn't."

"Strange. But no matter. They took everyone to the hospital here in Winston to check us out. I'm fine. Drake's fine. It's just the hotel that's in bad shape. Drake has been kind enough to let me bunk at his place in the spare bedroom. Are you still at the hospital?"

"Yes. But I want to see you with my own eyes, just to make sure you're okay and that nothing's happened to you. You're still at the Winston hospital? I'm on my way."

"Beth, really I'm fine. But I'm real tired. Why don't we catch up with each other tomorrow? But really, I'm fine. Okay?"

"Are you positive?"

"I'm fine. Go have your pizza. I'll see you tomorrow."

"Are you sure?"

"Yeah, I'm sure. Really, I'm okay. Go visit with Logan. I'll see you tomorrow."

Fire in the hotel? What's going to happen next? she thought to herself. *I'll check in with him again after dinner.*

Beth returned the phone to her pocket and, on her way out, she decided to make two final visits before leaving for the night. She would look in on Sweetie and the Colonel. The hospital was quiet. Outside Sweetie's room she saw Dr. Monroe about to enter.

"Good evening, Dr. Harding," he said, carrying a folder in his hand.

"Hi, Dr. Monroe. You're working late today."

"Yes, just on my way home, but I thought I would look in on our patient here and talk with her. I think we caught a break in her case."

They had tried everything, including an article in the *River Dale Times* and sending Sweetie's picture to the local police department and the regional television station. In turn, the photo was circulated to other local police departments and the state police, all in hopes that someone would recognize her. No luck.

"Care to join me?"

"Yes. Did you get her test results back?"

"Just got them an hour ago. Her psychological evaluation was fine, normal. Which is a relief. We have ruled out dementia."

"That's good," she said, sounding relieved.

"However, after a complete physical examination, she does have some contusions, possibly a concussion on the rear portion of her skull. One consistent with a fall and hitting her head on a hard object. This appears to have resulted in a case of retrograde amnesia."

"Retrograde?"

"Yes. I've consulted with some amnesia specialists as to the best way to proceed."

"Hmmm. I see," Beth murmured. "Let's go talk with her."

She was wide-awake, watching a game show on television when they arrived.

"Good evening, Sweetie," said Beth. "I was on my way home and just thought I would stop by and visit with you, along with Dr. Monroe. How ya doing?"

The old woman's smile never seemed to dim. "I'm fine. The question is . . . How are you?"

Beth chuckled as she read Sweetie's chart. She liked this old woman. Feisty. Sassy. "I'm okay, I guess. Your test results came back, as well as your PE. It all looks good."

"PE?" she queried.

"Psychological evaluation."

"I could have told you that. I may be forgetful, but I'm not crazy." Sweetie laughed at the thought.

"Well, I'm glad to see you've kept your sense of humor. Dr. Monroe will fill you in on the other results."

He moved closer to her, opened the folder, and then closed it, preferring a more direct and personal approach. "I know it is frustrating for you not to be able to remember certain things," he said, "but trust me, it will come back. It may be slower than you would like, but your memories will return."

"All of them?"

"Eventually, but complete recollection will take some time. Once you remember certain things, and then if you return to familiar surroundings, it will speed recovery."

"What happened to me?"

"You slipped on some ice in town, and when you fell, you hit your head. This resulted in what we call retrograde amnesia."

She sat up in her bed to listen to him. "Amnesia? But I feel fine. I'm ready to go home . . . if I only knew where home was." She managed a weak smile before becoming serious, asking, "If I have amnesia, why is it I can remember such things as what I had for lunch or breakfast, and the awful taste of the medicine they gave me this morning with no problem? It's just everything that happened before coming here to the hospital that I have a problem remembering."

Dr. Harding reassured her and explained. "Sweetie, retrograde amnesia is a loss of memory of things that happened to you before the fall. You should have no problem in remembering things that have happened since the fall . . . all the new things that you've learned since you've been in the hospital. It will begin slowly, and then soon the floodgates of memories will open for you. It is not to be confused with anterograde amnesia, which deals with the inability to form new memories following the onset of an injury or disease. Okay?"

She nodded.

Dr. Monroe patted her hand, "For now, all I want is for you to try to get some rest. I'll look in on you again in the morning. Good night. See you tomorrow."

He said goodbye to both of them, left the room, and headed for home.

Beth turned back to her patient and said, "He has a six-month-old baby girl with colic. Cries all the time. He's on his way home to help out and give his wife some relief so she can get some sleep." She patted Sweetie's hand and smiled. "At least now we know what we're dealing with, Sweetie. Which is a good thing, right?"

"If you say so, Doc."

"I do. Now try to get some rest. I'll look in on you tomorrow, okay? Good night."

As she walked toward the door, she heard the woman say, "Vicki."

Beth turned and said sweetly with a smile, "My name is Dr. Harding—Beth. Remember?"

"Oh, I know that," said the old woman. "But my name is Vicki. I can't tell you my last name, but I do know that my first name is definitely Vicki."

Beth hurried back to her bedside. "Vicki?"

"Yes?"

"When . . . how . . . what happened . . . Talk to me. When did all of this happen?"

"All of a sudden, tonight after dinner, I was dozing, and when I woke up . . . I knew my name. Crazy, isn't it?"

"Why didn't you say something to Dr. Monroe?"

"Because I wanted to talk with you first, and besides, all I remember is one word, one memory . . . my name. And only my first name. I wasn't sure if it was a good thing at first, but now after hearing all this . . . well, I feel better about it. I was afraid if . . ."

Beth patted the old woman's arm gently. "Don't worry, Vicki. We won't be releasing you from the hospital anytime soon, at least not until you remember more about yourself and maybe find some family members to help out."

Beth made a note in the woman's chart and buzzed the nurses' station. She felt happy for some reason. "I think we're on the road to recovery, Vicki. This is a first step."

"That's all I know, but I like the name Vicki. You know it's funny, I could have called myself any name in the world, but I think I like that name the best. Vicki. Has a classy ring to it, don't you think?"

Beth hugged the old woman and said with a smile, "It sure does. Get some rest; maybe you'll remember more in the morning. I'll see you tomorrow. Good night."

She walked past the Colonel's room and decided to look in on Johnny Ray. She saw they had upped the painkillers for Johnny Ray. "Hang in there, JR," she whispered. "Everybody's pullin' for ya."

She walked down the hallway and saw Dr. Crosby approaching.

"Pretty late hours for you tonight, huh, Doc?" she asked.

"I was just down in your office looking for you. Did you see my report on your desk?"

"No. What was it about? Or did you want to talk about it tomorrow?"

"This can't wait. I leave for New York tomorrow. It's my wife's birthday, and I promised her I would take her away for Christmas. It was about Logan Mitchell. The final report to the fire department requires your signature, but I think we should talk first."

"What's up?"

"It's like I said in my report. I received Logan Mitchell's scan and test results from the lab in California. It confirmed what I was thinking. He has evidence of past swelling in his cerebellar tonsil. Head trauma increases the risk by a factor of five. Ectopia may be present now but asymptomatic until whiplash causes it to become symptomatic. In his business, jumping out of planes and crashing into trees, well, it's not good. As a matter of fact, it's the worst thing in the world for him."

She stood before him in silence.

"Listen, Beth, I know the two of you are close, and with his condition he's fine now. But no football or jumping out of airplanes—ever again. He's had too many hits to the head, and the next one could be fatal."

"What about a fall or a stumble around the house?"

"He should be fine with something like that, just no more severe head traumas like he's had in the past . . . like those from smoke jumping."

"But that's his life. That's what he lives for."

"I understand . . . but he's young, and there are plenty of other things he can do. He just can't be putting his life and the lives of other smoke jumpers on his team in jeopardy. I tried to reach him, but I understand from the station house that he's out of town until tonight. Do you want to tell him . . . or do you want me to do it when I get back?"

Beth was silent for moment and then said softly, "I'll tell him. Thanks, Doc. Have a good trip to New York." The pain was obvious in her voice.

She wandered back down the hallway until she found herself outside the Colonel's room. It was dark and quiet, unlike the constant coming and goings outside his room. His chart showed no changes in his condition. She was still thinking about what she had just heard from Dr. Crosby about Logan. It was for his own good. He could still be a firefighter; he just could not be a smoke jumper any longer. She was troubled. That was what he lived for, but if he kept at it, it could cost him his life and maybe the lives of those who depended on him.

She stood by the Colonel's bed and watched his chest rise and fall. "Come on, old man, wake up. You hear me? Wake up."

The monitor kept its rhythmic beat, matching that of his chest, which rose and fell. The air tube was securely tucked inside his nose, helping him breathe. She stood over him and moved the hair from his forehead. "Take care, Colonel. See ya tomorrow." She turned to walk away.

"Where you goin'?" The coarse, quiet whisper was barely audible.

"What?" Beth asked in surprise.

"I said, where are you goin'? You just got here." It was a feeble reply.

"Colonel?" She gave him a cup of water with a straw. "Here, take some of this."

He sipped, then took some more. "*Aaaah.* That's so good."

"How do you feel?" she asked as she plumped his pillow under his head.

"I been better," he said, his weak voice straining as he tried to sit up in bed.

"Lay back down," she said sternly, then fluffed his pillow again and gently laid his head onto it. "It's about time you woke up. You just wanted to make sure you didn't miss out on all the Christmas presents, now didn't you?"

"You bet." He coughed, and then with that twinkle in his eye, he said, "Send in one of those pretty nurses with the short skirts they all

wear. I want something to eat. Steak. Rare. Beer or wine, I don't care."
He coughed again and then slid back deep into his pillows.

She laughed but could tell his strength was fading. "Hold on.
Only Jell-O for now," she said. "Lean back and take it easy. You need
your rest. You'll get a bigger meal tomorrow, maybe, but only after we
check you out. Your back wounds are still healing." She rubbed his arm.
"Welcome back, Bruce. Merry Christmas. I've missed you."

"Me, too. What day is it? Is it Christmas?"

"No. Christmas is Sunday, a couple of days away. Today's
Wednesday." She kissed his forehead. "Good night, old man. I'll send
in one of those pretty nurses to look after you."

When she turned around, he was sound asleep. She walked down
the hallway. Time to go.

CHAPTER THIRTY-FOUR

When Beth pulled into the driveway, she saw that Logan's rental car was already there. She sat in her SUV and thought about how she was going to tell him the news from Dr. Crosby. How would he take it? What would he do now? Would he stay in River Dale? Maybe work at the firehouse? *Will he* . . . She had to tell him he was healthy and okay, then take it from there. *First things first. Tell him the Colonel is awake and recovering. Then tell him . . . the rest.*

The light was on in his room over the garage, and she saw shadows move. She knew she had to tell him about his report. She just had to wait for the right time. It began to snow, small flakes at first, then larger ones fell on her windshield. She glanced toward the sky. *A storm is coming,* she thought to herself. *I love snow at Christmastime.*

Beth took in a deep breath and honked the horn to let him know she was home, then grabbed the pizza box from the front seat and made her way to the house. He waved to her from the window in his apartment above the garage.

Logan followed her inside a few minutes later and got a huge whiff of the pizza. "Boy, that smells good," he said, leaving his wet boots in front of the fridge to dry out. "And the Christmas music and the candles. Perfect Christmas dinner."

"You're so easy to please, Logan," she said, forcing a smile. "Oh," she said, trying to remain cheerful. "I have some good news. I was making my final rounds around the hospital tonight and I was in the Colonel's room . . . and he sat up and spoke to me."

"You're kidding? Wow, that's great news!"

"Still feisty as ever. Tired, but back to his old self. Said he wanted a cute, young nurse to bring him a steak." They both laughed. She had missed his laugh over the months he had been gone. She had missed him and could tell this was not going to be easy.

"Knowing him, he'll want to be up and out of bed for Christmas," remarked Logan, pouring some wine. He watched her reach and pull out some plates from the cabinet.

Logan took them from her and set the table. "And oh, by the way, I have something for you from Boston. Not much mind you, but something I thought you'd like." He stood, checking his jeans pockets, front and rear, then went to his still-wet jacket hanging on the hook. "Ah, here it is." It was the second small package he had bought in Boston, all neatly wrapped in Christmas paper. "Merry Christmas, Beth."

She held it in her hands, admiring the crisp corners of the wrap, a telltale sign of a professional. "But, Logan, I haven't wrapped your—"

"Don't worry about it. It's enough of a present just to be here."

"Well . . . from the looks of this beautiful wrap job, you bought it in either an expensive department store or an equally expensive boutique. And the lines of the paper are aligned so straight and the tape is—"

"Beth," he said with a grin. "Stop being so analytical . . . just open your gift."

She ripped off the paper and opened the box. He did not notice, but her eyes held a brief glimmer of recognition. She loved it. "Oh, Logan, it's beautiful." She held up a gold chain and the pendant that was in the shape of a piece of an old coin.

"It's an heirloom, the second part of three pieces of a coin. I gave one to Claire when I was there. Yours fits right into hers. The store didn't have the third piece . . . said it was missing."

She was nearly in tears. "Logan . . . I don't know . . . what to say." She swung her arms around his shoulders and kissed him. One long, hard, lingering kiss. Then, realizing what she had done, she pulled away from him. "I'm sorry, Logan. I don't know what came over me." An awkward silence ensued while they both stood there in the quiet of the old house.

"Let me help you with the clasp," he finally said to her, breaking the silence. He stood behind her and hooked the clasp, then his hand rested gently on her shoulder. She did not move it.

They both stood in the silent house, not moving or speaking to each other until Beth touched his hand and said, "Thank you, Logan. I love it. It's the best Christmas present ever."

"Good, I'm glad you like it. It had your name written all over it." He paused and then moved away, saying, "I'll get napkins."

She glanced at him as he set the table. *Good old, reliable Logan.* He was somebody you could always count on. The timer went off, she took the pizza from the oven, and they sat down to eat.

As she poured the wine, she said, "Tell me about Claire."

He let out a sigh. "She says she's happy. I know she was happy to see me, but he's a real controlling jerk, if you ask me. I think he's controlling everything about her—her friends, who she sees, and for how long, everything. I just don't think it's a healthy relationship. And what I don't understand is Claire is a bright, take-charge kind of girl and lets this happen. I was a little surprised, that's all." He did not say anything about the altercation he had with Roger as he was leaving or his rudeness. Maybe it was just a personality quirk or some jealousy on Roger's part.

"So? What do I tell her? How do I advise her?"

He looked at Beth, then said, "That's all I've been thinking about on my way home from Boston. Tell her to run as fast and as far away from him as she can—that's what I'd tell her. That's what I should have told her. I didn't even want to leave her there by herself with him. But I asked Claire, and she . . . told me she was okay and wanted me to leave."

"Well, I know I can count on you not to pull any punches. Thanks, Logan."

"Sure, anytime. I just wish there was more I could do. He seemed to dominate her, and that's not a good thing."

"I'll speak to her. As I recall, her shift finishes soon at the hospital, and then I can speak to her privately. Maybe even get her away from Boston to come here for Christmas."

"He doesn't celebrate Christmas."

"What?"

"I heard it with my own ears. After I gave Claire her gift, he said he doesn't celebrate Christmas. Maybe growing up his family didn't celebrate Christmas, or maybe his religion doesn't celebrate the holiday, but you think he'd do it for Claire. I saw the hurt look on her face. Some things you just do, and that's all there is to it. I don't know what to make of it."

"Hmmm. Thanks, Logan. I'll talk to her in my own way over the weekend." Beth watched him carefully when she asked, "Did Claire say if she was coming to the wedding?"

"She didn't say. We never really got a chance to talk about it once Roger entered the picture."

Beth was silent for a moment, carefully preparing her words. "What about you?"

He was quiet and did not answer.

"Will you give me away at my wedding?" she asked.

His head slumped to his chest and he could not look at her. "Beth, please don't ask me to do that. I'd do anything in the world for you, you know that . . . but I can't do that." He paused for a minute. "I'm sorry."

"Logan," she said. "Look at me, please."

Resigned to where the discussion was going, he slowly raised his head.

"What's going on here . . . between us?" she asked, almost pleading. "Logan, talk to me, please. We've always been able to talk things out between us."

"Beth, I can't—"

"Logan? Say it. For God's sake say it, say something . . . anything." Her voice was trembling.

Her mind raced and she thought, *Does he feel the same way about me? Logan, tell me what I want to hear. What I need to hear. Logan, for God's sake, say it if you feel it.*

"I just can't watch you marry some other guy. Don't ask me why. I just can't." He looked away.

"What? Why not? What the hell is going on here, Logan? I've known you for my whole life, and you're my closest friend. Talk to me."

He took in a deep breath and turned back to face her. "Do you love him?"

Beth halted and then stammered indignantly, "Well, we're getting married, aren't we? I would have to love somebody if I was going to ever think about getting married to him, now wouldn't I? I know he'd make a good father."

He was calm when he asked, "Is he the one you want to spend the rest of your life with? Is he the one you want to wake up to every morning? The last one you want to see before you go to sleep at night? To share all your secrets with? To laugh with? To have babies with? To grow old with? Do you love him?"

She felt that he had ripped away her veil of secrecy. He had seen right through her. Something she had kept hidden, even to herself, he had exposed. She had never asked herself the question he was asking her now. So simple a question, but one with so many answers. *Do I love him?*

Why did she want to marry Rory? Now, standing here, she could not tell him the truth. Something had changed in her feelings toward him. But if she told him how she felt, it would ruin everything. She would lose her best friend. And she was not going to be the one to lay her heart open. If he could not be honest with her, she could not open her soul to him. What gave him the right, after being away for so long, to come back home and turn her life upside down this way? To question her? Besides, she knew Rory was a good man. Now she felt an anger that surprised her.

"Those aren't fair questions, Logan," she shouted. "And you know it."

He said quietly, almost in a whisper, "I just asked you if you loved him and wanted to spend the rest of your life with him, nothing more. I thought it was a fair question. I'm sorry. Perhaps I better go. I'm booking a ticket for California, leaving on Saturday."

Her eyes grew much too wide. "Saturday? That's Christmas Eve. You're not even going to be here for my wedding?" she said, nearly screaming.

"No, I can't. I got a job to do. I'm a smoke jumper, remember? I better call it a day. Good night, Beth."

He stood and was putting on his boots and jacket, preparing to leave.

She was angry at him; no, she was furious. He had hurt her, cut her deep with his questions. She wanted to lash out at him, to hurt him the way he had hurt her. "You're grounded, Logan," she shouted at him. "You can't go jumping out of planes anymore, ever again." As soon as the words left her lips, she regretted it. The one thing he loved most, she had just torn away from him.

His head twisted toward her. "What are you talking about? What do you mean?"

She saw the hurt look in his eyes. *What do I say? I can't bring the words back,* she thought, furiously trying to remedy the hurt situation. She settled for the truth.

"Dr. Crosby came by to see me tonight. He got the results of the routine scan from California, and that's when he discovered you have a swollen cerebellar tonsil as a result of numerous traumas to the head. You're safe now. It was probably from hitting your head after too many jumps from the airplane. You can work as a firefighter . . . but not as a smoke jumper. Not ever again." She slumped in a heap on her chair. This was not how she had envisioned this. She had hurt him and could never forgive herself. Why had she done it?

He stood there in disbelief. "Tell me this isn't true. Tell me, Beth," he said raising his voice.

"I wish I could, Logan, believe me, I wish I could," she said, her eyes staring off into the distance, tears streaming down her cheeks. "You need some rest, and you need to stay away from parachutes for a long, long time. Forever."

He slowly turned and walked out of the room, the door closing quietly behind him as he left. "Good night, Beth," she heard him say.

She stood at the door and watched him walk away. Her mother's favorite rosebushes lined the backyard fence, once so green and filled with bright-red flowers, now snow covered and all dressed in white.

Beth watched him go. *Mom, what have I done? It's so confusing. Mom, am I doing the right thing? Give me a sign. Mom, please, let me know. I think . . . I love him.*

CHAPTER

THIRTY-FIVE

Drake's apartment was exactly as one would expect for a bachelor living away from home. Books, files, memos, and newspapers were everywhere.

Rory took it all in as he surveyed his new surroundings. He chuckled to himself because that was the way he had kept his place until Beth had come to visit one day. Never again was anything left out, lying around. She was good for him.

"Drake, I appreciate you letting me stay here. For some reason, I didn't want to intrude on Elizabeth. She already has one houseguest with Logan staying there. All the other hotels were fully booked for miles around because of the holidays. Besides, I need some time to think about a lot of things."

"Want a beer or some eggnog?" asked Drake.

"Eggnog sounds appropriate for this time of year."

"How about a little scotch to spice some things up?"

"Yeah, I sure can use it. And that was a good suggestion about the store," he said, looking at the large bags of clothes sitting on the chair near the television. "They had everything I needed, including a toothbrush, razor, and toiletries. Thanks again for letting me stay here. I really appreciate it."

"No problem, mate."

While waiting for his drink, Rory walked around the apartment and began glancing through the assorted binders and presentation materials scattered about. "Is this all for your copper-clad medical presentation on Friday?"

"Yep."

"Mind if I take a look? It sounded interesting."

"No, not at all. Help yourself. I'd appreciate your input."

Rory sat down after clearing away the stacks of newspapers piled on the old sofa. He picked up the presentation binders and began perusing them. "Is all this stuff in here true?" he asked a few minutes later, never taking his eyes off the material.

"Absolutely. It sounds like a fairy tale, but hospitals can use copper to ward off infection. It will kill ninety-nine point nine percent of all known bacteria in less than two hours. Dr. Harding's mother saw the ramifications of its use when she was still alive, and we tried it in the ICU on a test basis. The results were incredible. Unfortunately, it's a matter of money and educating the right people on the advantages of using copper on different surfaces. The next hurdle is, because copper is so expensive, finding somebody to pay for it and the right suppliers to fabricate it."

Rory was listening but still deep into the materials, reading page after page. He was lost to the world.

An hour or so later Drake told his guest, "I'm going to bed, Rory. I left out some fresh sheets and towels for you on the bed."

"Uh-huh, sure," he muttered without looking up. His salesman's curiosity was fully piqued. "Thanks again, Drake. I think I'll stay up a little bit and read through this stuff, if you don't mind."

"No, not at all. Good night. See you tomorrow."

The next morning when Drake awoke, Rory was still in his living room reading, sitting in the same location with a coffee mug in one hand and a red marker in the other. He used the marker to make notes on a flip chart he had set up. The room and dishes were clean, but the floor was now littered with pages of notes ripped from yellow legal pads.

"Morning," Drake said, reaching for the pot to brew some fresh coffee. "You been at this all night?"

"Yeah," Rory said with a huge grin. "I can't believe this stuff. Take a look. I have some wonderful things I need to show you."

As Drake walked around to the other side of the easel, he was shocked at what he saw. His presentation board was marked up with red and blue marks. Items on his flip chart were circled in red and blue, with arrows pointing from one bullet point to another.

"What the bloody hell are you doing to my presentation, mate? You've destroyed it." His well-hidden Cockney accent was finally evident.

"No, no, no. It's all right there. Trust me. I just put it into a PowerPoint presentation on my laptop. You can use it with a projector and make changes on it at will. Real easy to use. Even a . . ."

"A dumb Brit like me can learn how, right?" Drake said, his arms folded and his lips pursed.

"No, that's not what I meant. You're a genius. But there's no time to waste; come here and sit down. Let me show you."

An hour later, when he was finished briefing Drake, Rory sat down next to him and sipped his fresh cup of coffee. "Well, what do you think?"

Drake did not say anything at first, but after giving it some deep thought, he nodded and said, "I think you should make the presentation to the governor. We need to work on tying up a few loose ends, but I think it's bloody fantastic. Yes indeed."

"Me? No, no this is your show. I just tried to tighten it up somewhat, that's all. Make it clearer. Drake, you have a very compelling case here to make to the governor and the state board."

"Rory, you did a bang-up job. This may just work, if you know what I mean?"

"I do, but it still needs a lot of work."

"Work with me. Let me do the history; then, you can finish it off with your presentation. We can make the presentation together. What do you say?"

Rory eased back into the sofa and studied the flip chart. "I don't know, Drake. The company I work for sells antibiotics and is also in the business of curing infections. I don't think they would take kindly to another very viable competitor in the marketplace—which is what they would have if this thing takes off."

"Look, Rory, you've seen the numbers. The case you presented is compelling. If not you, then somebody else will get behind this thing and sell it like it needs to be sold . . . and make a lot of money. It's going to happen. Now Ascot is probably not interested, but somebody else will be when the feds start flexing their muscle and making hospitals use this philosophy to save lives, cut infections, and shorten hospital stays."

"For somebody who says he's not a salesperson, you sure do sell this well. All right, it could cost me my job, but . . . count me in. I don't know what Beth will say about all this, but I have to tell her."

Drake looked at his newfound friend and said, "She's a great lady, a good friend, a wonderful doctor, and a fantastic boss. You're lucky to have her."

"I know I should be, but . . ."

Rory's voice trailed off, but Drake did not seem to notice because he had launched into a new topic. "The presentation is tomorrow. Let's get the rest of your stuff from your car and then come back here and finish this. We've got a lot of work to do."

"Sounds good," said Rory. He sat for a while, not saying a word as Drake began his laundry list of items that needed to be done before Friday. *I need to talk to her,* Rory thought, *and the sooner the better.* "I'd like to stop by the hospital before we get started. I have something I have to do there."

CHAPTER
THIRTY-SIX

"Hey, old man. You still sleeping?" Logan asked his old friend. "Colonel? You awake?"

"I am now," came the groggy reply. "Can't a fella get some rest around here?" he responded as he slowly opened his eyes.

"Nope."

"Logan. Boy, are you a sight for sore old eyes. How'd you find out? When'd you get here?"

"I got a message from Royce and from the Doc right after it happened. They told me all about it. I had just finished up fighting a big blaze out at Los Lobos. We lost some good firefighters. But I'm here now."

"Logan, you're getting too old for all that nonsense. Like me." They looked at each other, words unspoken, but they knew what was unsaid. "Royce stopped by earlier to visit. Told me he offered you my job when I retire next year. You should take him up on it. I may not last that long before I put in my retirement papers. I want to enjoy life a bit. Margie and I have been talking about doing a cross-country road trip next summer in her RV."

"Margie? At the station? You . . . her?"

"Yeah. For about the last two months we've been keeping each other company, if you know what I mean. I like her a lot. She's like Beth, a good sort."

"Well, I'll be damned. Good for you." Logan stopped for a moment, then said, "You know, Colonel, I always thought I would end my career as a smoke jumper . . . in my old age, mind you. Not sitting at a desk in some fire station. But I have to tell you I've enjoyed working with the group you have here."

"Yeah, it's a good group. You can do a lot of good here, helping these folks, keepin' them safe." He paused for moment, then asked, "Tell me, Logan, what's the average age of the firefighters who work for you as smoke jumpers?"

Logan was slow to respond. "In their twenties."

"Royce also told me that the Forest Service is thinking about opening up a training area for Hotshots in New England." He glanced at Logan's red beeper on his belt. "Send them your 1038 leave papers. Do it now before something happens."

"It already has."

"What do you mean?"

"I had to take my annual workup, and the results finally came in—"

The old man finished his thought. "You got headaches, right? Neck pain, vertigo, sensory changes, and reduced coordination?" He shook his head slowly. "You got cerebellar tonsillar ectopia."

"Yeah. How'd you know? Did the Doc talk to you?"

"No, she didn't have to. It's the leading reason smoke jumpers leave the Forest Service. It doesn't mean you're dying, Logan, it just means you can't be crazy anymore and jump out of airplanes. You can still work at a station or with the Hotshots. You'd be great. Trust me, I know what I'm talking about."

The Colonel paused for a moment. "I never told you, but I got the same condition. I took a bad tumble early in my time smoke jumping.

That's why, years ago, I filed my 1038 to quit and came back here to New Hampshire. The best thing I ever did in my life. That's the reason I left. You need to do the same." He lifted his finger and pointed to Logan's belt. "Think about it, before that little red beeper on your belt goes off one day, just when you least expect it, and calls you back to California." He paused and looked past Logan toward the door.

"Good morning," Beth said to both of them. "What do we have here? What are you two up to?"

"Not much. Just having a conversation with my old friend Logan here, that's all."

"Hi, Beth," Logan whispered.

"Hi," she said without looking at him. She walked past him to reach the bedside of the Colonel. "Just thought I'd look in on you to see how you're doing."

"I feel better today. Will I be home for Christmas? I got some special plans."

"We'll see. Let's take it one day at a time. Okay?"

"Sure, Doc. Can I get some breakfast?"

"You bet." She turned to Logan, "Logan, you got a minute? I think we need to talk. My office, say, ten minutes?"

"Sure, Beth. Let me finish up with the Colonel. I'll stop by before I leave for the station."

They both watched her walk away. "She's a good lady," mused the Colonel. "You missed the boat not grabbing her when you had the chance."

"Yeah, but—"

"No buts about it. Still not too late."

"Colonel, she's already taken. Getting married here next week and sore at me that I'm not going to the wedding."

"Oh, now I understand. That's the reason for the chilly reception."

"Yeah. Hey, I had better go. I want to stop by and look in on Johnny Ray."

"Royce told me about what happened to him. How's he doing?"

"Not good. A lot of burns. I got roll call at the station house at ten. See ya later, old man."

Johnny Ray's room was dark and quiet as Logan entered. He lifted his hand and felt some movement but nothing else. "Hey, JR, it's me, Logan. When you going to get up and walk out of this place?" There was no response. He sat for a while, talking with his new friend. Not about anything special, just about the town, his friends, the station, and of course the Colonel. Still no snappy comeback from the young firefighter. He glanced at his watch and said, "Gotta go, JR. I wanna see you back at the station soon. You take care now," he said, finally laying his hand back down by his side. This was the tough part of being a firefighter.

He walked into Beth's office still lost in thought.

"Mornin', Logan," she said and hugged him.

She felt warm to his touch. "Morning," he said, still smelling the faint scent of her perfume from her embrace.

"Sit here," she said, pointing to the leather sofa. "I'm sorry about last night. I should have been more sensitive about the way I handled it. How do you feel?"

"I feel fine now. I just need some time off."

She glanced in his eyes. "Sometimes that's all it takes."

There was an awkward silence as they sat next to each other. He had so much to say, and he was afraid he would say it all. Finally, he stood, knowing it was time to go. "I have to be at the station soon. Ten o'clock roll call to start my rotation. I better get going."

He hugged her, and suddenly he realized he never wanted to let her go. Ever. He moved inches away, still holding her in his embrace. *Say it, Logan. You had your chance; don't blow it again. Now!*

"Beth, there's something I've been wanting to tell you for a very, very long time. I should have told you this years ago, but I didn't want to cause any waves or disruption in your life." He gently rubbed her arms, took a deep breath, and looked into her eyes. "Beth, I have always—"

"Ummm."

They heard a cough at the door and separated. It was Rory.

"Oh, hi, Rory. I was just getting ready to call you," Beth said.

"Yes, it certainly looks like it. Hi, Logan. Good to see you again."

Logan looked at Beth, stepped away, and reluctantly said, "Well, it sounds like the two of you have a lot to talk about, so I best be on my way."

"Logan, can you wait . . . so we can finish our conversation?" she pleaded.

"I'll leave you two be." He kissed her on the cheek.

She watched him leave and suddenly realized that Rory was still in the room, watching her. "He's going back to California Saturday," she said aloud to no one in particular.

Rory walked up beside her. "He's a good man, Beth. He'll make somebody a great husband someday."

Turning to him she said, "Rory, we need to talk." Beth stepped outside and told Carlita that they did not want to be disturbed, then returned to her office and closed the door. "I'm glad you came by; I've been wanting to talk to you since you came to River Dale. How are you doing, first of all? After the fire at the hotel. I was worried."

"I tried to get hold of you, but you were out of your office. But I'm good. Drake was kind enough to let me bunk with him for a while, as this all gets sorted out."

"You could have stayed with me. I have plenty of room at home."

"I know, but you already have one houseguest, and the dust and all, well, it's complicated . . . maybe it's just better this way." His eyes glazed over as he spoke. "But I must tell you, there were some very spooky moments in the hotel, with the fire and smoke, the sirens and noise, and everything else. I was never so happy in my whole life than when I saw that first firefighter come through my hotel room door and lead us to safety downstairs. Fortunately, no one was hurt. It looked a lot worse than it was—a lot of smoke."

Beth let him talk, then said, "Rory, please, I have a lot to say, and—"

"Me, too . . . but let me go first. Okay?" He sat down.

"All right." She sat down next to him on the sofa, still feeling the warmth of where Logan had sat.

"Where do I start?"

"The wedding?"

"Yes . . . the wedding. Going through all the details just so we could become man and wife, well, I thought maybe we—I was pushing it. Our courtship was a whirlwind. We met, we dated, we got engaged."

Beth smiled and said in a low, understanding tone, "But we never got to know each other; I mean, really know each other. Logan joked to me one time when I was describing how we met that it sounded more like a corporate merger than a courtship and a marriage."

"Yes, he's right." Rory laughed softly. "Marriage is tough enough without having things and places and history to share. I love you, Beth. You're the absolute best thing that has ever happened to me, but for us to ever work out . . ."

She took his hands into hers and looked at him. "Why don't we just part as friends? Good friends?"

"Of course," he said, a look of relief covering his face as he leaned forward to hug her. "You're the best, Beth. Whoever you marry will be one lucky guy."

"I know," she said with a mischievous twinkle in her eye. Then she became serious. "What are your plans for Christmas? Are you going back to Chicago? Staying here? I still have the spare bedrooms. Dusty but free of charge. You're more than welcome to stay with me. Friend?"

"Thanks, but no thanks. Drake and I have been working on his presentation together."

"You have?" she said, surprised.

"Yeah. He wants me to help him present it to the governor when he comes in town tomorrow. As long as you don't have a problem with it."

"No, not at all. Of course not. He's a great administrator, but sales presentations are not his forte. And you're one of the best that I've ever seen."

"I agree. So, since he doesn't mind putting up with me, maybe it's just easier for me to stay at his place. We've got a lot of work to do on this presentation. But I have to tell you, I find the whole idea very exciting. Could be very interesting. Using copper to stop the transmission of bacteria and for infection control. Wow."

"Yeah, I think so, too. One last thing, Rory. I won't be taking the job at Ascot Pharmaceuticals. It just never felt right for me."

He looked at her and said, "I understand. No problem, Beth. None at all."

They stood and hugged again, and she walked him out of her office. When she returned, she laughed. Beth could not help but notice three open drawers on her credenza and four open cabinet doors. *Thanks for stopping by to help, Mom,* she thought to herself.

CHAPTER
THIRTY-SEVEN

As Logan drove along the river road, he watched the frothy water churn over the rocks. Along the snow-covered banks he even saw one brave fisherman trout fishing. Logan honked his horn, and when the hearty angler looked up, he gave him a thumbs-up good luck sign. The mountains in the distance shone bright as the sun reflected off the white hills and valleys. He turned off on the road before the station to make a slight detour. He was going to visit Sarah and the Judge.

Logan made his way to the resting place of his adopted parents. Doc Sarah and the Judge, side by side.

He took off his wool hat and said, "Hi. It's me, Logan. Just came back to River Dale for a quick visit to check on the Colonel . . . and to see Beth. He's doing fine now, but . . . it's Beth I'm worried about. She's getting married to some guy, but I'm not sure she's really in love with him. I'm not sure she even knows what love is. Who does?" The snow began to fall and cover his peacoat as he whisked the snow off the bench and sat down.

"How did you two manage it all those years? I never heard you two fight, raise your voices at each other, or say a harsh word about anything. That's what I call love. And Claire, I'm worried about her as well. She's with some creep. I don't care for him at all, and I don't trust him. I wanted to just smack him and bring her back here, where it's safe. But as you always used to say to all of us, we have to make our own mistakes. That's how we truly learn." He looked to the sky, closed his eyes, and let the snowflakes hit his face before returning his gaze to the quiet monuments before him.

"I think Beth is making a mistake, but I can't stop her." He paused, then told her his secret. "I love her, Mom, but I guess you already know that by now. Sometimes love is just letting the person you care for go their own way and make their own mistakes. But it tears me up inside. He's not a bad guy, but . . ." He folded the outer flap of his coat over to the side to keep out the chill. "I better go now. I just had to say it to somebody. Help me if you can. I gotta go, I have roll call soon at the station and then a training session later. Merry Christmas, Judge, Doc. I love you and miss you both."

Once inside the truck, he turned the key and then sniffed the air; he swore he could smell the faintest aroma of cherry-and-honey pipe tobacco, the Judge's favorite. He smiled. *Time to go,* he thought to himself.

He drove to the station, still lost in thought.

Once roll call was over, the daily ritual of equipment and maintenance began. Checking pressures. Generator testing. Checking and cleaning hoses. Pumper trucks and EMT trucks needed to be serviced and restocked daily—all ready to leave on a moment's notice. Twenty-four hours a day, seven days a week. Cleaning, washing, and servicing of all equipment was paramount in their work—people's lives depended on it. When the service work was done, the hoses were taken down from the drying towers and reinstalled on the trucks. After the morning checklist was completed, the crew broke for lunch.

Fletch sidled up next to Logan and asked, "What's on the schedule for today?"

"I understand that there was a fire at the Holden Inn near Winston yesterday."

"Yeah, a real smoker I hear. Why?"

"Well, they're putting up another one west of here just off the highway, near West River Dale. They need a fire inspection for their certificate of occupancy. Want to join me to check 'em out?" queried Logan.

"Sure."

The two of them drove in silence along the river road until they saw a large bull moose hoisting a full rack of antlers meandering through the field on the other side of the fast-moving water.

"He wouldn't be showing his face around here in October, that's for sure," said Fletch, making a reference to the nine-day October moose-hunting season in New Hampshire. The big bull moose stopped along the whitewater to study them as they drove by before returning to his terrestrial scavenging.

"Right," Logan said.

"So, tell me something. I hear they offered you the Colonel's job. Are you stickin' around?"

"I have a plane ticket out of Boston for Saturday. Now that the Colonel is on the mend, there's not much more for me to do here."

"And there's so much more for you out in the foothills of California?" Fletch said with a sarcastic tone. "Working the hills and valleys, then just waiting for the next big one to hit. Ready to go fight fire with fire. I guess you're right. But let me tell you somethin', Logan, you're a good firefighter, and you're a natural leader. This town sure could use somebody like you. The Colonel might stick around for another year if we're lucky, then there'll be nobody here when he leaves."

"What about you?"

"Oh, me? I'll probably be around for a little bit, but this isn't home for me. I'm from upstate New York, and that's probably where I'll head back to next summer. Everybody goes home sooner or later."

"Not me," replied Logan as he parked the vehicle in the new hotel's parking lot. Changing the subject, he said, "Let's go see what we have here." They were greeted by a big, burly man in work overalls.

"Hi, I'm Robert Brooks, but everybody calls me Bo. I'm the general contractor here at the hotel," he said, extending his beefy hand and then handing them both hard hats. "This is still a construction site until we get your okay and the certificate of occupancy." He paused before continuing. "I need that CO soon, 'cause we got people checking in for the holidays startin' tomorrow. So the quicker we can get this done, the better. Where do ya want to start first?"

"Basement," said Logan, giving Fletch a sideways glance and pulling out his clipboard. They walked through the lower level, checking all the mechanicals, including the sprinkler systems. The pumps. The alarm systems. The converters. The elevators. "Everything seems to be in order here. Let's work our way up the building."

Everything had that new-car smell, from the fresh carpets to the new paint and all new fixtures.

"Nice place," Fletch remarked as they walked through.

"Yeah, the owners want the best . . . at the best price, if you know what I mean," commented Bo. He kept glancing at his watch and asking how much longer it was going to take. "Hey, guys, can ya give a fella a break? I got a deadline to keep, and like I told ya, I got people checkin' in tomorrow."

"Half hour tops, if you let us do our job."

"Okay, okay. I'll just settle in behind you and open any doors for you. Got everything locked until we have regular daily staff here. Ya know what I mean?"

Neither one of them answered. They just kept their eyes open and continued their inspection. They walked down the main hallway and turned left.

Near the end of the passage, the big man said, "Nothin' down there," and turned to walk away. The two firefighters continued down the hallway and stopped in front of an exit door.

"It's locked," said Logan.

"And chained shut," added Fletch. "Code violation of the first order."

Logan began to write it up on his code sheet.

Bo watched him scribble. "Aw, guys, come on, if I didn't lock the door, then things around here would start to walk away. Ya know what I mean? Come on. Gimme a break, will ya?"

Logan kept writing and walked up the stairs to the next floor, where he opened the door and walked down the hall. Halfway down the hallway he stopped in front of an unmarked door. "What's in here?" he asked.

"Just a housekeeping storage room, that's all," Bo said.

"Open it, please," Logan replied.

"Oh yeah, sure," Bo said, reaching deep inside his pocket for a long chain filled with assorted keys. He fumbled with them in his hand until one finally clicked in the lock. He swung it open and then began to close it. "See? Storage. Nothin' here," he said, closing the door.

"Put the light on, please," asked Logan.

The light illuminated the packed closet filled with extra toilet paper and stacks of white towels piled high on top of one another to the ceiling.

"Can never have too many towels in the hotel business. These guys like to have a lot of extras," Bo said.

Logan walked inside and looked around, then returned to Fletch and their escort.

Logan pointed to the closet ceiling with his clipboard. "Those towels are stacked way too high. They're blocking the sprinkler heads. Safety violation. And code violation." He stopped to look at Bo and said harshly, "And you know it." He continued to write on his clipboard before they walked away.

Bo raced to catch up with him and then stood in front of both fire-fighters. "Well, you know we're under the gun here and the owners . . . they want to have everything ready to open. We have a lot of people comin' in from out of town. I'll get this all taken care of today—now. I'll call in a crew from another job site to come and fix this stuff. Right away. Today. Okay?"

Logan looked at him and then walked around the big man. "I have an inspection to finish. Excuse me."

They walked up two more floors and found the same situation on each floor. Logan had had enough. He turned to face the man. "Sir, the reason we do these inspections is so people who stay at this hotel can have the same confidence here as they have in their own home. They want to feel safe. If there was a fire in one of those closets, the sprinkler would not be able to put it out in time, and the fire would grow out of control before activating the sprinklers."

"Possibly, but highly doubtful, don't you think, General?"

"Yes, possibly," Logan said, ignoring the snide remark, "but I sure wouldn't want to take a chance on that . . . would you?"

The man did not answer him.

"And by the way, I'm just a trained fire inspector, not a captain or a general. Just trying to do my job." He stopped in front of one of the hotel guest rooms at random. "Can you open this, please?"

"Yeah, sure." Bo inserted the key card, the door light lit up green, and they walked inside. Fletch checked out the closet and the bathroom while Logan walked inside the room. He glanced up at the sprinkler head over the bed. "Let's see a couple of other rooms on this and a few other floors."

In the last room they inspected, Logan climbed onto the bed and leaned in close to look at the sprinkler head. "This is only the second one in compliance that I've seen. All the other ones were painted over."

"Yeah, the owner requested it that way. Said his guests didn't like looking at sprinkler heads with green liquid in them," he said with a grin.

"Well, that's going to cost him, because those heads are SH250s, rated at two hundred fifty degrees and not one hundred seventy."

"So?"

"Believe it or not, the SH250s are cheaper, but it means that the temperature in this room or anywhere in the building would have to reach two hundred fifty degrees before the sprinklers would go off. People would die well before that happened. You should know that as a general contractor."

"Well . . . sometimes when you're in a hurry—"

"People die. Our job is to prevent that from happening. Another thing: the paint on those sprinkler sensors that have been painted over increases the temperature the room would need to reach before a head would activate and start spraying water to put out the fire. That's very dangerous." Logan finished writing and handed Bo his copy.

"My copy goes to the county fire marshal's office." He stood in front of the construction boss with his finger pointed at his chest. "I'm going to recommend that a full reinspection and declaration be done for this building. You can't cut corners with people's lives. When you fully meet the standards, then you'll have your certificate. Good day, sir."

The contractor stood there and watched them walk away, both of them shaking their heads in disbelief. He ran after them and caught up with them as they reached their car. "Hey guys, I'm under the gun."

"Not my problem," said Logan, fishing for his keys and opening the car door. Bo tapped his window, and, when Logan lowered it, the big man smiled.

"Okay, guys, I understand." His smile turned into an all-knowing grin. "Ah, I get it, it's Christmastime. One of you fellas must've dropped your Christmas shopping money in the parking lot back there." He handed them a bulging yellow envelope filled with what looked like hundred-dollar bills wrapped around his copy of the inspection report, then said, "Merry Christmas?"

Logan looked at it carefully and then at the smiling face of the burly man. "That's your copy of the report, sir. You're going to need it when the fire marshal comes by for a revisit. Good day, sir." He started to drive away, then stopped and turned to the contractor. "Bo, I gotta ask ya'—would you want your family to stay in this place? I didn't think so. Merry Christmas." Holding out his arm, he waved goodbye.

"Serves him right," said Fletch with a grim look.

They were both shaking their heads when they were interrupted by a loud buzzing noise—it was Logan's red smoke jumper beeper. It vibrated and buzzed three times to alert him. He glanced at the message. Fletch looked at him to see if he was going to say anything more as he drove down the river road back to the station. When Logan parked the truck, they stayed inside the still-running vehicle, Logan gripping the steering wheel until his knuckles turned white. Finally, he spoke.

"I gotta go," he whispered.

CHAPTER THIRTY-EIGHT

Beth looked out the bedroom window; tomorrow was Christmas Eve, her favorite time of the year. She felt like a kid again. Glancing outside, she saw snow falling gently onto the driveway. Her mother's favorite rosebushes were leaning over from the heavy weight of the fallen snow. She saw the tracks from the local deer and foxes as they made their way across the yard, but there was no sign of Logan's car.

Where is he? I have to talk to him. I have to tell him. She was excited and nervous at the same time. She would convince him to stay. He had to stay. He had said he was going to leave, but she had to talk to him before she went in to work. *Where is he?* She glanced at the clock on the wall.

She had made the decision that she was going to stay in River Dale. This was home—even if she could not save the hospital and her mother's legacy, she would still stay here. She could work here as a pediatrician. Perhaps she could talk Claire into moving closer to home, though for now her sister was not even answering her calls or texts.

She turned on the radio to listen to the ever-present Christmas songs. The music played in the background.

Shall I play for you . . .

Beth missed him. Try as she might to occupy her mind, Logan kept stealing her time and her thoughts. She glanced at her watch. She would wait for him. Then they could talk. Really talk. She decided she would tell him everything. How she felt, how she had always felt but only just now admitted to herself. She had loved him from the first moment she had seen him—a tall, gawky kid who had moved in next door. A sense of relief crashed over her like a warm wave of emotions; she had finally acknowledged it to herself. She smiled. That was exactly what she would do.

She saw in her mind what would happen. Soon he would walk through the door, and she would throw her arms around his neck, kiss him, hold him, and tell him to his face, "I love you, Logan." Yes, she could hardly wait. She showered, dressed, set the breakfast table, and prepared the coffeepot. She wanted it to go perfectly. *Help me, Mom . . . Dad. Please.* It was nearing nine o'clock. *Where is he? Please hurry.*

Her cell phone rang, startling her. It was Carlita.

"Dr. Harding, Beth, where are you? The governor and Mr. French are here, waiting for you in the conference room."

"What? Why?"

"Your nine o'clock meeting? Remember? You'd better hurry."

"Nine? I thought it was for noon. Oh no! I'm on my way."

She rushed to her car and looked in the driveway, asking herself, *Where's Logan?* She drove as fast as she could along the old river road— too fast. The car spun sideways on the icy street, nearly fishtailing before she was able to straighten it out. How could she forget a meeting like this? *Logan. Focus, Beth, focus.*

She parked the car in her reserved spot and noticed Drake's car already there. A quick touch of the car's hood told her it had been there awhile. *Good.*

"Merry Christmas," said Carlita, grabbing Beth's coat from her and handing her a stack of presentation materials and a hot cup of coffee.

She walked into the room, and the governor greeted her like an old friend. "Good morning, Elizabeth, so good to see you again."

"Yes, and you, too, Governor. So good to see you again, sir."

"And of course you remember Amanda Pelletier, my director of the state hospital oversight board. My right hand when it comes to health-care matters."

"Yes, of course, of course, we met during a previous presentation at the state capital. I must apologize. I had some trouble with my hot water heater at home, but I—"

"No problem," said the governor. "No problem at all. Young Dr. Corrigan has been regaling us with some interesting stories about his time with the National Health Service in England. Quite interesting. And Mr. Daniels here has been filling our minds with some grand illusions of finding a miracle cure for the common cold and doing away with all hospital-borne infections. Quite the staff you have here, Dr. Harding. Quite the staff," he said with a chuckle. He glanced at his watch. "So, if we are ready, perhaps we could start. I would like to look in on my old friend Bruce Devlin and see how the old coot is doing. Please proceed."

Ron French nodded to Beth as he sat at the other end of the conference table taking notes, watching, listening, and waiting to absorb all the facts. That was his way.

Beth stood and opened the folder in front of her. "Thank you all for coming here today and taking the time to listen to what I am sure you will feel is one of the most compelling stories in modern medicine. One that has been known for centuries but never acted upon to the extent it deserves. One that has been scientifically proven effective. Lifesaving. But rather than stealing anyone's thunder, I would like to turn this meeting over to Dr. Drake Corrigan and Mr. Rory Daniels. Thank you. Drake?"

Drake stood. He looked very impressive in his tailored Harris Tweed three-piece suit. "Good day, ladies and gentlemen. We have prepared some talking points for you to take with you, some facts and data. But rather than wasting your time reviewing all the information we presented before, I would like you to hear it from a fresh voice. A new perspective, from Mr. Rory Daniels. Rory, please."

Rory looked uncomfortable and annoyed when he stood in his new suit, shirt, tie. Beth noticed that the collar was tight around his neck, too tight for him to button. He managed a weak smile, but as soon as he opened his portfolio and began to speak, he was transformed. He was the consummate salesman, and now he had one chance to help Beth and Drake save their hospital.

"Good morning, ladies and gentlemen. Did you know that there are over one hundred fifty million antibiotic prescriptions written every year in America alone? It is estimated that at least fifty million of those prescriptions are unnecessary. How do I know this? Because until yesterday, I worked for one of the largest pharmaceutical companies in the world."

Beth watched him with a bewildered look.

"As most of you know, over the years, antibiotics have been overprescribed for many minor issues such as coughs, colds, sore throats, flu, cuts, and skin infections. Although antibiotics kill bacteria, they are not effective against viruses and especially not viral infections."

He leaned over and poured a glass of water, took a drink, and proceeded. He stood at his laptop, and, using a PowerPoint chart, he pointed to some information on the screen.

"We all know some things that many of our patients do not: that antibiotics will not cure the flu and will not keep other individuals from catching a virus. In fact, they may cause unnecessary, harmful side effects and may contribute to the development of antibiotic-resistant bacteria."

He stopped and looked around the room.

"Most of you in this room already know this. Misuse and/or overuse of these drugs has contributed significantly to a phenomenon known as antibiotic resistance. This resistance develops when potentially harmful bacteria change in a way that reduces or eliminates the effectiveness of antibiotics. Patients come into the hospital for treatment, and while they are here, they contract some other type of bacterial infection. It's what we call a readmit. Now, due to antibiotic resistance, we are finding that some of these patients' infections cannot be treated."

He stopped and looked at each one of them individually. "Antibiotic resistance is a growing public health concern worldwide. When a person is infected with an antibiotic-resistant bacterium, not only is treatment of that patient more difficult, but the antibiotic-resistant bacterium may spread to other people. Even our drug of last defense, Colistin, is now shown to be ineffective against the new strains of superbug bacteria. But our main concern here today is hospital-acquired infections, or HAI, and their impact on patient care and hospital budgets. When antibiotics don't work, the result can be longer illnesses, more complicated illnesses, more doctor visits, the use of stronger and more expensive drugs, and more deaths caused by bacterial infections. The annual cost has been estimated to be in excess of one hundred forty billion dollars. All paid for with taxpayer dollars."

He saw them all lean back, digesting what he had just told them.

"The federal government is now cracking down on hospitals that cause their patients to be readmitted for infections that they picked up during their hospital stays. Last year the government reduced by one percent what Medicare, Medicaid, and other insurance programs pay for excessive readmits. This can amount to millions of dollars in some hospital systems. So it is incumbent upon medical providers to try to prevent infections wherever they can for two reasons. One: for patient health and safety. And two: for financial reasons. The government has set a guideline that more than ten readmits per one hundred hospital stays will result in a penalty assessment. Three years ago, River Dale General had a readmit rate of fourteen percent. Dr. Harding's mother, the late Dr. Sarah Harding, decided to do an experiment to reduce that number. She brought on board Dr. Drake Corrigan, a noted British expert in bacterial infections at the London Institute, to help oversee what she called the Copper Infection Reduction Program, or CIRP for short. Copper was used on some high-touch surfaces in the ICU to help reduce readmit rates in that unit."

He pointed to Drake, who passed around some additional literature.

"Copper? CIRP? How does it all work?" asked Amanda.

"Good question. I'm going to ask Dr. Corrigan to step back in for a minute to give you the technical specifications."

"Thanks, Rory," Drake said as Rory returned to his seat. "In the green folders you have in front of you, all of this information is spelled out in a thorough and boring presentation."

They laughed.

"But let's take our toughest bacteria: MRSA and MSSA. There are over eight hundred cases of MRSA and almost ten thousand cases of MSSA reported annually in the United States. Copper damages the bacterial respiration and DNA of these bacteria, resulting in irreversible cell breakdown and death. To put it simply and not bore you with all the technical details, when it comes to bacteria, copper kills everything. How? Research shows that copper targets various cellular sites, not only killing bacterial and viral pathogens but also rapidly destroying their nucleic acid genetic material so there is no chance of mutation occurring and nothing to pass on to other microbes, a process called horizontal gene transfer. Consequently, this helps prevent breeding the next generation of superbug. Copper is the holy grail in our fight against HAI."

Drake looked at his audience to make sure he had not lost them.

"Bacteria have been shown to stay alive on our traditional stainless steel surfaces for up to eight days, but on the other hand, the EPA has certified that copper begins killing the bacteria in less than ten minutes and completely destroys them within two hours."

He knew he had them now. Why hadn't he done this last summer in his presentation at the state capital?

"When a bacterium comes in contact with a copper surface, a short-circuiting of the current in the cell membrane occurs. This weakens the outer membrane and creates holes."

They were nodding their heads in agreement. They had all heard the rumors of the effectiveness of copper in a hospital setting, but none had seen hard data about its effectiveness.

"Now that the outer membranes are full of holes, copper ions start rushing into the single-cell bacteria, overwhelming them and grinding their metabolic activity to a halt. The bacteria can no longer breathe, eat, digest, or create energy, and so they die. The real question we have been asking is . . . what *won't* it kill? It seems to kill all bacteria."

"Thanks, Drake," said Rory, returning to the podium. "The idea is simple; copper is a known antibacterial material, but it has never been fully used before in a hospital setting due to its cost. Here at River Dale General, they set about slowly at first, due to budget constraints, to equip and retrofit surfaces in the ICU that are most frequently touched by patients, visitors, nurses, doctors, and other staff. But first they had to ascertain what surfaces were touched most frequently. This was done rather ingeniously by requiring everyone in the ICU to use a motion-activated, nontouch, automatic sprayer mixed with quinine water."

"Why quinine water?"

"One reason is it's safe and nontoxic. Second, the residue glows in the dark in the presence of a black light. So, after a few days of using quinine water, we moved a portable black light around the ICU and saw all the surfaces that received heavy use. Next, the hospital set about copperizing as many of those surfaces a possible. Bed handrails were first, then cabinet knobs, doorknobs, chairs, IV poles, and other heavy-use surfaces."

French raised his hand and asked, "You mean to say that you covered these surfaces with one hundred percent copper?"

"No, sir. That would be way too expensive and a certain amount of overkill, no pun intended. The EPA has certified that materials need to be only sixty percent copper to be effective against bacteria. There are only two companies in the world that make these products for hospitals; one company is in South America, called CRH. There's also an American company, south of Chicago, called E. J. Royster. The hospital obtained copper samples from the American company and proceeded with the experiment. The results in the limited survey were astonishing."

He flashed a PowerPoint chart on the wall showing the sharp decline in readmissions.

"The readmission rate due to HAI dropped significantly in the test. As more copper-clad items were installed, the readmit rate dropped even further. We initially reached a three point four percent readmission rate, and once all the items were installed it dropped to . . . less than one percent for that ICU area over the past twelve months."

The governor nodded. "Wow. Very interesting."

"This copper technique is effective against all known bacteria, including MRSA, MSSA, CRE, and C. diff, as well as norovirus and a host of other infectious monsters we find lurking in and around our hospital units. What we propose today is to equip the entire hospital with these bacteria-fighting copper items."

"Wait just a minute," said French. "Mr. Daniels, that's going well beyond our budget, especially for a hospital that is scheduled to close soon." He shot a questioning glance at Dr. Harding. "Perhaps we should try it at a different hospital, say, the new hospital in Winston."

Beth stood to plead her case. "With all due respect, Mr. French, the initial trials for comparison purposes were conducted here, so to ensure that we are comparing apples to apples and to save time—and money—I suggest we continue to do the study right here at River Dale General."

"That makes a lot of sense," the governor chimed in in support of her idea.

"There is still the question of cleaning the surfaces. Correct? And the expense, Dr. Harding," interjected Amanda. "No matter where the trials are held, from what I am hearing here today, it's going to be very expensive to install and maintain a full copper hospital."

"Excuse me, if I may?" Rory interjected. "I think I have the answer to that question."

"Of course," Amanda said.

"The copper kills bacteria in two hours or less, however, all surfaces still must be cleaned regularly just like any other surface in the hospital. And now the elephant in the room—cost. I have arranged to have the entire hospital fitted out with all of the latest copper antibacterial technology, down to wall switch plates, elevator panels, keypads, doorknobs, and the like—all at no cost to the hospital."

"What?" French was on his feet. "How is that possible?" he blustered to everybody in the room. "Nobody can afford those kinds of expenses."

Rory saw a small grin grow on Drake's face as he continued. "I have been in touch with the folks at E. J. Royster, and they agreed to fund and donate everything we need to have River Dale General be a guinea pig for this retrofit test project. They only ask that we acknowledge their participation in our findings and the part they played in the program. They also volunteered to help fund the monitoring of the program. They are willing to partner with us to see if we can reduce the number of readmits hospital-wide at River Dale General."

"Are you sure about this?" asked an unbelieving French.

"Positive. It was authorized by their new vice president of sales just today, and the company's senior management is fully on board." He smiled. "The company is convinced it is a good idea to fund a test hospital, and I was able to convince upper management at the firm that this would put them at the forefront of bringing hospital-borne infection rates down and under control. They are looking at it from a global perspective."

"And greatly increase their copper sales," joked the governor.

"Yes, sir. They see a great potential in using the same copper-clad pieces to stop noroviruses on cruise ships, in clinics, at public sports stadiums, and the like."

Rory knew he had the audience right where he wanted them. He added, "The only other item we need is state approval for emergency funding of two million dollars to buy the equipment needed to bring this hospital up to code and keep it open. River Dale General is scheduled to begin closedown procedures starting tomorrow. So time is of the essence. We need to have a commitment of the funding by the middle of next week to remain in compliance with state laws. Thank you for your time and questions."

The governor smiled. "I think we've heard everything we need," he said, closing his portfolio and nodding his approval to Amanda. "Fine presentation. I will ask Amanda here to put the program on the fast track and recommend the results be followed nationally by the National Hospital Association"—he winked—"where I am on the board. That's the good news."

He looked at Beth and held up a blue binder. "Now for the bad news. Dr. Harding, I received your written request for a onetime emergency funding for your equipment needed to bring the hospital into compliance." He sighed deeply before looking at her. "Doctor, I'm afraid I can't approve this. You see, if I did it for you, I would have every hospital, clinic, and school throughout the state asking for additional funding. This state does not have the budget to do that sort of thing for everyone."

He paused. "I can get the approval for your copper project with no problem. Either for your hospital or perhaps the new Winston hospital, but in regard to the two million dollars . . . I'm afraid you're on your own. I'm sorry. You will need to get the two million dollars for your equipment. But I need to know soon if it's going to be River Dale

General or Winston Regional. Let Amanda know when you've reached your decision. Good luck, and merry Christmas."

Beth slumped back in her chair. She had support from the governor and the hospital board, but she could not get the approval for her funding? Not from the state, not from the county, and not from the city. She needed $2 million. What was she going to do? Her dream was turning into a nightmare.

French approached her and said, "Dr. Harding, I'll support you in any way I can. After listening to this presentation and the favorable spotlight it would put on River Dale, well . . . But you need a commitment for your two million dollars, and fast. And you need to keep away from Sidney when he returns from his cruise. I tried to cover for you yesterday. I didn't answer his e-mail when he asked how the shutdown was going. But he's going to find out sooner or later that you haven't even started it yet. He's due back soon."

Governor McKerney turned and shook Rory's hand. "Good presentation, yes indeed. I liked it. I liked it a lot. Good job. You should be in sales."

"Ah, but I am, sir. I now work for E. J. Royster," Rory said with a huge grin as he shook the governor's hand. "I'll send you my business card in the mail just as soon as I have one. So glad to meet you, and I appreciate you coming all the way here today."

"No problem at all, son. You see, I came to see how my old friend Bruce is doing and to visit with my mother. She lives just outside of Conway, which is not far from here. I'm going there to spend Christmas Eve with her just as I have always done for the last sixty-two years. Merry Christmas, son."

Rory shook Amanda Pelletier's hand. "Merry Christmas, sir. Nice to meet you, ma'am." Rory helped the governor on with his heavy wool topcoat and asked, "By the way, sir, if you don't mind me asking, which hospital does your mother use?"

The big man turned to look at Rory with a shocked expression on his face, nodded with a sly, knowing smile, and headed toward the door on his way to visit with the Colonel. "Merry Christmas, all," he said as he left.

The room cleared slowly, and Amanda approached Drake. She did not say anything at first but extended her hand.

His face grew red. "I must apologize for my behavior and remarks that I made on the phone the other night. I'm afraid that I had too much good cheer . . . and one too many eggnogs."

She smiled, still holding his hand. "No apologies necessary. I thought it was charming. Don't worry about it. I'm glad you called, and I'm sure that we'll be seeing a lot more of each other, especially if we work on this project together. Either way, you must come to Concord someday and let me show you around. It's such a quaint town. I think you would enjoy it." Still holding his hand, she said, "As a matter of fact, I know you would."

His face brightened. "I'll make a point of it . . ."

Drake and Amanda walked to the elevator, talking in subdued tones.

"I was very impressed, Rory," said Beth. "You did a great job. Thank you for everything." She shook his hand and then drew him in close to hug him and give him a friendly peck on the cheek. "Now I just have to find a spare two million dollars and keep away from Sidney until I do."

"Sidney?"

"Sidney Milner, my boss. I expect him back from his cruise any day now."

As they slowly trooped out of the conference room, her cell phone vibrated in her jacket pocket. It was Sidney. He was direct and to the point: "Harding, be in my office tomorrow morning at ten o'clock . . . sharp."

CHAPTER
THIRTY-NINE

Early Saturday morning, busy people rushed by the hospital's conference room, but they all paused to listen to the beautiful sounds coming from inside. Sweet, angelic Christmas voices. They stopped, listened, smiled, and then proceeded on their way, humming as they walked away. Inside the room, Stephen Collins raised his hands in the air, and again the choir began to sing.

> O Holy night, the stars are brightly shining
> It is the night of our dear Savior's birth

"Very good," said Stephen as he held up his hands, stopping them. He turned over the sheet music on his stand to redirect them the first line. "Let's try this first line at just an octave higher." They began to sing again, their glorious voices ringing true, and he began to smile. *Yes, now they have it.* He glanced at his watch. "Everybody be here early this evening. Merry Christmas. See you tonight. Good luck."

His sister was enjoying all the festivities, and he waved at her before he left and ran up the stairs to visit his parents. Their room was dim as he came in and stood by their beds, listening to the rhythm of their machines.

"Mom, Dad, come back. It's me, Stephen," he whispered. "I'm home. We miss you. We need you. I don't know how much longer I can hold up without you two. Please. Come back."

The sound of the pumps never stopped or even slowed. They kept beating in tune with the rise and fall of their chests.

He leaned forward and touched each of their hands; he held them in his and squeezed them tight. They seemed so cold, so lifeless. "Oh sweet Lord, if it be your will I understand, but if we can keep them here just a little while longer, please . . ."

"Help us," came his sister Lisa's response behind him.

She rolled her wheelchair up beside him. He saw the tears in her eyes, and they both watched the heart monitors as they bounced up and down.

After watching for over an hour, he said, "Come on, sis—let's go. I'll buy lunch, and if you're good, maybe some dessert."

"Yummy," she said, brushing the tears away.

He turned one last time to look at his parents lying in bed, motionless. It was all his fault. The death of the tiniest member of the Collins family was all his fault. Last summer, Kerri had been only four years old when the two of them went to a local pool to swim. She had stayed in the kiddie pool as he sat on the bench behind her, watching. He had only looked away for the briefest of moments to see who was calling his name. When he had turned back around, she was floating facedown in the pool. He had screamed and rushed to her, but he was too late. She was gone. After the funeral, his pain had grown and he could no longer carry the grief or watch the pain in his parents' eyes. He had to leave, but the unbearable guilt followed him everywhere no matter how far away he went. Putting his head in his hand's he moaned. "It's all my fault."

He heard Lisa's squeaky voice. "Stevie, it's not your fault."

His head snapped backward. "What do you mean?"

"You know . . . Kerri."

He smiled a knowing smile. "I'm sure."

"No, Stevie, really. Daddy told me. It wasn't your fault, really."

"Whatever you say." He knew she was just trying to look out for him, as always. In her eyes, he could never do anything wrong.

"But Stevie, I'm telling you the truth. Really I am."

"Sure, Lisa. I understand. Come on, let's go."

She stopped her wheelchair in the middle of the hallway. "Don't treat me like a little kid. I'm not a baby. I know what I'm talking about. The doctor . . . he came to our house to talk with us about three weeks after the funeral. You had already gone, and there was no way to contact you. He told us what happened to Kerri. He said she . . . had something in her head . . . something went wrong . . . bad . . . a stroke, and then she died in the pool."

"What? What are you talking about?"

"He said it could have happened anywhere, at any time. You didn't cause it, Stevie. You didn't cause Kerri to die. He said it was a rare blood condition and there was nothing you could do. You couldn't have saved her."

He nearly fell into one of the nearby chairs in the hallway. "What? What are you saying? Are you sure? Lisa?"

She slowly wheeled herself to his side and hugged him. "I'm sure. That's what the doctor told us. It wasn't your fault, Stevie. Really, it wasn't. Daddy had made the decision this week to come and find you no matter what it cost or how long it took. He wanted you to come home, to be part of the family again. We all missed you so much."

He brushed away the tears from his eyes and hugged her. "You're the best sister in the whole wide world. Did you know that?"

"Of course I know that. I'm a Collins, aren't I?"

They went down the hallway, him pushing her wheelchair and holding her hand, whispering Christmas carols to each other. He felt as if a tremendous weight had been lifted from his shoulders; nothing could hurt him again. They waited at the elevator, and he heard a voice.

"Excuse me, Mr. Collins? Could I speak to you for a minute, sir, please?" Dr. Stone had a troubled look on her face. She glanced down at the young girl. "Hi, Lisa. Want a piece of candy?"

"Sure."

She handed her a mint, then another, and said with a smile, "Why don't you enjoy that candy . . . over there by those chairs? You might be more comfortable there."

"Oh, I get it, that's just another way of saying that you want to have an adult talk . . . without me. I'll have you know I am ten years old and very capable of—"

Stephen intervened. "Lisa, why don't you rest for a minute? Then we'll go and get something to eat. Okay?"

She took in a loud, deep breath and said, "Okay, okay. I can take a hint."

"Mr. Collins," the doctor said in a low tone as the little girl rolled away, out of earshot. "There's been no change in your parents' condition. I'm afraid if this continues we will have to arrange transport to a continuing care facility. It's for their own good. There they will receive the best and most appropriate care."

"Why can't they stay here? They're comfortable here, they're getting good care; my sister is here and is going to be discharged tomorrow. Just a few days longer, please, Doctor. I know they'll come out of this, please. Just a few days more."

"I'm sorry, Mr. Collins, but I'm afraid it's out of my hands. Besides, the hospital is scheduled to close soon, so beds at other hospitals in the region will be at a premium as patients get moved. So it's best that they be moved as soon as possible. I wish there was something else I could do for you, but unfortunately my hands are tied."

"Dr. Stone, Alicia, please can't we—"

"They'll be moved tomorrow morning to Clifton Continuing Care. It's not far from here. Very clean and comfortable. It's for the best, believe me. I have to finish my rounds now. I'm sorry I didn't have better news for you."

His shoulders slumped as he walked away, but he tried to put on a happy face for his sister.

"Why the long face?" she asked.

"Oh nothing. She said she was sorry she hadn't bought me a Christmas present and wanted to make sure I wasn't upset."

"Yeah, right. You never were a good liar. How much time do we have?" she asked as her hand reached for his.

"They want to move them tomorrow, to Clifton."

"On Christmas Day?" She was nearly yelling.

"Yes. Come on, let's get you something to eat. Then we'll come back to visit until it's time for the Christmas carols."

"I'm not hungry anymore. Lost my appetite."

"Me, too. Let's go outside and see the snow."

"Okay," she whispered, and clung to his hand. "Stevie, don't ever leave me again."

"I won't."

"Promise?"

"I promise." He held her small hand in his and they went outside to watch the snow fall. He hoped tomorrow would never come. He felt it was the beginning of the end.

CHAPTER FORTY

Beth could tell that Sidney was angry; the small veins on the side of his neck were turning purple and beginning to bulge and throb as he addressed her formally. "Dr. Harding, is there anything that was unclear in my instructions to you about preparing the hospital for closedown?"

"No, sir."

"Anything you did not understand?"

"No, sir." She fidgeted awkwardly in the tall black leather chair in front of his desk. She kept sliding down to the front and had to pull herself back up with her elbows.

"Any reason why you did not notify the board and follow proper procedures before you submitted your emergency request to the governor's office?"

"No, sir," she said, and then proceeded to try to explain. "I thought I would make one last attempt to obtain the money we needed to—"

He held up his hands to silence her. "Please, Doctor. I've heard it all before. I know what you were trying to do, and it was very noble of you." He leaned back in his chair and sighed. "However, Dr. Harding, Beth . . . you put this hospital in potential violation of state law by not following my instructions. Very specific instructions, I might add."

"But, sir, if the governor or the city had approved the funds, as I understand it, with that approval we would have been technically in compliance by having identified a funding source and—"

"Except they didn't, and we don't have the funding. It's that simple." He stood and walked over to her, settling his hefty weight in the chair next to hers. "I know what you were trying to do. You're stubborn, just like your mother was when she had your job. But sometimes you have to play by the rules. Sometimes you have to know when to call it quits."

She'd had enough. "And sometimes you have to toss the rules aside when you're fighting for a cause you believe in. I would do the same thing all over again if I had the chance."

"Beth, that might work in Hollywood, but what you and Dr. Corrigan did was insubordinate. And I'm afraid that—"

"Leave Drake out of this. It was all my choice. It was my decision to try to save this hospital. He was merely following my orders and direction."

"I see. Have it your own way. Beth, my hands are tied, and you leave me no choice." He paused for a moment before saying, "I'm sorry, Beth." He stopped, then lowered his voice. "I'll expect your letter of resignation on my desk by noon. Make today your last day. Clear out your desk and pick up your final paycheck at the accounting office. It will be waiting for you. I'm sorry it had to end this way, Beth, really I am. I am bound by the by laws of the state. I'm sorry." His voice nearly choked as he spoke to her.

Beth stood in defiance. "I'm not sorry. No disrespect, Sidney, but I'll keep on fighting for this hospital until I leave." Her voice began to rise and tremble with emotion. "It means more to me than just my mother's memory. The people of River Dale mean more to me. Good day, sir."

Her adrenaline was pumping, but she had run out of ideas. She had asked everywhere for the funds—the board, the county, the city, and the state—with no luck. She walked aimlessly about the building and suddenly found herself outside the hospital chapel. *Why not? It never hurts to ask for help,* her mother always said.

❉

Beth was distracted as she left the chapel and was nearly knocked over by Fletch Morgan in the corridor.

"Hiya, Doc," he said with a broad grin. "I was just on my way to visit the Colonel. He goes home tomorrow."

"Yes, I know. I signed his release papers. Just make sure he doesn't go back to work anytime soon. Speaking of work . . . have you seen . . . uh . . . Logan?"

"Oh. I know he tried to call you when we were out on a run." Fletch stumbled, not really knowing what to say. "His red beeper went off . . . and he said he had to go . . . he left."

"His smoke jumper beeper?"

"Yes."

No! With his condition, he should not be smoke jumping. He knows that. What is he thinking?

Fletch paused for a minute. "He's on his way to California. Sorry. I don't want to get in the middle of any of this. I gotta go and visit the Colonel. See you at the memorial tonight?"

"Yes," she said absentmindedly, and wandered away. She needed to sit down, and fast. She felt light-headed. What was she going to do? She put her head on her hands between her legs.

What am I going to do now? My whole world is falling apart. The hospital. Logan. Claire. Rory.

Sitting there, she heard footsteps and then saw two feet on the floor in front of her in an old pair of black shoes. A familiar voice rang out.

"Merry Christmas, Dr. Beth."

Beth looked up and saw Vicki standing before her in a robe, steadying herself with a cane.

"What's up, Doc?" Vicki asked. "You know, I've always wanted to say that, but it never seemed appropriate until now."

That brought a gentle smile to Beth's face.

The old lady gently glided her ancient frame onto the bench beside her. "Talk to me. You look like you could use a friend."

What the heck, she thought. *Why not?* "Well, where do I start?"

"The beginning is always a good place."

"Right. This has not been a good couple of days for me. My best friend, who I adore and now finally realize I'm in love with, is on his way to California with a condition that could kill him. I moved here to be close to my family, and then my sister moved to Boston. She's not even coming home for Christmas, and I found out that the guy she's living with might be abusing her. Now she won't even talk to me. The hospital is closing if we don't come up with two million dollars today. I turned down a big job in Chicago paying a lot of money to stay here in River Dale. Oh, and along the way, I was fired from my job for not following orders. So, today is my last day at work. In short, I have no family, no job, no prospects—nothing."

The old woman smiled at her. "It's what you have inside your heart that matters. Follow your heart and don't worry about the money. Heck, I'll give you the money, the two million," Vicki said sweetly. "You've been so good to me, so why not?"

Beth played along. "Thanks, Vicki. I appreciate it. Really I do."

"I'm serious. I can—"

"Beth! Dr. Harding, come quick." It was Sidney. "Carlita called looking for you. It's Nancy. The little girl with cancer in Room 300. She's failing, and she asked for you. Quick!"

Beth was on her feet in an instant.

"You go," Vicki said to her. "Then we'll talk about the two-million-dollar donation later and . . ."

"Who's she?" Sidney asked as they walked away.

"Her name is Vicki. She's an amnesia patient . . . but she may also be delusional."

"No," she said. "My name is Haddie. I . . ."

Sidney gave her a puzzled look, then whispered, "I thought you said her name was Vicki?"

"See what I mean? Gotta go, Vicki."

They both rushed off toward Room 300. For some reason this little girl was special to Beth and the entire staff. She hoped they would get there in time, before it was too late.

Not on Christmas Eve, please Lord, not on Christmas.

CHAPTER

FORTY-ONE

Larry addressed the two remaining members of his entourage. The small group assembled at the nurses' station. Michael and Maria were the only ones left. They watched the comings and goings of patients, family, and doctors.

"Today is the last day for you two. I hope that you've found this experience to be helpful and eye-opening. You can see what is required and how you can help people make their journey easier. I'll be seeing you both later, back here at the end of your shift. Stay out of people's way and don't get involved. Do you understand what I'm saying? Michael? Maria?"

"Sorry, Larry," Maria said, sounding exhausted. "I was just saying we don't know if we can do this anymore. All the people, all the hurt, all the pain, all the—"

"I understand, Maria. You must be strong; today is your last day. I need you to do your best. And now . . . I need you in Room 300."

"Room 300? Isn't that—"

"Yes, it is. Nancy. She's there and waiting for you. Be kind and gentle. She's been through a lot. I know that I can trust you to know what to do. You two have done this so many times before throughout the week. But hurry. And, Michael, I need you in Room 401. I'll see you both later. Okay?"

"Yes, sir," they said in unison.

They both went their separate ways, and they turned to wave and catch one last glimpse of each other. Maria made her way to the third floor, Room 300, and quietly walked inside. Young Nancy was there waiting for her, on the bed, a contented smile on her face.

"Hi, Nancy," Maria whispered.

"Hi," Nancy responded in a low tone.

Maria lifted the girl's hand into hers.

Nancy was quiet, then asked, "I have to know . . . will the pain go away when I leave here?" she asked. Her eyes begged for an answer.

"Yes, it'll be all gone," came Maria's consoling response.

"And, my hair? I know this sounds awful, but my hair, will it come back?" she asked, gently touching her bald head. "I miss it," she whispered, nearly in tears.

"Yes, it will," came the tender reply.

"How long will it take? I mean to leave here and get there . . . to heaven."

"Not long at all. A blink of an eye. But we have time to talk."

"You know my mommy and daddy never talked to me like this, they always just say—"

"Nancy, who are you talking to, sweetie?" came a voice in the distance.

The little twelve-year-old girl turned to look at her parents huddled nearby and smiled a tiny grin. "Oh, nobody really, Mommy. Just my new friend. That's all." Turning, she giggled, making a funny face at her new companion, overjoyed at the secret that just the two of them shared.

"Are you an angel?" she whispered.

254

"No dear, not yet anyway. I'm an escort to heaven. You have to be asked to be an angel, and they haven't asked me yet. I'm here to answer any questions you have and then lead you to heaven."

"What's your name?"

"Maria. But we're all called Maria or Michael . . . until we become angels."

"Maria, what's heaven like?"

"Oh, it's a very special and wonderful place. You'll like it a lot, and you'll have many friends there."

"Like who?" asked the now-excited young girl. She attempted to lean on her elbow to sit up and listen to Maria.

"Your brother will be there, many of your other friends, your grandma and Pop-Pop, and lots of others."

"Can Mommy and Daddy come?"

"They'll join you there soon enough, dear. The wait will feel like a blink of an eye."

"Do you have any children, Maria?"

For once, Maria was without an answer. "Well, I . . ."

"Nancy! Nancy! What are you doing sweetheart, lifting up like that? You'll hurt yourself," said her father, rushing to her bed to ease her back down to the mattress. "You have to build up your strength before you can sit up like that. Come on, now, it's time for your medicine. Let me call the nurse. You wait right here, baby."

Her mother could hear the sound of his heavy footsteps on the tiled hallway floor as he hurried away.

"Just wait for a minute. Daddy will be right back, okay, baby?" her mother told her.

"Sure, Mom. But I'm okay now, really I am."

"Is your friend here with you?" her mother asked quietly, placing a cool towel on her forehead.

It felt cool to the touch but did not make the mounting pain go away.

"Maria? Yes, she's right here, waiting."

"Waiting?" her mother asked, her voice now trembling. "Waiting? For what, dear?"

"For me to say it's okay to go, Mommy."

Her mother turned away to hide the tears that were now streaming down her cheeks. She began to sob, unable to hold it back any longer. "Jack!" She screamed when she could take it no more. "Jack . . . I need you." Footsteps sounded at the doorway.

"What's wrong?" asked Nancy's father, nearly out of breath from running.

"I need you here," her mother said, her hand reaching out for his and squeezing it tight. She turned to her one and only daughter and said, "Oh, baby, please don't go, please don't leave me. I'm going to miss you so much if you go. Please don't leave your mommy. Jack, talk to her."

He squeezed his wife's hand tighter and said softly to her, "Rachel, when it's time, it's time. Then her pain will be all over. It'll be gone." He reached down and ran his finger softly across the forehead of his tired little princess. For years, he had wanted her pain and struggle to be over, but he had dreaded this very moment. "I love you, baby," he whispered through his tears.

"I love you, too, Daddy, Mommy," came the weak response, barely audible in the silent hospital room.

She turned away and said with a weak smile of anticipation, "I'm ready, Maria."

"Are you sure?"

The little girl's face brightened as she nodded her head. "Yes, I'm sure. It's time."

Maria reached out and helped the girl from her bed. They walked hand in hand down the hallway, the little girl's long, streaming blonde locks flowing behind her. She was going home. Dr. Harding and Sidney arrived moments later.

"She's gone," said her father, his tears washing his face as he clutched his wife tightly in an embrace. "She's gone," he repeated.

Beth felt the life drain from her as she collapsed into a nearby chair. Tears formed in her eyes. It was finally over.

❋

Michael made his way down the hallway until he reached his destination. The sign on the door said, **Room 401—John Mason.**

"Hi," said Johnny Ray, looking away from the window. "Do the nurses know you're in here?"

"No, but it's okay. How ya doin'?"

"Good. I'm doing really good. A little surprised." Then he paused for a minute. "You're not with the hospital, are you?"

"No. I'm not."

"From the station house?"

"I think you know who I am. I'm here to help you in any way that I can, that's all," said Michael.

"Oh, like how?"

"You're going on a journey, Johnny Ray. To heaven. It won't take long at all, and when we get there you'll see a lot of familiar faces."

"Like who?"

"Old buddies from River Dale, like Teddy McElroy, Pat Janderson, and of course Jimmy Civiletti, you know—the whole crowd. It'll be just like old times."

"Wow. When do we leave?"

"Whenever you're ready."

"Now?"

"Sure, why not."

Dressings and bandages fell away and disappeared as the tall, young, good-looking firefighter stood from his bed, now dressed in brand-new bunker gear. "I'm ready," he said with a proud smile.

Bryan Mooney

"Let's go, then."

As they made their way to the corridor outside Johnny Ray's room, a small crowd milled about, waiting, all dressed in bunker gear. They were young and fresh-faced, smiling for the world to see. His band of brothers had come to take him home.

"Jimmy!" Johnny Ray shouted when he saw him. His old friend. Then turning to face the others he said, "Teddy. Wow! It's so good to see you and all the other guys."

"Wouldn't miss this for the world, buddy boy."

The tallest one, Jimmy, said to Michael, "We can take it from here . . . if that's okay with you?"

"Sure," he said. "Take care now, Johnny Ray."

"So long, Michael," he said as he disappeared among a crowd of old friends, and then he was gone.

Michael turned suddenly and looked around. *Where's Maria?* He was lost without her. *I have to find her, talk to her . . . before it's too late. Maria! I have to tell her.* He stopped. *I know where she is.* And he rushed off to find her. As he expected, he found her standing outside Room 313. The sign on the door read, COLLINS.

"Michael?" she said when she saw him. She was so happy to see him that she embraced him, afraid to let go. "I can't do this anymore. I don't want to do this anymore. I thought I could do this, but I just can't. I don't want anyone else to die."

"I agree," he said as he took her in his arms.

In front of them, Stephen and his sister, Lisa, were at their parents' bedside watching the monitors and continuing to pray. They held each other's hands and closed their eyes.

Maria shouted, seeking his help, "Lord, I can't do this anymore. Lord! Please help me and Michael. Lord, where are you?"

"I am always here," said Larry Of River Dale. He looked different. Sometimes he looked old, sometimes young, but always when she looked at him, he made her feel special. She looked at his name tag and suddenly realized the answer was there right in front of her—Larry Of River Dale . . . L.O.R.D.

He smiled that gentle smile of his. "You both have done very well in your assignments," he said. "I understand your concerns, and since it's Christmas Eve, you have a choice. You can choose to become angels and come to heaven with me." He paused to look at both of them with his kind eyes. "Or you can stay and return to your old life here," he said, pointing to the motionless figures on the hospital beds with the brother and sister huddled close together. "Your choice. And since it's Christmas Eve," he said with a smile, "you can make a wish. A glorious wish or a simple one. Your choice. Now, what do you wish to do?"

Maria stood tall with Michael at her side, looking at him, holding his hand as tight as she could. "I don't want to be an angel. I want to stay right here. I don't care what I have to give up, please," she pleaded, nearly in tears as she looked at Michael, then at the still figures and the brother and sister beside them. "I have a wish. My wish is that we both stay here . . . together . . . and that no one else dies here tonight. That's my wish."

"Merry Christmas," Larry said with a twinkle in his eye, and then he was gone.

Maria reached out for Michael's hand, but he drifted away from her, fading from sight.

"Michael!" she screamed. "Michael!" It was no use, he was gone. Sadly, she turned to watch what was happening in Room 313 and drifted above the brother and sister.

The monitors in Room 313 beeped and clicked loudly, almost out of control, as if someone had won a jackpot. The nurses came running to the room, checking the charts and monitors.

It was she who opened her eyes first . . . then him.

"Michael!" she said, reaching across the distance between the hospital beds that divided them, stretching. She had to touch his hand, to hold him, to kiss him, to comfort him. To make sure he was real.

"I'm right here, Maria. I would never leave you."

Their eyes met.

"I love you," she said.

"I love you, too," he whispered.

"Maria, you were in my dreams. Strange dreams, so real. I was working in a hospital and—"

"I had the same dream! And I fell in love with you all over again," she whispered.

They heard a cough and turned to find their children by their side.

"Stephen! Oh my God, you've come home," he said. "I was on my way to find you. To bring you home."

"I'm home, Dad, Mom. Home for good. Merry Christmas."

"This is the best Christmas present ever," the parents said in unison.

Maria's hand stretched across the divide, reaching for her husband. "I love you, Michael."

"I love you all—Maria, Stephen, Lisa. I love you now more than ever." The family was together again, whole again.

CHAPTER
FORTY-TWO

Young Mayerle held the baby called James in her arms. She cuddled him, held him, and sang to him. The little one was her favorite, and she was concerned when he got quiet. Something was not right; she sensed it as she began to rock him softly in her arms. "Sweet baby James," she cooed to the motherless child, softly touching his short, curly black hair.

Nurse Abrams watched the young woman holding the baby that nobody else wanted to hold or try to manage. Too cantankerous. She had to admit that young Mayerle had a special knack for the rowdy ones, calming them down and soothing them. Little James was a perfect example of her ability.

She returned to her paperwork. It was late on Christmas Eve, but she had nowhere else to go, no one to visit, no gifts to exchange. Tonight she was on her own, and that was fine with her. It was just the way she liked it, the way she always liked it. Her replacement would be there soon to relieve her for the night. Then she would go home and reheat her chicken dinner from the night before.

Some way to spend Christmas, she wryly thought to herself.

Bryan Mooney

The head nurse heard a Christmas song play louder for a brief moment.

> What Child is this
> Who laid to rest
> On Mary's lap is sleeping?

She had always loved that song; it was one of her favorite Christmas songs. She smiled, thinking back to growing up with her sister in Detroit. They would always go caroling in the neighborhood. They had not had much at that time, but they'd had one another. Christmas was special then, before the accident, before the funeral, before the orphanage. She missed her sister and her parents even now. If only they had not gone out that Christmas Eve night to sing Christmas carols . . . if only. But now . . .

"Ummm, excuse me."

She heard Mayerle clear her throat and looked up to see her standing in her doorway, still holding young James.

"Nurse Abrams?" Mayerle asked with concern obvious in her voice.

"Yes," she responded, not even bothering to look up from her desk.

"Nurse Abrams?"

"Yes. What do you want, Mayerle?" she said sharply while still intent on reviewing her reports.

"I think there's something wrong with James."

"There's always something wrong with James. Just put him back in his crib. And if you can't handle him, then go home. Your shift is over."

The young woman did not move; she held her ground. *"Nurse Abrams,"* she said emphatically. "Can you please look at this baby, *now!"*

The startled middle-aged woman looked up at Mayerle, marveling at her insistent and forceful way.

"Please! I think something's wrong," Mayerle repeated, almost pleading.

262

The nurse pushed the chair away from her desk and walked to the young woman holding the baby in her arms. He looked fine to her, and she began to turn away. Normal, except he was sleeping. She looked closer; a hint of blue appeared around his lips. His breathing was shallow, and just then he began to twitch. He was having a seizure.

"Let me help you, Mayerle. I'll take him now, okay? Everything's going to be just fine," Nurse Abrams said with warm encouragement.

She gently took the baby from Mayerle's arms and sat on a chair while turning the baby on his side. She checked to make sure that there were no obstructions in his mouth and looked at her watch while she massaged his back. She needed to time the duration of the incident and then added fifteen seconds for the approximate time that Mayerle had held the baby.

Mayerle stood by like a loyal confidant, asking, "Is there anything I can do to help?"

"Yes. Get me a blanket to keep him warm." Then she added, "You're doing good, Mayerle. Real good."

The young woman returned with a warm blanket in record time. Soon the twitching stopped, and the baby's breathing returned to normal.

The door opened. "Is everything all right? What's wrong?" Mayerle's mother asked, arriving to pick her up and take her home. She immediately sensed something was wrong.

"Everything is fine," said Nurse Abrams, turning the baby around. "Thanks to your daughter . . . Mayerle. She saved this baby's life," she said, nearly in tears. "She recognized something was wrong, and she was right. He was having a seizure. Thanks to her quick action little James is fine now." She picked up baby James and offered him to Mayerle. "Here, Mayerle. You did good—real good."

"Thank you, Nurse Abrams. I think I'll get him ready for bed. It's late." She turned and walked back to join the other babies in the nursery, then changed him and bundled him. "Time to sleep, little one. See you tomorrow, baby James. Behave now, you hear me," she whispered.

Her mother watched the scene unfold and saw a difference in Nurse Abrams.

"We're going to the annual memorial dedication at the town square in a little while, and then we're coming back to listen to the choral group in the cafeteria," Mayerle's mother said to the head nurse. "Would you care to join us?"

"Well, I don't normally go for that kind of stuff, and I have to go home to . . . ," she blustered, but then she softened. "Yes, I would love to go with you, now that Agnes is here to relieve me. Thank you for asking."

CHAPTER FORTY-THREE

"Dr. Harding, Beth, you're going to the memorial service at the town square, aren't you?" Carlita reminded her.

"No, I don't think so. I think I'm going to finish packing some things and then head home. Get drunk on some five-day-old eggnog."

"You should go. I am. The whole town will be there." Then, glancing at her watch, she said, "It's time to leave."

"Yes, you should go," Sidney chimed in as he walked up behind Carlita.

Beth had always liked Sidney and could never stay angry with him.

"Beth, walk with me to the ceremony," he said in his fatherly way.

She took a deep breath and set her box of personal things back on her desk. "I suppose these things can wait. Logan was supposed to be here tonight to present the memorial wreath representing the fallen firefighters."

"I'm sure he'll be there," said Sidney.

"I don't think so. He's gone. Back to California." She put on her boots, and he helped her with her coat. "I'm ready," she said.

While they waited for the elevator, Sidney said matter-of-factly, "I turned down the job at Winston Memorial Hospital. River Dale is home for me. I think I'm just going to stay here. I'll find something to do, I hope."

"Good," Beth said, holding tight on to his sleeve. "Very good. This town needs you."

"And you."

They walked through the hospital, out the front door, and down the street a short distance to the town square. A white limousine slowed, then pulled up next to them, stopping. The rear window rolled down, and a sweet voice from inside said, "Dr. Harding, Beth?"

Beth leaned forward, looking inside the big stretch limo. It was Sweetie. "Hi, Vicki. So good to see you. I heard you were being released, but you were already gone by the time I got to your room to say goodbye."

"Yes. My nephew came by early to pick me up," she said, pointing to the fresh-faced young man sitting next to her in the backseat. "You were very kind to me, Beth, and you looked out for me when no one else would have. You touched me. It's a kindness that I will never forget nor ever be able to repay . . . but I can try. I was going to mail this to you, but I thought you could use it sooner rather than later. Plus, you saved me the postage."

She handed her a blue envelope. Beth opened it, then looked at Vicki without saying a word. The envelope contained two items: a check for $2 million signed by Victoria Haddington and a note.

> Dr. Harding—
> Beth, you deserve the best. You gave me help when I needed it. And hope for the future when I had nothing else. For that I will be forever grateful.
> Thanks for everything,
> Vicki

She was speechless, first looking at the check and then at the elderly woman she had grown fond of during her stay. "Oh, Vicki, I don't know what to say."

"You can say 'Merry Christmas,'" she said with a jingle in her voice.

Beth stared at the name on the check saying, "Haddington. Haddington? That name sounds so familiar."

"Haddington Chocolate?" Vicki said. "The largest chocolate company on the East Coast. And the best I might add. That's my company. No wonder I liked the name Sweetie so much." She paused, smiled, and said, "Thanks again for everything, Beth. And now you should go find that young man of yours and never let him go. I'm going to Schmidt's Bakery. I never did get my *Pfeffernüsse* cookies. So long and bye for now, Beth. Merry Christmas."

She raised the window, and they waved goodbye to each other. Beth turned to Sidney and handed him the check, sporting a very large Christmas grin.

"Merry Christmas, Sidney. Now you can keep the hospital open," Beth said. She began to whistle.

He could not take his eyes off the check.

"Wow! No, now *we* can keep the hospital open."

Beth began to whisper Christmas songs as they made their way to the festivities. *So this is what cloud nine feels like,* she thought to herself.

Sidney walked beside her, still holding the check and marveling at their good fortune. They stopped walking when they reached the area for the annual memorial.

Beth turned to him and said, "For years I have always done everything for other people, for my job, my father, my mother, my friends, my coworkers . . . everybody. I've never done anything just for me. I've never minded it before, but . . . now I do. I pushed all my feelings to the background and only focused on my job. Well, now I'm going to do something for me."

"You're going to California? To find Logan."

"Yes. If he's dumb enough to have me."

"But what about your job? Your life here? And what about—"

She interrupted him. "After seeing Vicki, I realized something. Here's a woman who a few days ago had nothing in the world, not even her identity. But she once told me it's what you have inside your heart that matters. Nothing else. Well, I have Logan in my heart, and now I'm going to find him and try to make up for some lost time."

They heard the mayor make an announcement from the podium. "Ladies and gentlemen," Royce said loudly, "if you would all please have a seat, we will be starting our annual police and firefighter memorial program shortly. Thank you."

Everyone took a seat.

"I want to thank you all for coming here on this snowy night. It looks like the whole town has turned out again this year. I know it's Christmas Eve, and everyone has a million things to do before the holiday. However, I hope you won't forget to stop by the hospital and join in with the Christmas choir. I understand they'll be serving German cookies, eggnog, and homemade fruitcake—all donated by Elsie Schmidt of Schmidt's Bakery."

Everyone in the crowd stood and clapped.

"I understand this year the choir is better than ever under the tutelage of our new music director—singer, songwriter, and composer, Mr. Stephen Collins. I heard them today when I stopped by the hospital. They sounded wonderful."

The entire crowd clapped again.

"I know it's a little strange to be honoring our fallen heroes at this time of the year, but it is our tradition here in River Dale. It goes back over a hundred years. Every year at this time we honor those firefighters and police officers who have died in the line of duty, coming to our aid.

"Police Chief Mark Richards, who you all know, will join me to place a Christmas wreath at the police officers' plaque."

The two men walked together slowly, then solemnly placed a pine wreath with a black ribbon draped over it in front of the plaque. They both stood at attention and saluted before returning to their positions.

Royce took the podium again. "Usually we have the Colonel join us to place the second wreath to honor our fallen firefighters. However, since he is still in the hospital—getting out tomorrow, I might add—we had asked Logan Mitchell to help us with this honor. But I have not seen him here tonight, and I understand that he is on his way to—"

"Present," a deep baritone voice boomed from the back of the square.

Beth turned around . . . it was Logan. He walked down the middle aisle of the makeshift memorial. Their eyes met.

"Are you ready, Logan?"

"Ready, sir."

They each took a side of the wreath and slowly walked to the memorial. After placing it, they followed the same routine, standing at attention and then saluting. Logan whispered to the mayor and Royce nodded his head in agreement and stepped aside. Logan turned to face the crowd.

"Ladies and gentlemen. It is with a sad heart that I must also recognize another fallen firefighter. Johnny Ray Mason died today from injuries suffered on the job. It was a job he loved, and we ask that you remember him."

He turned and placed Johnny's silver shield on the black banner, then saluted again. Logan returned to his position of honor at the front of the crowd, while Royce concluded the ceremony with a prayer for the fallen heroes.

Beth was waiting there behind him when he returned. The crowd was leaving, on their way home or to the hospital.

"I tried to reach you. You didn't answer your phone," she said, moving closer to him.

Those around them whispered, "Merry Christmas" as they walked by.

"I know. I didn't answer it. I had to have some time to think things through."

"Logan, I have so much to tell you. I missed you. I'm sorry about . . . everything," she blurted out in rapid succession. Tears dribbled down her cheeks. "I'm no longer engaged. I broke it off with Rory. We received a huge donation for the hospital, so now we can stay open. And I . . ."

"I love you," he said as he slowly put his arms around her, pulling her close. It sounded so natural, words that he should have said so long ago. "And I won't leave you ever again."

"I love you, too. I always have, ever since that first—"

She never finished the sentence as he kissed her the way she should be kissed, the way she wanted to be kissed, long and slow . . . with love. She put her arms around him and placed her head on his chest.

"I'm just sorry it took us this long to get to this point. So much time wasted, so much . . ."

He kissed her again. "Shhhhh," he whispered. "I agree. Let's go join the others for the caroling. Then we can go home and talk. We have a lot to talk about."

CHAPTER FORTY-FOUR

The hospital cafeteria had been transformed into a Christmas wonderland. Christmas lights hung from the ceiling, pine garland wrapped around the columns, and young girls dressed as Santa's helpers served up platters of cookies, cake, and other Christmas treats. "Merry Christmas and welcome," they each said politely.

Rows of wheelchair-bound patients were seated in the first and second rows. Those with crutches were seated directly behind them. Candy-striped nurse volunteers walked around with cups of spiced eggnog on trays.

"The whole world is here," Beth whispered, grabbing two plastic cups of eggnog from a passing volunteer's serving tray.

"Merry Christmas, Dr. Harding," Mayerle said as she passed by them. "See you at church tomorrow?" She glanced quickly at Logan, raising her eyebrows in a show of approval.

"Yes, of course."

"Of course. Merry Christmas. See you tomorrow."

The proud choir director tapped the microphone to get everyone's attention. "Good evening, ladies and gentlemen. And merry Christmas.

Thank you all for coming out tonight to hear your River Dale choir and ensemble. Most of these songs you hear tonight you will recognize as old favorites, but we've thrown in a few new songs as well. These are ones I wrote as a tribute to my hometown, River Dale. I hope you enjoy the program."

Beth stood up on her tiptoes to survey the crowd and saw Stephen's mom, dad, and little sister all proudly resting in wheelchairs in the front row. The lights dimmed, and the star on top of the Christmas tree in the corner began to twinkle. The music began. It sounded heavenly.

> It came upon a midnight clear,
> That glorious song of old,
> From angels bending near the earth

Beth tugged on Logan's hand and pulled him closer. Life was good, almost perfect. The choir sang three songs, each better than the one before. She loved it. If only . . .

She felt movement beside her, and when she looked up, she saw it was Claire. Her eyes, face, and smile were glowing like a Christmas star.

"Claire!" Beth nudged Logan, who was just as happy to see her as Beth.

"What are you doing here?" he whispered. "Are you alone?"

"Yes, I'm alone. And I'm home. For good."

They all hugged, and Claire could not help but notice the two of them holding hands. Beth held Claire's hand with her free one.

"Isn't that Stephen Collins?" Claire asked, sitting up in her seat. "Hmmm. He had a crush on me in high school. This is going to be a good Christmas. No, this is going to be a great and wonderful Christmas."

CHAPTER FORTY-FIVE

As the three of them opened their gifts on Christmas morning, the sun came out to shine brightly on the freshly fallen snow.

Logan sipped his coffee while looking out over the backyard. "You know, I could build a large garden for you this summer. You would have lots of vegetables, and we could move some of the rosebushes so that—"

"Move the rosebushes?" both women screamed in unison.

"Never!" Claire exclaimed. "Mom loved those roses. You should know that better than anyone. You loved them, too, and if you ever . . ."

He laughed at both of them in his own genial sort of way. "I'm kidding. Just wanted to see if you two were listening to me at all."

"Breakfast is ready, but first I have a gift for you, Logan," Beth said, holding out a small green box. He looked at it with great interest but did not move.

"Go on, open it. It won't bite you."

He peeled back the brightly colored Christmas paper and removed the lid. It was the third piece of the coin pendant. Now all three of them had one, and when they brought their pieces together, they all fit to make one whole coin. The inscription now could be easily read—Love.

Logan was in awe. "When? How? Where did you find it? I bought two pieces in Boston, but they said the third piece was missing."

"I bought it for you right here in River Dale before you had even bought our gift. But that just goes to show you that you can find anything you want in River Dale. Even me."

He pulled her close and kissed her.

Claire looked at her watch and then rushed up the stairs. In a few minutes she returned all dressed for church. "I'll see you at church. I'm meeting someone at the hospital before services," she said, throwing her coat over her shoulders.

"Who are you meeting?" asked her big sister warily.

"Stephen Collins. He remembered me and asked me to go to church with him and his sister today. His folks are still too weak to travel just yet. Bye. See ya later." She kissed them both on the cheek, saying, "Merry Christmas" as she ran out the door.

They laughed as they watched her vanish outside.

"I have one place I would like to stop on the way to church later . . . if you don't mind?" murmured Beth.

"Me, too. We'll leave a little early, after breakfast."

The cemetery was quiet and deserted as they trudged through the snow and made their way to visit Beth's parents. She held Logan's hand tight; she never wanted to let him go.

"I'm so glad you came back. It saved me a trip to California to track you down."

He stopped and kissed her.

"I love you," he said.

It was just a few feet in front of them, and they both saw it at the same time. There were no footprints in the snow surrounding the grave site, but on top of Sarah and the Judge's granite headstone was a fresh red rose.

Logan brushed off the new snow from the bench, and he and Beth sat down and began to talk.

"Merry Christmas, Mom, Dad. The family is all back together again. We miss you. It's not the same without you, but I think you know that already," Beth said, eyeing the rose. They had their own ways of letting her know that they approved.

Life was good again.

"Doc Sarah, you always loved your roses. Merry Christmas to you and the Judge!" said Logan. They walked away, arm in arm, through the softly fallen snow. They were going to have another white Christmas after all. It was a very good Christmas.

ACKNOWLEDGMENTS

A huge thank-you goes out to all firefighters across the country. Thank you for your service; we truly appreciate all that you do.

A special thanks to Captain Bruce Cavelleri, Firehouse #42-WPB, Delray Beach, Florida, for his invaluable time and input. A big shout-out of thanks to Danielle Goetzinger—thanks for all your help. And, as always, thanks to Dr. Robert Johnston (Dr. Bob) for his medical insight in researching this book.

Finally, a very special thank-you to my wife, Bonnie, for her patience, insight, and guidance throughout this and all my other books. Thank you, sweetheart!

AUTHOR'S NOTE

Dear readers—I hope you enjoy my books. If you do, please feel free to post a review on your favorite reader website. Thank you!

—Bryan Mooney

ABOUT THE AUTHOR

Bryan Mooney is the author of *Christmas in Vermont, Once We Were Friends, Love Letters, A Second Chance,* and other romance novels, as well as the Nick Ryan thriller series. He spent years traveling the globe for both business and pleasure, and he draws upon those experiences in his writing. Originally from the Midwest, Bryan now lives in sunny South Florida with his childhood sweetheart and longtime wife, Bonnie. When he's not penning romance novels and thrillers on the beach, he and his wife love to travel. Connect with Bryan at www.bryanmooneyauthor.com.